D0050808

WILDSEED WITCH

MARTI DUMAS

Cataloging-in-Publication Data has been applied for and may be obtained from the Library of Congress.

ISBN 978–1–4197–5561–3

Text © 2022 Marti Dumas
Page 79: image courtesy Pavel Talashov/Shutterstock.com
Book design by Hana Anouk Nakamura and Deena Fleming

Amulet Books are available at special discounts when purchased in quantity for premiums and promotions as well as fundraising or educational use. Special editions can also be created to specification. For details, contact specialsales@abramsbooks.com or the address below.

Amulet Books® is a registered trademark of Harry N. Abrams, Inc.

ABRAMS The Art of Books
195 Broadway, New York, NY 10007
abramsbooks.com

To all the people who have ever loved me—
know that I have felt it and needed the strength of it,
and know that I love you, too

CHAPTER ONE

TINGLE AND BLUSH

The first time I did magic was the third day of summer vacation. I hadn't seen my dad in forever, and everyone I hang out with had already left town. But I didn't mind. With everybody gone, I had time to make more videos for my YouTube channel, MakeupontheCheapCheap. At that point, I had only one video— a dollar store makeup haul I did over spring break—but my channel was already up to 18 subscribers anyway, and, thanks to my favorite YouTuber, AnyaDo0dle, I had a plan to make it to 100 before school started.

Don't get me wrong. I got inspiration from lots of YouTubers. Nobody did contouring better than JeffServesFace, and I wouldn't have known anything about eye shadow at all if it weren't for TheRealCorinaSparkles, but AnyaDo0dle, a goddess among mere mortals, had posted a video called "Love Them and They Will Come:

6 Ways to Grow Your Channel," and you better believe I took notes. Lots of notes. The checklist I made out of them filled up most of my whiteboard.

- **Camera, Stand, and Lighting**
- **Backdrop**
- **Edit Intro**
- **Plan Your Content**
- **Post Daily**
- **Love Your Subscribers**

The main ones I had left to do were Post Daily and Love Your Subscribers, which was kind of the same thing. AnyaDo0dle said loving your subscribers meant three things: make promises, keep promises, and show them the real you.

I was always the real me, so that part was easy. I'd already made my first promise, too: posting a new video every day all summer. Now all I had to do was keep it.

Filming and editing a video every day would be a lot of work, but I was actually excited for it. I had already recorded myself doing a $3 Lavender Look for Summer and Makeup Removal Hacks So Your Mom Won't Freak out about Her Sheets, and even though it took a long time to get an hour of video down to seven minutes, cutting stuff out and speeding stuff up was weirdly satisfying, like the moment when you finally get the piece of popcorn out of your teeth. I had a plan and, even if the plan didn't work, at least it kept me from thinking about the suitcase staring at me from the corner.

It was just a regular suitcase. My suitcase. The one I packed the last time my dad was supposed to come pick me up. He didn't show, just like he hadn't the three times before. My mom said he was "going through some things" and that I should be patient. I shoved the suitcase in a corner and left it there to remind me how mad at him I was.

But when he finally did show up in his new car, I wasn't as mad as I thought I would be, so I clicked Publish on my first summer video, grabbed the suitcase that I had never unpacked, and hopped into the car.

It was a convertible, but the way it got quiet but kept driving meant it was also electric, like my mom's.

"You got an electric car?" I said, adjusting the air to blow on my face. Mom would be so excited when she found out.

"A hybrid plug-in," my dad said. "Best of both worlds."

Then he pulled a latch and pressed a button and the top went down. It would have been cool, too, if it weren't so hot. New Orleans in the summer is no joke, but I was too excited to be mad about the heat. My mom was going to freak over this car. It was basically the exact one she had been dreaming up for forever. She loved having the sun on her, even in the summer.

"I didn't know they made cars like this," I said.

"They don't. It's custom," my dad winked. "I know a guy."

"Yeah, right," I smiled, pulling out my phone to check my You-Tube. This was the part of the car ride when, if my dad wasn't grilling me about whether Mom had made any "friends," we would settle into quiet. His new house was across town. Plenty of time for quiet. Except my dad wasn't quiet.

"YouTube, huh?" he said, glancing at my phone as he slowed to stop at a red light.

That's when I noticed him smiling. Big. Really big. Too big. I tried to ignore it, but once I thought about it, I realized he had been smiling like that the whole time. Weird.

"Yeah," I said, refreshing my profile page. Still 18 followers, but the video view minutes were up by three. I smiled to myself.

"Sandy is big on social media, too."

"Who's Sandy?" I said, refreshing the page again. The video view minutes were up by four. Someone was watching my video right at that very moment. If I could have, I would have reached through the Internet and hugged them. I hoped they left a comment so I could tell them so. I had already favorited the perfect GIF.

"Sandy is my good friend. YouTube's not her big one, though. Her big one is Instagram. Look her up. Sandyandfree83." He was still smiling with all his teeth. I hadn't seen him in more than a month, and it was like he had spent that whole time turning into a cartoon version of himself. Everything he said sounded extra.

I refreshed the page one more time—seven minutes, they had totally watched the whole video—before opening IG. I never posted on Instagram, but my friends were always posting funny animal pictures that I loved, especially the ones with puppies wearing hats or puppies that looked like a box of fried chicken. When Sandyandfree83's page loaded, I blinked and turned the phone so my dad could see.

"Her?" I asked.

"Yep!" my dad said, smiling even bigger, if that was possible. "That's my Sandy."

When my dad said "friend," I was expecting somebody parent-ish. Sandy did not look like a parent. She had curly blondish hair and 374,000 followers, about one for every shot of her in a bikini or making a kissy face at the camera.

"Her??" I asked again, showing a picture of Sandyandfree83 tossing her hat into a sea breeze. He must have said the wrong one.

My dad nodded. "It's a play on words. Sandy loves the beach. I can't wait for you to meet her. The two of you have a lot in common. You'll like her."

I stopped on a pic of Sandy wearing a bikini on a mountain instead of on a beach. Bikini was the common denominator here, not sand, but whatever. What could the two of us possibly have in common?

"She'll be at the house when we get there."

"Why?" I asked.

"Well, Hasani, sweetheart, that's something I've been meaning to tell you. Sandy lives there, now."

That's when I felt it—the magic.

It was this weird, tingly feeling somewhere between blushing and your foot falling asleep. I didn't know what was happening. I just knew that under no circumstances did I want to go to my dad's house anymore. Then the tingle spread from my chest up to my face, and the St. Claude Avenue Bridge went up.

"There aren't any boats coming," someone shouted from the car behind us, but at the time I didn't think anything about it, because the stupid St. Claude bridge was always going up and at least this time I wanted it to. At least this time the bridge was helping me instead of making me late.

"Is that why you didn't come get me last time? You were helping Sandy move in?" I didn't look up at him. I just kept scrolling through Sandy's feed. Apparently, she had also had a bikinis-in-wildflowers phase.

"No, sweetheart. Sandy and I were out of town. We went on a little trip to Nevada."

The car engine went silent. Cars piled up behind us, blocking us in. I didn't bother to ask him about why he hadn't shown up the week before that or the week before that. I knew. He had been too busy hanging out with Sandy to come see me. The tingling in my skin turned into buzzing. When he'd finally shown up, I hadn't even told him I was mad. I'd even let him put the stupid top down on his stupid new car. It was summer in New Orleans! That was basically a death sentence. Now we were stuck on a bridge with the sun beating down on us and I was sweating, but I didn't care, because being stuck on that bridge was better than whatever was on the other side of it, especially if that something was Sandy and free.

"You didn't get this car for Mom?"

He made a weird face. "Your mom wouldn't want this car. She said the wind drag would ruin the mileage and defeat the purpose of getting a hybrid in the first place. Sandy likes to ride with the top down. I thought you would, too."

"So, you're just quitting?" I said. My skin was buzzing so badly I thought I must be getting a sunburn, and I never get burned.

"What are you talking about, Hasani?"

"On Mom. You said y'all were trying to work it out."

"We were," he said. "It just didn't work."

My teeth clenched. The bridge operator climbed out of her booth with a radio in her hand. There were vines growing up through some of the grates. The vines didn't seem too weird, because in New Orleans everything is always growing over with something.

7

I was baking but refused to ask my father to close the top and put on the air conditioner. I refused to say anything to him ever again.

My dad kept talking, but I sat in silence for the next half an hour before the bridge operator started directing cars to drive over the neutral ground to turn back the way we came, because the bridge was now closed for some reason. I didn't notice how big the vines had grown or that they had sprouted morning glories, but I had scrolled through all of Sandy's Instagram pictures and forced myself to move on to puppies in hats. Puppies in hats always made me feel better and, thanks to Cartoon Dad, I definitely needed them.

CHAPTER TWO

SANDY AND FREE

There were three bridges going to the Lower Ninth Ward, where my dad lived. Only two of them were drawbridges. My dad picked the one that wasn't to drive us the rest of the way to the house he had been living in since Christmas. The house barely had anything in it the last time I went, but a lot had changed. There were flowers planted out front, and we pulled into a fancy carport that hadn't been there before.

"Solar charging station," my dad said, gesturing at the plug under the carport. My mom had always wanted one of those, too, but where we lived there wasn't space for one. We charged her car at Whole Foods. "Six solar panels. Totally off-grid."

I didn't say anything. I just took a baby wipe out of my bag to clean the sweat off my face.

"I know you're mad and I know I did this all wrong, but give Sandy a chance, OK? You'll like her."

I still didn't say anything. I just grabbed my backpack and followed my dad up to his front door. The door flew open before he'd put the key in the lock.

"It's so good to meet you, Hasani! Welcome! Come in. Come in."

Sandy's hair looked more sandy brown than blond like it did on her Instagram, but it was long and thick and wavy just like the pictures. Perfect mermaid hair. Even standing in a doorway in a plain white sundress, she looked like some kind of beach goddess.

"Your dad has told me all about you, but I'd rather hear it from you." Sandy had somehow hooked her arm into mine and pulled me into the house. "Let's go talk on the back porch. I have everything set up and I just want to hear all about you."

Sandy led me through my dad's house as if I'd never been there before and couldn't find my own way to the back porch. The rocking chairs were there, thank goodness. I picked those chairs and the little table, but I barely recognized them mixed in with the vases of flowers and the pitcher of lemonade and tray of cookies. It looked like something out of a magazine. The ice in the glasses wasn't even melted.

"Sit, Hasani, sit!" Sandy said, flipping her mermaid hair to the front as she sat down. "I just love your name, Hasani. I've never heard anything like it. It's so unusual."

"I'm named after my dad," I said.

Sandy looked from me to my dad, confused. Then she laughed. I guess she decided I was joking. I wasn't joking. "Your dad's name is Bobby. How do you get Hasani from Robert?"

"It wasn't Bobby when I was born," I mumbled.

My dad jumped in. "I changed my name to Hassan when Nailah and I got married, but I changed it back to Robert when we split up."

The way he said it made it seem like it was a long time ago. It had only been a year since they broke up. Their divorce wasn't even official yet.

Sandy changed the subject. "I just watched your video, Hasani, and I have to tell you, I love it! You have such a great camera personality."

That was Sandy who was watching my video? The disappointment pushed my eyebrows even closer together. No one had ever accused me of having a good poker face.

"You should have way more followers. I can help you with that, if you want."

My dad looked at me, hopeful.

"No, thank you," I said. Unlike my dad, I had no desire to betray my mother.

"Oh. OK," Sandy said.

"Can I go home now?"

"But you were supposed to stay through the weekend," Dad said. "Sandy was going to help you set up a studio in your room."

I was looking forward to decorating that room, but that was when I thought my dad had bought this house to make room for my mother to plug in her car and have a garden and that we'd all live in it and be happy again.

"My room's Uptown," I said, my skin tingling.

"Hasani—"

"No, Bobby. Don't make her."

I could have called my mom. She'd have come to get me. I might have had to wait an hour for her car to finish charging, but she'd have come to get me.

Instead, my dad got up from the table and walked back out to the car. I grabbed my bag and followed him. He drove me home with the top up, mad at me the whole way. I expected him to just let me out on the curb, but he walked me to the door and, when my mother answered, he smiled and they hugged and for a second everything felt like old times, so I slipped inside as fast as I could so I wouldn't mess up their flow. Before long I could hear them laughing then talking then laughing again.

I had already texted everything to my friend Luz by the time my mom came inside and sat on the edge of my bed.

"We'll discuss this tomorrow when you've had a chance to calm down and remember what kind of person you want to be."

"But, mom—"

"Tomorrow," she said.

I didn't press her. She probably would have taken my phone away. And the minute she walked out the door, Luz FaceTimed.

"They can't really be together," Luz said. There were a lot of trees in the background. I would have thought they were camping if she hadn't already texted me that they were in a giant mall in Minnesota.

"I don't know. He's being weird," I said. "He was smiling for, like, an hour straight."

"Doesn't matter. I checked all her accounts. They don't have any pictures together. No pictures, no relationship, no problem. He's probably just trying to make your mom jealous."

Luz's little brother, Miguel, shoved his face into the picture, then started doing some dance where he kept smacking his forehead.

"I gotta go," Luz said, shutting down the video on her end.

Talking to Luz made me feel better. My dad didn't need to make my mom jealous. She was already pretty miserable without him. She cried a lot, but whenever I went in to give her a hug, she pretended she wasn't crying in the first place. But you can't have allergies *all* the time.

The only time my mom ever seemed like herself was when she was with my dad. That's why I had to get them back together. I thought helping dad get his act together would be enough, but apparently it wasn't. I needed a real plan, but the only thing I could think of was the one from *The Parent Trap*. Too bad I didn't have a long-lost twin.

I checked my video views—no more since the last time—then opened my Instagram for some cute puppy action. Mistake. Sandy's name was still in my search bar. I clicked it. Of course she had uploaded a new picture. The angle made it look like it was in a jungle somewhere, but I knew it was my dad's backyard. She and my dad were leaning toward each other over the perfect pitcher of lemonade. She was feeding him a cookie and he was smiling that stupid smile again. The stupid picture didn't even have a caption, but in less than five minutes it already had 147 likes.

Love your followers. Show them the real you. Well, there was nothing more real than how mad I was right at that moment. All I wanted was to show my dad how ridiculous it was for him to be eating cookies at sunset with someone who wasn't my mom.

My camera was already set up in front of a glitter poster board. I sat down in my chair and pressed GoLive.

"Sorry, you guys. I know this isn't about makeup, but I just had to get this off my chest . . ."

My face was flushed and tingling the whole time I recorded, and the eyeliner I'd put on in the tutorial that morning was smudged, but I didn't care. I posted it before I could change my mind.

CHAPTER THREE

PETALS AND PARASOLS

The next day, a woman with a little pink umbrella showed up at my house at the crack of dawn. My mother always gets up that freakishly early, and I was up because something kept dinging even though my phone was on silent. It took me a few minutes to figure out that the sound was coming from my computer. I must have left YouTube open when I collapsed after my rant. The dinging was notifications for MakeuponetheCheapCheap. I had 81 new followers and 147 new likes, and the count kept climbing.

Pretty much all the likes were on the rant video, but my eyeliner tutorial had exactly one new like and comment from a user named _AnnieOaky_.

"New subbie here! Love your stuff. I did a vid of me doing your tutorial."

I picked up my phone and replied to _AnnieOaky_ with the link to the hug GIF I had been saving. I was so happy I could have cried.

Another ding. My follower count went up by 1, and I ran into the living room shouting, "Triple digits! I broke into the triple digits," only to realize that my mom was not sitting alone in her pajamas with a cup of tea and her journal. She was fully dressed, sitting next to a plump lady with dark brown skin and straight black hair. The lady was wearing a pink suit with a matching hat, and a pink flowered umbrella rested against one knee.

My mother was dressed, too. She had even put out an arrangement of purple flowers and put saucers under their mugs on the coffee table. It looked nice. I, on the other hand, was still wearing the same jeans and T-shirt I had worn to my dad's house, my hair was all stiff and smushy because I had fallen asleep without a satin scarf, and I was pretty sure the right side of my face was plastered with drool.

"Sorry. I didn't know you had company," I said.

The two of them stood up, the pink lady rising so gracefully that she didn't disturb her umbrella.

My mom gestured toward the guest. "Actually, she came to see you, Hasani. I wasn't going to wake you, but since you're up, this is Aimee Lafleur. She's from Les Belles Demoiselles: Pensionnat des Sorcières in Vacherie."

I raised an eyebrow. My mom spoke French?

"Belles Demoiselles is a finishing school for talented young ladies like you," Miss Lafleur said. "I came to offer you a position in our program this summer."

I blinked. Even in English it didn't make sense. Me? Talented? I was good at a lot of stuff—math, comics, finding my mom's keys—but nothing you would call a talent except . . .

"Like, for makeup?" I blurted out. Miss Lafleur had seen my eyeliner video.

"For magic," my mom said. She said it gently, like maybe I might be afraid or something, but legit, I was thinking what a shame it was that she wasn't there because of my Dollar Store Eyeliner 101 video. Miss Lafleur's makeup was perfect, but she was probably using really expensive products. It's hard to get perfectly smooth lines when you're working with stuff from the dollar store, and I can do it pretty much every time. Skillz, yo. The trick is you have to kind of roll it around in your hand to warm it up, but leave the cap on until—

"Hasani." My mom's voice popped me out of my eyeliner reverie. "I just want to make sure you understand that Miss Lafleur isn't talking about pulling a rabbit out of a hat. Belles Demoiselles isn't like circus camp for stage magicians."

"I beg to differ," Miss Lafleur said smoothly. "Our girls can do anything they choose to. If Hasani wants to be a stage artist or street performer, that would be entirely up to her."

"Yes," my mom said, "but my point is that Miss Lafleur isn't talking about sleight of hand. She says you can do real magic."

My mom was holding my hands, looking into my eyes. I was looking back at her, but I wasn't.

Real? Magic?

I shook my head. Separately those word made sense, but together? Nothing.

"I'm still trying to wrap my head around it, too, but Miss Lafleur showed me some videos and you should see them, too."

Miss Lafleur pulled an iPad out of a purse that looked too small to hold it, tapped the screen, and showed it to me. "Yesterday, our satellites picked up an impressive display on St. Claude Avenue."

I looked down at the screen the fancy pink lady was holding in front of me. It was a bird's-eye view of a bunch of cars driving. The footage was good. Better than Google Earth. But it didn't look like it had anything to do with me. Then I spotted my dad's convertible rolling up to the St. Claude Avenue Bridge. With the top down, I could see both of us as clear as if I were sitting there.

"Your school has drones?" I said, mostly to stop myself from getting mad at my dad all over again.

"No, but our satellite images are quite sophisticated. Take a look again with these."

She handed me a pair of rose-colored glasses and played the video back again. Everything in the video looked black and white except for a bright purple spot in my dad's car and another one on the bridge.

"The amethyst aura you see is your magic at work. Our satellite imagery clearly shows your magic acting on a bridge that is still quite a distance ahead. There is no mistaking it. Hasani, you are a witch."

I stared back at the screen, dumbstruck. The purple spot in the car was me.

Miss Lafleur kept going like what she was saying was the most normal thing ever. "We were quite surprised as well. You must be quite a powerful little witch for your aura to be so bright without algorithmic enhancement. There are many magic users in the area, of course. Most of whom don't know they're using magic at all. It creates a lot of noise in the system, so we've been training our technology to differentiate between incidental low-level magic users and witches."

"What's the difference?" I asked.

"We call low-level magic users kismets. While it is technically magic, a kismet is essentially good luck. Unlike witches, they can't use it intentionally to change the world around them. Mind you, even witches can't do the impossible. I like to call witchcraft the art of the improbable." Miss Lafleur laughed. I guess she had made a joke? I didn't get it, but her laughter was the kind that makes you laugh along with her. "Apparently, it took several hours to clear all the flowers and vines and get the bridge back in working order, so I'd certainly say that you can affect the world around you. Had you ingested anything? Herbal tea, perhaps?"

I pulled out my phone and googled the St. Claude bridge. It was all over the news. TikTok. YouTube. Instagram. Honestly, I might have thought that was fake if I hadn't also had a text from Luz.

Yo!!! Did you see the vine thing? New Orleans summer is NO JOKE. Good thing you didn't get stuck at your dad's.

Luz sent a link, too, to some kids who went live on the levee watching the workers pull the vines out of the bridge. Even on the video Luz sent, the vines glowed when I looked at them through the pink glasses. That's when I knew something was up.

"How do you know it was me?" I asked. I was looking at Miss Lafleur, trying to see if I could see a glow on her, but there was nothing besides the hint of sparkle in her foundation.

Miss Lafleur smiled. "We were fairly certain from the satellite images, but this clinched it."

A few taps later, Miss Lafleur had pulled up my YouTube rant. Had my mom already watched this? I felt the heat rising in my cheeks, but that time it wasn't magic; it was just plain old embarrassment. I purposefully kept my eyes glued to the screen and off my mom's face. Thankfully, the volume was turned off.

"Pay careful attention to the plant on the table to your left."

It was hard to look away from myself yelling. Did I really look like that? I looked bad, even through the rose-colored glasses that added a magic glow on my skin. But when I tore away from the horror that was my face, I saw the plant Miss Lafleur was talking about. It was the rosemary plant my mom kept sneaking into my room to "cleanse the air." I must have bumped the camera when I sat down, because it shouldn't have been in the shot, but it was and it was glowing, too. And growing. Like, a lot. When the video started, it was about the size of my hand. By the end, it was the size of my head and covered in flowers. Purple flowers.

I looked down at the coffee table. My mom hadn't made a flower arrangement at the crack of dawn to make our coffee table fancy enough for this fancy lady. She had gotten it from my room to check Miss Lafleur's story.

I looked at the plant, rubbing the stiff leaves between my fingers. Same pot, and the flowers didn't budge, but there was no mistaking the rosemary smell on my fingertips or the faint trace of amethyst aura. It was on the flowers and leaves and on my hands, too. I pulled the glasses off. The glow on my hands disappeared, but the weird feeling in my stomach didn't.

"You're saying I did this?"

Miss Lafleur nodded.

"And I stopped a bridge? With magic?"

"Yes. The art of the improbable in action. And you are capable of much more. I understand it may come as a shock, Hasani. It was quite surprising to us as well. It is unusual for such a strong display to come from a child whose family has no real witching legacy, but that is precisely why we felt it was so imperative that we step in. Without someone in your immediate family to guide you, in some ways a school is even more important for you than it is for any of the other girls who will attend."

I looked at my mom. She looked almost as confused as I did. Like she had a thousand questions, a thousand things on her mind that needed answering.

Then my phone dinged. It must not have been the first time, but it was the first time I heard it. The notification banner said I had 87 new likes and 47 new followers just since I had been standing there. It was unreal. No. It was magic.

I stuck the phone in my pocket. "Tell me about the school?" I said, plopping down on the couch. My mom sat with me. "Bell Dimwazell, right?" I didn't speak French, but I tried to copy the way my mom had said it. She sounded so smooth.

Miss Lafleur sat, too, using the lightest touch on her pink umbrella to keep it in place. "As I was saying before, Belles Demoiselles is a finishing school for talented young ladies."

"Witches," I said, squeezing my mom's hand.

"Yes, but only the most talented of witches. For generations, Belles Demoiselles has been one of the finest, most sought-after programs in the world."

"Like Hogwarts?" I said.

Miss Lafleur's smile froze but only for a second. "That is fictional. And in England. Belles Demoiselles is right here in Louisiana. In Vacherie. I understand from your mother that you have family in Vacherie?"

At the mention of Vacherie, my mom looked a little more like herself. "My mother was born there," she said. "She grew up here in New Orleans, but we still have family in Vacherie."

Miss Lafleur's smile warmed up again. "Good. It might make you more comfortable to send her knowing you have family nearby. We're very proud of our Vacherie connection, and along with that we're very proud to have the most selective finishing school for witches in the country right here in Louisiana. We have no application. Offers are by invitation only and there is quite a lengthy waiting list, but we're bypassing that waiting list to offer you a place. If you accept it, you'll find there's no better way to hone your magic. Everything is already arranged. Since your family has not had time to financially prepare for your attendance, we are offering you a full scholarship, including room, board, and supplies. Term is typically six weeks and it begins in three days."

I looked at my mom, but she was already looking at me.

I took a deep breath. It all sounded too good to be true. "So, I just go and learn about magic and my mom doesn't have to pay anything and that's it? There's no, like, blood pact or vow of silence or anything?"

"You are free to talk about Belles Demoiselles with your immediate family but, due to the selective and delicate nature of our program and admissions process, we would require that you not mention the school or any of your studies in public. That's it."

I'm not gonna lie. I was really nervous. I had a good vibe off Miss Lafleur and, honestly, my mom must have, too, or she never would have made it into our living room. The thing that made me nervous was that if I went, I'd have to do whatever I did to the bridge again, and I didn't know what I had done in the first place. But that's the point of school, right? To teach you stuff you can't figure out on your own?

"OK. I'll go," I said.

"Are you sure?" my mom said.

"I can leave and give the two of you some time to discuss it in private," Miss Lafleur said, putting a hand on her umbrella.

"That's OK," I said before my mom could say something different. "It's like you said. If I have magic, it would be stupid of me to not learn how to use it. I want to go. I want to go to Bell Dimwazell."

My mom nodded when I said that, but I knew she'd probably be crying the second I walked out the door. I squeezed her hand. With me gone, she didn't have anyone, not even my dad. I expected her to say no or at least look concerned about me leaving, but she squeezed my hand right back and said, "Six weeks? I guess I can part with you for that long."

That's when I hugged her. Like a for real, tackle hug. She really was the best. And six weeks wasn't all that long. I'd be back before her birthday, before Luz got back from Minnesota. I'd probably be back before my dad even realized that I was gone now that Sandy was there grinning in his face.

"Should we call your dad?" my mom said, standing up to get her phone.

"No. I'll do it," I said, pulling my phone out of my pocket. My mom would be too nice and we'd end up talking to him for, like, twenty minutes. The last thing I wanted to do was talk to him after he had basically declared his undying love for Sandy on the Internet.

Going to camp, I texted. He didn't need to know any more than that. Then, because apparently I love torturing myself, I opened up Sandy's Instagram page again. The pic of her in my dad's yard was gone. Gone. That right there is when I knew that my magic was real. That picture probably had thousands of likes on it. Sandy wouldn't have deleted it, but it was gone. I must have done that with my magic, and I didn't even know what I was doing. Imagine what I could do if I learned.

"So, you agree to the terms?" Miss Lafleur said, waking up her iPad again.

"Yes," I said.

Miss Lafleur smiled. "Then let's make it official. Nailah?" She showed my mom a QR code.

"Oh, right. I guess a minor can't really enter into a legal agreement. Do I sign with my finger, or . . . ?"

"This is more of a pre-agreement. You'll sign the official document when you're on campus. You're not allergic to cats, are you?"

"Cats? No." My mom shook her head.

"Verbal agreements are technically binding, but we do like to back it up with something a little more solid. Scan here, please. Mother first, then daughter."

Miss Lafleur held out her iPad. My mom had to get up and get her phone anyway, and I talked her through opening her photo app and lining up the focus. Then I did the same on my phone. There was a chime, and Miss Lafleur's smile softened even more. She looked just like Glinda in *The Wiz*, only browner.

"There now," she said. "That is so much neater than it was when I was a girl. And painless, too. Welcome to Belles Demoiselles, Hasani."

The idea of it really washed over me. Magic! I didn't know what else it could do, but MakeupontheCheapCheap would probably have a million subscribers by the end of summer, not a hundred.

Maybe I'd even get to meet AnyaDo0dle. We could partner up. Swap makeup routines.

I was smiling so big I probably looked like AnyaDo0dle had asked me to take a selfie.

Miss Lafleur beamed. Her lipstick was the perfect shade. Petal Pink.

"I am so happy you'll be joining us. You'll be an excellent addition. A car can come to collect you any time from today at noon to three o'clock on Sunday."

"Today is Friday!" my mother said, suddenly looking to-do-list frantic.

"It's fine, Mom. I can go at three o'clock on Sunday."

My mom looked relieved. "We just have so much to do, and I'll need some time to get her packed and—"

"I understand." Miss Lafleur rose from her seat. "I'll leave you to it. Sunday at three o'clock. Please do not be late."

Miss Lafleur left with a nod that bordered on a curtsy, and my mom hugged me tighter than she had in a long time. I thought she was going to say "I love you," but what she really said was, "If you're going to be gone for more than a month, I guess I have to braid your hair," which, honestly, is pretty much the same thing.

CHAPTER FOUR

MINT AND MISGIVINGS

My mom agreeing to braid my hair was a minor miracle, but before I tried to talk her into using actual braiding hair instead of just braiding my own, I needed to tell Luz what was going on. Not about the magic stuff. Luz is family, but since we're not actually related, I was guessing she wouldn't have counted as a person I could tell about Belles Demoiselles. I couldn't have told her about that anyway, at least not until she got back. "I can do magic" is kind of a ridiculous thing to say and, unless Luz could look me in the eye in person while I said it, she was definitely going to think I was messing with her, and Luz HATES when people mess with her. So I was only going to say that I was going to summer camp after all, but I didn't get the chance to because when I unlocked my phone, there was a long beep. I thought for a second that it was a flash flood warning or tornado watch or something. It was coming from my mom's phone, too. But instead of it flashing a message about severe weather, the screen filled with flowers and a single instruction: Swipe right.

When your phone tells you to do stuff, you do it. I swiped right before I even thought about it. Sky blue flowers danced and flowed and reformed into a kind of a silhouette like the ones on those old-timey brooches. Words appeared underneath the figure and my phone read them out. "Miss Villere," it said. It was Siri, but my Siri was set to an Australian guy because, I mean, that's funny, right? But in that moment I wished I hadn't done that, because when Siri said vill-er-ee I didn't know if that was how it was supposed to be pronounced or just his accent. My Siri couldn't say Tchoupitoulas right, and that street was two blocks from my house.

The flowers moved and reformed and turned a shade of pink for Miss Lafleur. Well, I had met her, so I knew Siri said that one right. The silhouette kind of looked like her. Then came Miss Lavande, whose flowers were all lavender, Miss LeBrun, whose petals were a golden bronze, and Miss LaRose, whose petals were all white.

It went fast, so fast that the whole thing sounded like one smooth sentence. "Miss Villere, Miss Lafleur, Miss Lavande, Miss LeBrun, and Miss LaRose welcome you to Belles Demoiselles, Hasani, la première pensionnat des sorcières."

My name was spelled in vines, but it faded into a house shape covered in birds and flowers and honeybees. It was so dope that I didn't even think to take a screenshot until right at the very end. That was mistake one.

"Screenshots and other functions have been temporarily disabled in accordance with our privacy policy. Full functionality will be restored at the close of this message. Do you wish to proceed?"

I tapped yes and, no joke, words started scrolling up the screen like the opening of *Star Wars*, but double time. The font was prettier, but still. It was way too fast for me to read. I was just catching things here and there.

- **Those with cat allergies should not enter the main campus.**
- **Cell phones and other devices are permitted.**
- **Magical enhancements strictly prohibited.**
- **Maintain appearance of hair and clothing.**
- **Be courteous.**

For every sentence I caught, there were at least five I missed. Some of what I caught weren't even whole sentences, but they were obviously important stuff, so I tapped the screen to pause the scrolling. It kept going, so I kept staring at it while I tried to make it to my room without tripping. Harder than it seems. I caught glimpses of things like "on gold" and "showcase" and "qualifying exam" as I grabbed a marker. My walls were covered in list paper. I needed to take notes. But by the time I got the cap off the marker, the message was over.

Breathe, Hasani, I said to myself. No one can read that fast. It's definitely going to play again.

It didn't play again.

I tapped. I double tapped. I pinched. I spread. I even shut the stupid phone off and turned it on again. Nothing.

My mom, who had stayed put where she was in the living room, had had better luck than me. Apparently, she got the same message. Well, not the same message. Hers was for parents. The same kind of message. And for the next three days, she kept dropping things about Belles Demoiselles, almost like she was fan-girling.

Mom: Did you know seventeen senators and at least one queen of England have been Belles Demoiselles?

Me: Uh-hunh.

Mom: They didn't name them of course.

Me: Of course.

Or—

Mom: It's so good that they invite parents to the closing ceremony. As long as you're not allergic to cats, of course.

Me: Of course.

Sometimes I asked her to clarify. Most times, I didn't. She'd asked me to tell her what was on my message a bunch of times, but the only thing I could remember were the names at the beginning. I don't know why I remembered Miss Villere, but Lafleur, Lavande, LeBrun, and LaRose sounded like the components of a bomb eye shadow palette.

My mom wasn't into makeup, though, so she wouldn't have cared about any of that. She was really getting excited about the whole me-being-a-witch thing, and I didn't want to squash her spirit. I especially didn't want to tell her that no matter how many times I'd tried to make the magic happen again, I couldn't. Even my YouTube follows had slacked off. I was up to 213, but by Saturday night I had practically forgotten what a follower notification sounded like. No magic, no follows.

So when I was on hour four of sitting on the floor to get my hair braided and my butt hurt and I couldn't get my mom to put on something for us to listen to that wasn't Sweet Honey in the Rock, and my mom mentioned for the umpteenth time that it didn't matter what Miss Lafleur said, magic did run in our family because, "according to the history in the parent information," Vacherie had a long history of people who could do magic and, even though I'd only been to Vacherie a few times, it was obviously in my blood, and didn't I remember that time my grandmother had left a gallon of milk in the car overnight in August and it hadn't even spoiled, I snapped.

"Those are all kismets, Mom. It's just luck. At best. It's probably just coincidence."

You know how they say, it's not your words, it's your tone? Well, it wasn't my words. It was my tone. My mom stopped with the comb mid-part. Then she was quiet. Real quiet. Long enough for me to get nervous. But when she finally talked, she surprised me again.

"You're worried that you're not really a witch," she said. "You're worried you can't do it again."

Instant tears from me. Not, like, boohoo crying, but I definitely couldn't have wiped them away without her seeing.

I don't know why I was surprised that she wasn't mad and yelling at me for being flip or disrespectful. My mom never yelled, at least not by raising her voice, and she was always doing stuff like this: saying exactly what I was thinking but was afraid to say. She says it comes from being a parent and knowing a person from before they could really know themselves, but every time she did it, everything I was trying to keep inside would just come pouring out of me. This time was just the same.

I told her everything. How I had been trying to make things happen with my magic ever since I found out. How I hadn't had a single new subscriber. How I didn't want to leave her alone. How magic was one thing, but I was sure everyone else there had to be speed-reader super-geniuses, because otherwise why would they have made the welcome message go so fast and then disappear?

I told her everything. Well, almost everything. I didn't say anything about my dad, but, honestly, I just wasn't thinking about him. He had his thing. I had mine.

"Oh, baby. I couldn't read all of the parent message, either."

"You read more than me," I mumbled, "and I'm supposed to be the witch. What if this whole thing was just a big mistake?"

"You know what?" my mom said, but she didn't finish the thought. She got up and left me there with the comb still wedged into my hair and came back with two cups of tea and THE PLANT. The rosemary plant that was huge and covered in flowers because of my magic.

"The more I think about it, the more I realize that this is a gift, Hasani. You are gifted. They wouldn't have found you and given you a place in their school if you weren't. I already knew you were special. Now they know it, too. But the real question is, do you?"

My tea was minty and supersweet, just the way I like it. I gulped it down, let out a minty breath, and reached for my phone. There was a ding. My follower count had gone up to 214.

CHAPTER FIVE

HEARTS AND SWANS

My braids came out exactly like I wanted them. Well, not exactly-exactly. If we had had time, I would have asked to go to a real salon to get microbraids like a bunch of the girls at my school had, but even if my mom could have magicked up an appointment, microbraids take forever to do and we didn't have that much time. Instead, my mom braided my hair into cornrows with the braiding hair I managed to talk her into using so they would go all the way down to my butt. My mom is a short Afro, no makeup person, so she didn't love the idea of the fake hair—or my YouTube channel, for that matter—but she let me go with both when I said it was part of my "art." Art was something my mom did understand.

After my hair was done, we only had a couple of hours left to finish packing. My mom was worried about the laundry, so we packed way more T-shirts than I could wear in a whole summer, along with shorts, jeans, and a sundress. The sundress was a compromise. My mom wanted to pack the sparkly purple dress I'd worn to my friend Julie's bat mitzvah. I didn't. That dress had long sleeves. No one with half a brain would wear anything besides shorts, maybe jeans, and a T-shirt in the summer. A cute T-shirt for sure. I usually ironed mine and made sure I had earrings and lip gloss to match, but still a T-shirt. My mom insisted I pack something fancy anyway, "just in case." We settled on the sundress, but I was mainly concerned about saving enough room in my suitcase for my makeup, camera, lighting kit, backdrops, laptop, and emergency hard drive. My mother had other ideas. Every time I put something in, she took something out.

"Mom, I need this," I said, putting my tripod in for, like, the eleventh time.

"You need bug spray," she said, taking my tripod out and putting a bottle of citronella bug repellent in its place. "YouTube can wait. It's only a few weeks."

YouTube couldn't wait. So what if my channel wasn't growing as fast as it did with my magical rant? I had posted a video every day since, and somehow after my mom and I talked, I had gotten 17 new followers. Magic or not, there was no way I was abandoning it. It was the one good thing I had going.

I didn't say any of that, though. What I said was, "It's a camp. They probably have bug spray."

"It's a summer school for gifted young ladies," my mom corrected, "and even if they do, theirs probably has DEET in it."

I knew better than to argue with my mom when there were chemicals involved. She was so all-natural that I'm pretty sure my first word was "organic."

By the time we were done packing, she had filled my suitcase and hers with towels, bathing suits, water shoes, organic lemon-citronella insect repellent, a sewing kit, a first aid kit, and bags of dried fruit and raw nuts in case I got hungry. Thankfully, I had a portable ring light and tripod for my phone from when I was first trying to figure out my YouTube setup. They weren't as good as my studio setup, but they were good enough. I had the two videos I'd already scheduled to auto-post, and after that I'd just have to do it vlog style from my phone. My rant video was my most popular one, anyway.

On Sunday, a black limousine arrived exactly at three o'clock. There was a driver in a uniform and everything. His name was Mr. Paul and he carried my bags and held the door open for me to get in. My mom cried and hugged me and cried and apologized about a thousand times for holding us up.

"I'll follow you in Daisy," my mom said, kissing the top of my head. "I just hope they have somewhere for me to plug her in when we get there."

Daisy was my mom's electric car. It got seventy miles to a charge, which was great for the city, but not so good for road trips.

"I can bring you back whenever you're ready," Mr. Paul said. He didn't smile, but he didn't seem unfriendly, either.

"I wouldn't want to trouble you," my mom said.

"No trouble at all, ma'am. That's my job."

My mom ran to pull her suitcase out of Daisy's hatchback. Mr. Paul was there in a flash, taking her suitcase from her. "I think you'll be more comfortable in the car, ma'am. Leave this to me."

She did an airflip of her hair before climbing in next to me. I laughed. She was carrying the rosemary plant, which I was pretty sure I didn't need, but she seemed so happy I didn't want to spoil it. She was so happy, in fact, that I took advantage and got her to take a selfie with me. I even got her to poke her head into the mini-vlog I recorded in the car. It was only for a second, but still. It was my first one. Second, if you counted the rant—but I didn't. That was more of a confessional. A popular confessional. It had almost 10,000 views and I was up to 233 subscribers. I didn't think my car vlog would do as well, but it felt profesh to tell my followers about my temporary switch to vlog style. Some of them might even care that I was on my way to "summer camp." And of course I included a shout-out to _AnnieOaky_ for being my first commenter.

I uploaded the video, set it to auto-post, and checked to see if my dad had answered my text. He hadn't, but Luz had sent me a pic of her and her brother on a roller coaster. Sandy had posted a new picture, but it was an old picture—#flashbackfriday—of her in a bikini top and shorts holding a sun hat on her head with one hand and a garden spade in the other. I doubt whatever was going on was funny enough for her to be laughing so hard. The new caption said, "Getting in the mood. 'Tis the season! #blackgirlgreenthumb #gardening #greengoddess #fbf," and it had 1,142 likes. I closed my phone. The signal was bad, anyway. I'd watch the scenery.

When my family left the city, we usually took the interstate. Mr. Paul didn't. He started out on River Road, a street I had been on a thousand times, but then we were driving and driving, and everything started looking different. I had no idea River Road went so far. It took us from our house in the city all the way out to the country. The river was right next to us, but I couldn't see it unless we were crossing a bridge. We passed giant plantations I had double-toured—once on field trips and again with my family when my parents corrected whatever history the tour guides had taught us—until we turned away from the river, down a road that was barely a road with enormous fields of grassy bamboo on both sides.

"Sugarcane," my mom said. She was only half talking to me, but I was glad she said it because . . . duh. Sugarcane. How many times had my mom and dad, separately and together, told me about how many of our family members had been forced to work and grow that stuff? It looked peaceful, though. Beautiful, even, once I knew it wasn't an overgrown lawn.

Despite all my parents' history talks about American and Creole plantations, none of which were what you would call "happy," I was a little disappointed when the car didn't stop in front of one of those enormous houses on the main road. We slowed in front of what I already knew was a Creole cottage. I recognized it as a Creole cottage because my grandmother lived in one before she died and this little house had the same pointy roof and barely any front porch. Mr. Paul stopped right alongside a ditch. The house wasn't shabby or anything, but it did not look like it should have a limousine parked out front, let alone a row of other fancy cars that filled the space next to us. It did look like it should have a ditch.

"I'll wait right here for you, ma'am. Sorry I can't help you in. Young ladies and family only," he said after he helped us get our bags and plant situated.

It took only a few seconds for the summer heat to eat away the cool left over from the car's air-conditioning. Little beads of sweat were popping out along my hairline as I silently prayed the little cottage had central air. A little cottage was one thing. A little cottage without air-conditioning was too much.

My mom squeezed my hand. "You belong here, you know. You might have been born in New Orleans, but you're from here. All that Back Vacherie magic is inside you. Remember that."

I nodded, trying to decide how to stop the suitcases from flipping on the gravel walkway. At least it wasn't far. I walked forward, awkwardly gripping the handle of the big suitcase with one hand while I tried to hold my mom's elbow with the other. The next thing I knew, there was something sliding over my face. I thought it was a spiderweb and dropped the suitcase and my mom's arm to swipe it out of the way. Whatever it was, it was impossible to see, just like a spiderweb, but it was too thick and heavy to be one. More like if Spanish moss and velvet curtains had a baby. I felt it swing closed behind me, but I was still flailing my arms around, trying to figure out what had attacked me, when my mom put her hand on my back and said, "Hasani, look."

The first thing I noticed was my mom pulling all the suitcases while still cradling the rosemary in the crook of one arm. The second thing I noticed was that it wasn't hot, not even a little. The air was cool and dry with the softest, gentlest breeze. No spiderwebs in sight. I looked up to see where the cool air was coming from. One of those misting fans like they have at Disney World, maybe? And that's when I saw the house. It was four stories tall with long windows and balconies like iron flowers and a porch that wrapped all the way around and a perfect arrangement of clouds behind it sparkling in the afternoon light. As if on cue, the clouds let loose a light, glittery rain.

"No. Way." I said. "Is that a rainbow?"

One rainbow? Cool. Two rainbows? Really cool. A rainbow that arched from one cloud to another, perfectly framing the house at the end of the walk? Possible—but probably magic. I pulled my phone out to take a video of myself with the house and the rainbow in the background, but my arms weren't long enough to get all of it in the shot, and I needed to see it all. It was totally going to look photoshopped and I was living for it.

My mom frowned at me.

"I'm not gonna to post it. I just want to show dad later," I said. Not true. Until I saw the look on my mom's face, my dad was the furthest possible thing from my mind. "Miss Lafleur said I could share with family."

"She said 'discuss,' not video. They're clearly trying to keep this place hidden. Don't get sent home before you even get inside, Hasani."

I looked back. There was a faint shimmer between us and the limousine, like patches of wavy light on the highway when it's sunny but all in a straight line.

"You're right, Mom," I said. If I couldn't get any shots of where I was, I needed to change strategies for my channel. Mentally I adjusted my checklist from vlogging to confessionals. No problem. My subscribers would understand.

"Good girl," my mom said, squeezing my hand again.

It wasn't a good sign that I was about to mess up before I had even walked in the door, but I tried not to let it get to me. I'm not gonna lie—my hands were shaking as we walked toward the house. I couldn't believe it was real. My mom just squeezed tighter as we walked under the pink magnolia trees that arched overhead, shading us from both sides. Every one of those flowers was in perfect bloom. I looked at the plant my mom was carrying, the one I had made bloom with my magic. It looked stupid and messy.

I stopped. "Mom. What if I'm not a good witch?" I said.

She stopped and turned to look me straight in the eye. "You're already a good witch. You have nothing to do but be you. I'm not worried."

"You're not?" I said. My voice was smaller than I expected.

"If you weren't already a good witch, they never would have found you."

I nodded, but it must not've been convincing because my mom kept talking.

"Listen to me, Hasani. Your magic is not a fluke. I don't care what Miss Lafleur says. Our family is from right here where this school was founded. That's not an accident, and neither is your magic. So what if you're the first witch in the family. Somebody had to be first, right? I bet you're the best witch in here. And here's the proof," she said, turning her body so the rosemary was front and center.

I nodded again. She was right. Or at least I wanted her to be.

There was a chime, and the rainbow disappeared right before we walked inside.

"Bienvenue aux Belles Demoiselles: Pensionnat des Sorcières. You must be Hasani," a woman in a lavender suit said as soon as we walked inside.

"And you must be Miss Lavande," I said. She had to be. In the intro video, Miss Lavande was the only one with purple flowers, and this woman's suit was the exact same shade but with just a touch of shimmer.

"I am," Miss Lavande smiled, tucking a wispy blonde curl behind one ear. "Someone's been doing her homework."

I smiled, too, but it felt more like a sigh of relief. This was going better than I thought it would.

"This must be your mother, Nailah. I've heard so much about you both and this powerful signature flower of Hasani's. Stopping bridges. My, my."

My mom smiled, holding the rosemary plant up so Miss Lavande could see all the flowers in the light. The entryway was already filled with flowers, some in vases, some climbing up the walls and hanging from the ceiling. My little rosemary looked sad next to all that, but Miss Lavande smiled right back.

"Impressive," she said. "We're very excited to have you with us, Hasani. May I show you up to your room?"

"I don't see any other children around," my mom cut in nervously. "Are we the first ones here?"

"Oh heavens, no. It's several minutes past chimes. All the other girls are getting ready for our welcome soiree. You'll see some of them when we go upstairs."

For the record, stairs and wheels do not go together. That includes suitcase wheels. Miss Lavande led us up a staircase with mossy carpet and white flowers growing all along the banister. My mom couldn't balance all the suitcases going up the stairs, so she gave me the smallest one. It was way heavier than I remembered and made a loud clunk on the first step, which, honestly, scared the heck out of me, a butterfly, and three tiny birds that I had no idea were loose inside the house. They kind of blended in with the flowers and, if the butterfly had flown away like the birds did, everything would have been fine. Unfortunately, the butterfly had other ideas. It flapped right in front of my face. I leaned back, not wanted to inhale it or have it land on me or something, which knocked me backward off the step. The suitcase landed on its side while I was still holding on to it and somehow managed to get tangled up in my braids on the way down, so when my mom and Miss Lavande looked back, I was bent over sideways trying to get the handle of the suitcase to let go of my hair.

"I should have warned you that there are pollinators through-out the house and grounds," Miss Lavande said patiently. Maybe too patiently. "I forget that you've come to us from the inner city. Pollina-tors help the flowers grow."

I don't know if I would have called where we lived the "inner city," but whatever. We had a container garden at our Uptown house, and I definitely wasn't afraid of some tiny birds and a butterfly. I just hadn't expected them inside, that was all.

"I'm OK," I said, smiling so she'd know I meant it.

Miss Lavande nodded and continued up the stairs. My mom raised her eyebrows like, *you want me to take the suitcase?* I pulled my braids around to the front, fixed the suitcase, and started back up the stairs, which meant, *nah, I got this.*

More pollinators flew out with every clunk, but since I knew what to expect, I could now notice their beauty. The birds and the butter-flies both seemed to land on flowers the same color as they were. It was forever before I realized that the walls behind the flowers were white, because there were so many colors flying around.

"This is the residence hall," Miss Lavande said, leading us down a long hallway on the third floor. It was just as colorful as the staircase, but instead of butterflies, it was the doors that did it. They were all double doors with flowers across the top, but each side had a different color and flower.

"Here we have daisies and peonies, lavender and roses, Louisiana irises and fleurs-de-lis, silver bells and passionflowers. Yours is room ten, but as soon as you settle in, we can call it its proper name."

A few of the girls looked up when we passed their rooms. One smiled and gave a little wave. I smiled back, then turned back to Miss Lavande. She had stopped in front of a set of double doors that was not like the rest. One side of it had a hint of yellow, but the other side was just plain wood.

"The color will change when it accepts your voice key," Miss Lavande said. "No one else will be able to open your door once it's set. Just hold the handle and say the name of your signature flower."

My heart fluttered as I put my hand on the knob. "Rosemary," I said. For the first time since my YouTube rant, I felt the tingle of magic rising to my skin. Nothing happened.

Miss Lavande wrinkled her forehead, but my mom nodded and smiled, so I did it again.

"Rosemary flowers," I said, thinking maybe I needed to be specific, like when they make you put uppercase letters in your password. The tingle came again, but still, nothing happened.

"This is a rosemary plant. It would ordinarily grow a rosemary flower but, thanks to your extraordinary interference, the flower growing on it is a morning glory." Ms. Lavande said it slowly, like maybe we didn't speak the same language.

My mom stared at me and nodded like I was already supposed to know.

"Morning glories are quite common in the city, so I thought you would have been familiar with them," Miss Lavande said. "Not to worry. Just try again."

The heat of embarrassment rushed to my cheeks, but I tried not to let it show. "Morning glories," I said, my skin tingling. The wood blushed bluish purple on my side of the door and the side that was already a little yellow got brighter and brighter. The tingle of magic turned into a buzz and leaves began to grow at the top of the door until I felt a little pop and the tingling stopped. I smiled up at the door, relieved my magic was back again. On the yellow side, the cutest little yellow flowers were mixed with the leaves. On the purple side, there was only a vine. A scraggly one at that.

I blinked. "There aren't any flowers on it. Maybe I said the wrong key?" A little bit of magic still tingled in my cheeks and fingertips.

"The flowers will grow in the next hour or two. These things take time, my dear. In the meantime, let's take a look inside, shall we?"

I opened the door just a crack. A breeze oozed out, ruffling the hair on my neck. It was soft and cool like the one outside, and when I opened the door all the way, I knew why. My room had a balcony, and the balcony doors were open, letting that delicious outside air in.

"It's beautiful," I said, my mouth hanging open, but I wasn't talking about the room. The view was magic. I was magic. The whole place was magic. My mom was right. I did belong at Belles Demoiselles.

"We hoped you would enjoy it. Your room offers a spectacular view of the grounds," Miss Lavande said. But I had already dropped my suitcase and run out onto the balcony to see for myself. The Japanese magnolia walkway looked even more perfect, and there was a pond we hadn't seen, with swans swimming on the surface.

"Mom! The swans are doing the heart neck thing! This place is amazing," I said. I was really thinking, "this place is markers, not crayons," but since even I didn't know why I thought that, I didn't think anyone else would get it, either.

"Swans are Miss Lafleur's specialty. You met her a few days ago, but you'll get to spend more time with her in Animal Affinities."

I mentally took note. Since the only thing I really remembered from the welcome video was the teachers' names, I was determined to remember as much info as I could.

"Usually, that swan formation signals the dinner hour," Miss Lavande continued, "but tonight is a special night. We're having a sunset social in the garden so all you girls can get to know one another. Celeste will tell you all about it, won't you, Celeste?"

Celeste?

I looked back into the room. There was a girl with fluffy reddish-brown hair and medium brown skin sitting on one of the beds. She was wearing shorts and a yellow T-shirt with a headband to match. The headband was the same color as the tassels on her throw pillows, which were the same color as the flowers on the bedspread and the curtain hanging on her side of the room. I don't know how I missed her.

"Buttercups?" I guessed, feeling bad that I had rushed right past her. The flowers above the door weren't daisies, and buttercups were the only yellow flowers I knew the name of.

"Yes, that's one name for it, but I like 'coyote's eyes' better," Celeste said.

"That's cool," I said. Understatement. Coyote's eyes was an insanely cool name for a flower. "Mine's the morning glory," I said, glad my flower wasn't something plain-sounding like lavender and relieved that I figured out the right name for it before I met this girl.

"I know," she said, nodding toward the plant my mom was still holding. We both smiled. She seemed nice.

Then she turned to Miss Lavande. "I know I'm supposed to show the new girl around, but I didn't know she'd get here so late and I already promised Angelique that we could get ready for the soiree together. She said she'd do my makeup."

"Oh! I could help you with your makeup," I said, rummaging through a suitcase to find the Ziplock bag of makeup I had packed. "I have a YouTube channel. MakeupontheCheapCheap."

The tweezers had poked a hole in the side of the bag, but the hole wasn't that big, so I just shoved them back in.

Celeste smiled. "I already promised Angelique. You might not have enough time, anyway. Looks like you have a lot of unpacking to do."

"I have time. My mom already did my hair and she's staying, so she'll help me unpack, right, Mom?"

"Your mom is staying?" The shock in Celeste's voice said that, no matter what the school's rules were, moms definitely did not stay.

"Just to help her unpack," my mom said.

I looked up at her, alarmed. I knew she wanted to stay. She always wanted to stay. I didn't blame her. Our house was little, but it still felt extra empty when you were there all by yourself, especially now that Dad was gone.

My mom gave me a look, angling her eyebrows toward the balcony. I looked out past the swans and the trees to the curtain on the edge of the grounds. It looked like lace the way the light folded together, but you could still see the road on the other side of it. There was only one car left. All the others had gone.

"Since we were coming late, I thought I would stay just long enough to help Hasani get settled in. Now, tell me your name again?"

"Celeste."

"Well, Celeste, you go ahead and meet your friend. You and Hasani will have plenty of time to get to know each other now that you're roommates."

"Thank you," Celeste said to my mom, grabbing a yellow bag off a hook by the door. "See you later?" she said to me.

I smiled and nodded, but I had no idea what was going on. My mom cleared it up when Celeste closed the door.

"None of the other parents are staying?" my mom said to Miss Lavande. "The message said that parents could stay."

"And you can. Parents usually come early and stay a day or so to get the girls settled, but most leave before the term officially begins. It was all in the welcome materials."

"Oh. I didn't realize." My mom looked awkward. I guess she didn't catch as much of that welcome video as I thought.

"Not to worry," Miss Lavande said. "Most of the families at Belles Demoiselles have been coming here for generations, so they already feel comfortable. In fact, Celeste's mother stayed in this very room. It was bougainvillea primrose that year if I remember correctly. But there's a cottage right on the edge of the grounds especially for parents. You should feel free to stay as long as you like. The house is fully equipped. The kitchen is stocked. There is a pool, Wi-Fi, and all the normal amenities. If you don't enjoy cooking, you can join us at meal times and of course you're welcome at tonight's soiree. Should I send word to Paul that you'll be staying a day or two?"

My mom looked at me. I didn't know what to say. I didn't want to hurt her feelings.

"A week?" Miss Lavande nudged, after a gulf of silence.

"No, no. I'll just help Hasani unpack and then head back to the city."

"Whatever you'd like. The soiree begins at sunset."

Then Miss Lavande left, closing the door behind her with a click.

"Mom, you should stay. I don't mind."

It's never cool to be the only kid there who brought their mom, but I honestly felt like I could manage it. Magic was running through me full force. I was sure if I had a pair of those rose-colored glasses, I would have been shining like Bruce Leroy in *The Last Dragon*. I definitely had the glow.

I checked my phone. Luz and Miguel had gotten s'mores. MakeupontheCheapCheap was up to 487 subscribers. 487! No message from my dad. Whatever.

My mom was furiously unpacking, refolding the towels and putting them on a shelf in the empty closet. "We already stick out a little,

Hasani. Different is good, but I don't want you to have trouble making friends. You'll be fine on your own."

"I know, but . . ." I didn't want to add "will you?" She looked stressed as it was, arranging towels on a shelf like it was in a store display, not a closet you could close.

That's when I saw Celeste's side of the room. I mean, like, really saw it. Everything matched. Celeste's suitcases were white and shiny with giant buttercups on the front. Unlike mine, hers were actually meant to be stacked together. They looked more like decorations than luggage. Her desk was all set up with books and pencil holders and a vase of buttercups. There was even a little rug next to her bed with matching slippers on top. On my side of the room, my mom was pulling my Miss Piggy pillowcase out of our mismatched suitcases. The plaid flannel sheets she had put on the bed were the only clean ones left in our linen cabinet at home. When we were packing, that had seemed perfectly fine. In this room . . . not so much. Compared to Celeste's, my side of the room looked awful. Even the morning glory blossoms on my rosemary plant were hanging their little heads in shame. Maybe my mom was right.

I checked my phone. No text from dad. 489 subscribers. No new posts from Sandy.

"I'll call you every night," I said.

"Call me if you need me," my mom said. "You probably won't, but if you do, I'll be here in a heartbeat, even if I have to ask your dad for a ride."

We both laughed and rolled our eyes, even though I kind of liked the idea of the two of them driving together. It'd give them a chance to talk.

"Now let's hurry up and finish so you can get ready for this fancy party and I can get home to brag about my daughter getting a full ride to a fancy summer program because she is so incredibly talented. I'm so proud of you, baby."

"Proud enough to not be mad if I wear makeup tonight?" I blinked innocently. "It'll be subtle and natural and age-appropriate," I added, sticking in as many of my mom's words as I could.

She laughed. "Fine, Hasani. This is your time to shine."

I hugged her and, once we were done unpacking, I shooed her out the door. I needed time to get ready, after all. My makeup was about to be on and popping. Celeste and her friend would freak at my transformation and I'd probably have a line of girls begging me to do their makeup like every morning. I could even record it for Makeuponthe-CheapCheap. Everybody loves makeover videos.

I pulled out my list. I had copied it onto a piece of paper, but so much had changed since we got in Mr. Paul's car that I had to fix it. Some of it was still OK. Like, my little phone-holder ring light thingie clipped perfectly on the edge of the desk. That was a good camera and lighting setup. And when I angled it just right, there was only the closet in the background. Nothing that would say I was at a secret magical witch summer camp. And when I tested it, the light was so perfect that I just went ahead and recorded myself doing a full face. It'd be the first in the new series, "MakeupontheCheapCheap: Camp Makeovers."

I gave a little kiss to the camera when I was done. My mom was right. It was definitely my time to shine.

CHAPTER SIX

GODDESSES AND GARDENS

I ended up recording two new intros—one with a full face, and one without. I wasn't thinking about time. I thought Celeste would come back to the room or that I'd hear people walking around or something, but it was just me and the buttercups and the touch of pink glitter I had set to give my eye shadow more sparkle. It looked pretty cute, too. I was itching to scroll through the recording to find some stills for before-and-after shots, but I stopped myself. I was losing the light and, honestly, what got me out of the chair was wondering what the sunset would look like from my fancy, magic view balcony. I was out there watching the sun set and wishing I could take a picture of it when I remembered Miss Lavande saying that's when the soiree started. Sunset.

I'm not gonna lie. A little panic set in. I didn't actually want to be late. I threw on the sundress and ballet flats—thank goodness my mom made me pack them—and headed out the door. The girl with glasses from across the hall was coming out of her room, too. She looked at me and smiled.

"I thought I would be the last one. I forgot my sweater. Come on," she said, rushing ahead. Her voice was tiny. Not quite like Minnie Mouse, but not far off.

We raced to the end of the hallway. She stopped running when we got to the landing. I guessed it was because she'd probably twist an ankle running down the stairs in those stack-heel sandals. They were cute, but I was quietly grateful to my mom again for making me wear flats. My shoes were cute, too, and you could run in them. Still, I stuck with the girl when she slowed down. Being late together was better than being late alone.

"I'm Hasani," I said.

She shushed me. "LaToya," she whispered. "They already started."

We joined the crowd of girls at the bottom of the staircase just as a woman with a bronze dress and big gold earrings said, "The rooms on the main floor show off the perfection of the Creole cottage. The house was built entirely without nails and, as you can see, each room flows purposefully into the next."

Definitely Miss LeBrun. Her flowers in the intro video were the same shade of bronze as the dress she was wearing, and from the side she had the exact same silhouette.

"Our ancestors used only a small portion of their genius when they built for outsiders. While they were imprisoned here, they poured the bulk of their magic into this place. The structure has been added to over time but always with those principles in mind. Le Chateaux des Belles Demoiselles is our refuge from the outside world."

I looked to my right, meaning to give LaToya a look like, *am I the only one expecting a party, not a museum tour?*, but LaToya had moved herself up to the front of the crowd and was nodding so hard it looked like she wished she were taking notes.

Should we be taking notes? But I let that go. No way was there a class about old houses at a witch school.

LaToya kept nodding like she was drinking in every word. I guess she really liked architecture.

Miss LeBrun moved and the crowd followed her into a dining room with a long, fancy table and different shades of blue all around.

"Later on, the influences of the French made their way in. Much of the main floor was decorated and furnished in the style of Versailles. Of course, our ancestors used their own special magic, carving the chairs from solid blocks of cedar without the use of tools and incorporating natural motifs from both Louisiana and their native Senegal. As in Versailles, one color dominates each room. This room was originally red but was changed in the 1990s because of research about color and digestion."

Miss LeBrun moved again. I tried to get closer to LaToya but only got about halfway. I ended up by Celeste. It took me a second to recognize her with her hair all pinned up in little spirals, but she didn't notice me. A girl on the other side of me said, "Isn't Miss LeBrun the best?" I turned to nod my agreement—it wasn't a party, but it was interesting—but that girl was talking to another girl, and neither of them noticed me trying to smile and nod my way into their conversation.

Miss LeBrun led us through a room she called the Evening Salon, through a wall of glass doors, and into the most spectacular garden I have ever seen. Everywhere you turned there were goddesses surrounded by flowers, some long and spindly with elaborate head ties, others round and glowing with the last of the sunlight. They were so beautiful it took a second for me to realize they were statues.

Miss LeBrun joined a line of teachers at the bottom of the patio steps. Weirdly, even though they were all different heights with hair and skin all in different shades of brown, it was kind of hard to tell them apart once they were all standing together. The only thing that really made them different was the color they were wearing, like markers in a fresh pack. They all looked alike except the woman in blue. Miss Villere. It had to be. Something about her reminded me of my grandmother. They were about the same size and had the same kind of thick, gray hair, but my grandmother looked like someone you wanted to hug. Miss Villere did not. She wasn't the tallest one there, but from the way she was standing, hands clasped under a string of pearls, she was most definitely in charge.

Miss Villere stepped forward, the silver in her hair glinting. "This here is Miss Lafleur, Miss Lavande, Miss LeBrun, Miss LaRose, and moi, j'uis Miss Villere." I knew it! It was hard for me to understand her accent, though. It helped that every woman nodded delicately when Miss Villere said her name. I'm decent with Photoshop, but whoever made those silhouette animations was at god status. All the teachers looked just like them, which was crazy because those silhouettes were made out of flowers. "Bienvenue a Belles Demoi-selles: Pensionnat des Sorcières, shès petites. We welcome you here to learn from us and hone your gifts. You will work very hard, but this evening it's our turn to work. You enjoy yourselves and be in by nightfall as all young ladies should. Have fun. Your lessons begin in the morning."

I suddenly regretted not listening to my grandma more before she died. She talked just like that, like she might be saying something in Louisiana Creole even though your mom swore she was speaking English, and I had no idea what she was saying, either. The only part of Miss Villere's speech I was sure I caught was "have fun."

Waiters appeared with champagne glasses on trays.

"Sparkling fruit juice, mamzelle?"

I nodded and took a glass. It was bubbly and sweet. There were tables of food, but that could wait. Celeste was standing by a statue of a woman growing out of tree roots, and LaToya was near a statue of a woman with a turtle shell on her back. I went for Celeste. We were roommates after all, and she did look great with her hair all pinned up in puffy swirls with gold leaves on the edges. And whoever did her makeup did a pretty good job. Mine was better, but hers was still good. It was the natural look my mom was always talking about.

Celeste was laughing with two other girls, one of whom had the thickest, coiliest, most beautiful hair I had ever seen. It went down to the middle of her back. If she stretched it, it would probably have gone all the way to her waist.

"This is the girl I was telling you about," Celeste said. "What's your name again?"

"Hasani," I said.

"Right. Hasani. Sorry. I couldn't remember. Desirée, Angelique, meet my roommate. Y'all have to come see how she decorated. You won't believe it."

"Your makeup really stands out. Did you do it yourself?" Desirée said, flipping her shoulder-length brown locks to the back.

I grinned. "Thanks! I could do yours, too. I have a YouTube channel. MakeuponttheCheapCheap."

"My parents won't let me wear makeup. Too young," Angelique said. She didn't need to toss her hair over her shoulder. It looked luxurious enough staying still. "I wouldn't even wear much if they'd let me, though. What kind of a witch has to draw a fake face on top of her real one?"

Witches who like to have fun?

Witches who want to be silly?

Witches who like glitter?

That's what I should have said, but I didn't think of any of that. I just laughed along with the rest of them, hoping there wasn't enough light for the glitter on my lids to shine.

"We're just joking," Angelique said when the laughter died down. "We love your makeup."

"And your hair," Celeste smiled.

"They're both so . . . plastic," Desirée added.

Celeste elbowed her in the ribs, but all three of them burst out laughing. Hard. Like, can't breathe hard.

A knot tightened in my stomach. I turned away. They didn't try to stop me.

"They're annoying. Don't sweat it."

I had practically walked into a girl on the other side of the tree roots. Her hair was short like my mom's, but unlike my mom, she had, like, five earrings in each ear. She nodded for me to follow her, and we started walking around the garden. It was probably beautiful, but I could barely see it. I was trying not to let the stinging in my eyes turn into actual tears. Dollar store mascara is not waterproof.

"I'm Dee," she said. "You're Hasani, right?"

I nodded.

"Don't worry about them. They're stupid. They talk a big game, but really they're just too scared to be different."

"No, they're right. My mom is always saying the same thing. My real face is good enough. My real hair is good enough. Well, maybe it would be if it looked like Angelique's. Hers is perfect."

"I like your hair."

"It's fake."

"So?"

"So, they're right. What kind of witch has to wear fake hair? I can grow plants, but I can't grow hair?" I hadn't really been able to grow plants, either. Not since I did it by accident, but that wasn't the point.

Dee shrugged. "It's not a big deal."

I looked over at Celeste and Desirée and Angelique. All so

different. All so perfect, like someone should make statues of them or at least post a pic. It'd probably get a million likes.

"Don't you ever wish you were perfect like that? Girls like that get everything." I thought of Sandy and her bajillion Instagram followers, then I tried not to.

"No, I don't. But I guess you do," Dee said. She didn't sound judgy or anything. I guess that's why I said my real answer.

"Kind of," I said. "I mean, it would be cool to have long hair like that for real."

"So why don't you grow yours out, then?"

"My hair doesn't grow. It never gets past my shoulders."

"You never let it."

"What's that supposed to mean?"

"You're a witch, right? If you want to have long hair so bad, you could just use your magic, right?"

"But I thought it didn't work like that. What about the whole 'art of the improbable' thing?" I said, holding my air quotes up a little longer than I needed to.

"Growing hair isn't impossible. Besides, what do you think potions and incantations are for? Sip a little, say a few words, bam! Hair all the way down to your ankles, if that's what you want."

"OK. Yes!" I said. I'd have settled for butt-length. Mid-back, even. But I could work with ankle. "How do we do it?"

"You serious?"

"I'm serious," I said. "What? You don't want to? You'd look great with long hair."

"Nah. I like mine how it is," Dee said, rubbing a hand through her tiny curls. "But I was joking. Potions and incantations are a bad idea. How you gonna go from 'I never even heard of potions and incantations' to 'let's go squeeze our magic' in, like, three seconds? Just take your braids out if you don't like them anymore."

Angelique and the others were still where we left them, but the crowd around them had grown. Angelique tossed her head back laughing. She looked more like a goddess than the statue.

Lanterns switched on all over the garden. Girls started to put their champagne glasses on passing trays and head inside.

"See you tomorrow," Dee said.

"Bye," I mumbled. Or maybe I just said it in my head. I was still staring at Angelique, wondering how she got her hair like that. It must have been magic. There was no other explanation for hair like hers to be so long.

"I could help," a voice said from my left.

I looked over, expecting Dee, but I should have known it wasn't. The voice was too small. It was LaToya, the girl with the glasses, looking at me extra serious. "If you want to get your hair like that, I can help. All we need is lavender and chicory."

CHAPTER SEVEN

LAVENDER AND CHICORY

"Were we supposed to bring books?" I asked.

"You didn't bring books?" LaToya looked at me sideways. We were in her room. It was smaller than mine and didn't have a balcony, but she also didn't have a roommate. After the way Celeste had acted downstairs, that seemed like a very good deal.

"No," I said, suddenly embarrassed that I sounded like a person who doesn't read books. Why didn't I bring any books? "I don't have any magic books. Where do you buy them? In the French Quarter?" There were lots of witchy-looking shops down there.

"We don't need spellbooks for our classes, if that's what you mean." She'd found the one she was looking for and was flipping through it. It looked more like a scrapbook than a spellbook.

"Good," I said, relieved. "Thank you for helping me."

"Oh, no problem. Us new girls have to stick together."

"You're new?" I said, looking around the room in disbelief. Everything about it, from the tall vases of flowers to the perfectly arranged bookshelf, made it seem like LaToya knew what was up. "How do you already know about incantations and stuff?"

"Oh, all my family are witches. I'm just the first one to go to finishing school. Daddy has been working on this for years."

"I just found out Friday."

"That you got into Belles Demoiselles?" LaToya's French accent was even better than my mom's.

"That I'm a witch," I said. "And that I got into Belles Demoiselles."

"Seriously?" LaToya raised an eyebrow.

"Seriously."

"Oh! So you're really a wildseed, then. And you already got a spot in Belles Demoiselles? Your family must be super rich. This place costs a fortune."

"I got a scholarship."

"Oh. Well, don't feel bad. Anyway, I don't know that much, either. I collect spells, but I don't have many, and this isn't an official spellbook. I think my granny wanted to teach me more, but my mom and dad got pretty mad whenever they thought she was. She wasn't, really, but I learned a bunch from her anyway because I started listening whenever I heard the old people talking, then I'd write down the stuff I could understand. Here," she said, propping the book open. "I used this one on my hair a little bit, but my mom noticed when I kept needing a new relaxer, so I had to stop. Yep, all we need is lavender and chicory."

I didn't feel bad that I got a scholarship, at least not until LaToya said don't feel bad about getting a scholarship. But I didn't say any of that because LaToya was picking things out from inside a trunk that had little shelves and bottles and bundles of dried plants hanging from the inside of the lid, and I didn't want to say anything that might make her think I wasn't cool enough to help.

LaToya pulled an electric kettle off the shelf and gestured for me to go fill it in what I thought was a closet but turned out to be a tiny, private bathroom just for her room.

"I usually use spring water, but we'll have to settle for filtered," she said.

Once the water was hot, she crammed a dainty-looking teapot full of dried leaves and flower petals, poured the water over the top, closed the lid, and said, "So, how much of that is your real hair?"

"Why?" I asked.

"I need to know where to cut. If we have to unbraid them starting from the bottom, it's going to take all night and we have class in the morning."

"It's about to my shoulders," I said.

LaToya nodded, took out a pair of scissors, and set to work. I didn't get nervous until she actually started cutting. I didn't say anything until she got around to the ones by my ear.

"That's too short," I said in a panic. "You're cutting my hair, too."

"It'll grow back," she said. "This is easier. Trust me." And she snipped the last braid.

The braids came out easily, but so did chunks of my hair. I blinked back tears as I unraveled the plastic hair from my own. In the mirror my hair was short and puffy with a little wave from being in the braids. It was sort of like an Afro, which would have been cool, except mine didn't go all the way around, which was definitely not cool. It sat like a sad semicircle, poofing out in jagged chunks around my ears. My grandmother would have called it paillé, then sucked her teeth. I know this sounds stupid, but honestly, that was the first time I thought it was a bad idea. All I could do was hope this girl wasn't punking me. It was too late for anything else. My magic already tingled as tears stung the backs of my eyelids, but when I took a sip of LaToya's hair grow tea, it was like it roared to life.

Too bad the tea was gross. I almost spit it back in the cup.

"Ugh, this is disgusting," I said, trying not to let the tea dribble out as I talked.

"You don't have to drink it. You could just put it on your roots." Now she tells me. "That's what I did, but I didn't want mine to grow too fast."

My lumpy half-fro stared at me from the mirror. I swallowed the tea down in one gulp. The magical buzz moved down my throat and around my shoulders before it started moving up to my scalp.

"It's working!" I squeaked.

"Did you think it wouldn't?" LaToya said, her eyebrows squished together.

I didn't answer. What was I supposed to say? No?

"This is so cool," I said. My scalp was tingling all over. I looked in the mirror, expecting to see it already growing. Maybe the half-fro was a little less lumpy?

"You have to soak your hair. Say this while you do it," LaToya said, handing me a spray bottle and an index card.

Sint-Añès mo priyé li

Shvé pousé vit lanwi

"I can't read French," I said.

"It's Creole," LaToya corrected. "Just repeat after me."

She must have corrected me nine times before it was good enough.

"Sant ahn-yes mo preevay lee. Sh-vay poosay veet la newy."

I could tell from her face that it still wasn't perfect, but that was the best I could do.

"You spray, I say?" I asked, thinking it would make LaToya laugh, but she stayed serious.

She shook her head. "It might get on me," she said.

I understood. LaToya's hair was already pretty long. It hung to her shoulders even in that high ponytail. And if she got new growth overnight, there was no way her edges would still be slick in the morning, even if she gelled them down.

So I held up the bottle and started to spray, saying, "Sant ahn-yes mo preevay lee. Sh-vay poosay veet la newy" the whole time. The tea dripped down my face and stung my eyes, but I didn't stop because I swear I could actually feel it working. It was a miracle. No—it was magic.

A weird music started playing. It wasn't music exactly. More like music sounds. And wind. Definitely wind. And it got louder every few seconds.

"What is that?" I said.

"Oh, no. That's the sleeping soundscape. I wanted to make the rounds during social hour, but it must already be bedtime. There was supposed to be a warning chime. You should go back to your room."

I wasn't looking forward to seeing Celeste, especially in a wet dress with tea dribbling down my face, but we did have school in the morning.

"See you at breakfast?" I smiled, hoping it made up for the weird blinking I was doing to keep the tea out of my eyes.

"Oh, don't take this the wrong way, OK? But don't sit with me tomorrow. You're nice and all, but my dad sent me here to make friends with real witches, not wildseeds. He'd freak out. So, don't mention this stuff and . . . um . . . maybe we should pretend that we don't know each other at all. We can still be friends, just, like, on the side. You understand, right?"

I hoped she was joking. Her eyes said she wasn't. I nodded, because what else could I say?

"Great! OK. So, say the incantation as much as you can tonight while the potion is still active, and leave your hair out when you go to sleep," she said, then she closed her door with me on the other side of it.

The hallway was empty. There was just enough light to see, like moonlight, but without windows. The flowers had grown in above our door. Morning glories on the left, buttercups on the right. Celeste's flowers were perky and bright. Mine looked half dead.

I put my hand on the left knob and whispered, "Morning glory." My hand tingled and the door clicked open. It was completely dark inside. I felt my way across the room, the buzzing on my head getting stronger with every beat of my heart. Thankfully, my phone was right where I left it. I clicked it on, hoping to see how many more followers I had or, at least, a message from Luz or my mom. No signal. I sighed. At least the phone made a good flashlight.

Celeste was curled up in her bed, hair tied up, sleep mask firmly in place. Either she was sleeping or pretending to sleep. I was glad either way.

There was a box on the floor on my side of the room, but I couldn't deal with it. I fished some pajamas out of the drawer, glad my mom had showed me where she put them, even though I had rolled my eyes and said I'd figure it out. It would have been hard to figure out by cell phone light. The dry clothes felt good, especially with a wet head, and I was so tired. Between the buzzing and the pulsing and the soundscape, all I wanted was to go to sleep. I pulled out the list I had tucked under the pillow. Everything I had written so far had come true. Maybe the list was part of the magic. I scribbled "long hair" and "make friends" just before I fell asleep.

When I woke up, the room was bright, Celeste was gone, and my bed was covered in vines.

CHAPTER EIGHT

COFFEE AND CREAM

I'm not gonna lie. I kind of freaked out. There were little green claws gripping my arm. I shrieked, busting through vines like the Hulk or the Kool-Aid Man or something, except yelling, "Oh, no!" instead of "Oh, yeah!" Or maybe I was just yelling.

There were ripped-up vines and purple flowers all over the place, plus a really bushy one clinging to my head. I tried tugging them off, but the vines were not having it. They were in there. Like, all the way in there. I ran over to Celeste's full-length mirror and almost shouted again.

My hair!

My entire life my hair had been somewhere around shoulder length, which some people said was long, but I was forever tipping my head back in pictures so it would look like my hair went past my shoulders. Now it really, really did. Yes, it was full of vines and torn-up petals, but none of that mattered as I flipped and turned to see how far my hair went down my back. LaToya's incantation worked!

I pulled at one of the coils and grinned like a fool when it stretched past the middle of my back. I could have cried. Sure, it took a while to slowly untangle the vines from my hair, but I got most of them out and left one in for effect. There were three flowers on it that were perfectly in bloom, and I arranged them so they would look like a headband or one of those fancy hairpins. We hadn't packed any hair stuff except a few hairbands, but there was no way I was cramming all that glorious hair into a ponytail. The morning glory vine was perfect. After all, it was my signature flower.

The box from the night before was still on the floor, but in the light of day I could see that: A. It was addressed to me; and B. The handwriting was my mom's.

I tore open the box, and I swear I heard a choir of angels singing. Without shifting stuff around, I could already see a glittery purple comforter, purple slippers, a purple rug, and purple vases. They were plastic, but they looked ceramic. And there was a note from my mom right on top.

Hasani,

There was a big box store not too far away, so Mr. Paul took me there before he brought me home. We can return what I bought if you don't want it, but I thought it might be good. I'm heading back to New Orleans, but Auntie Nette says she'll check in on you at the school. Mr. Paul says if she knows, she'll know, and she says she knows, so call her if you need her.

Love,

Mama

p.s. I couldn't find the right flowers, so I stuck to purple.

I wasn't sure which one Auntie Nette was—a great aunt? A cousin too old to call by their first name?—but I dove into the stuff from the box like it was Christmas. There was a lot of purple, but I definitely wasn't complaining. I knew how my mom felt about WalMart, so the fact that she went there for me anyway made me love her even more.

Soon my side of the room looked amazing with fluffy purple pillows and a mirror that stood up like a picture frame. My mom had even bought me a desk set and a curtain. OK, technically it was a shower curtain, but it was a sheer fabric, not plastic, and she had bought the cutest little hooks. Celeste's curtain was thick and heavy and wide enough to spread all the way across the balcony doors, but I pushed hers over to one side and hung mine up on my side singing *Let the sunshine in* in my head the whole time.

At the bottom of the box, there was a striped sundress in blueish purple and dark pink that perfectly matched the flowers in my hair. I popped the tags on the sundress and pulled it on with a pair of jean shorts underneath before examining myself in the mirror. I was cute. Really cute. I wiped the sleep crust out of my eyes, then snapped a pic. My full body selfie game was not as good as Sandy's, but it was still pretty good, especially in this light. I only had one bar, but I sent it to my mom and Luz, anyway. #firstday #summercamp #dormlife. Of course that one bar changed to zero bars as soon as I clicked Send.

That's OK, I thought. A little corner of the box had gotten in the shot, anyway. I moved it to retake the pic, and what should I find underneath but another piece of paper with my name on it.

The paper had flowers all around the edges. They were printed on, but the art looked so real it was like they were popping off the page. Morning glories, of course.

Hasani Marie Schexnayder-Jones 001

Breakfast		Dining Room	Circling Swans to 1st Chime
Greetings	LaRose	Grand Foyer	2nd Chime to 3rd Chime
Art & Architecture	LeBrun	Library	4th Chime to 5th Chime
Fragrance	Lafleur	Sculpture Garden	6th Chime to 7th Chime
Luncheon		Dining Room	8th Chime to 9th Chime
The Art of Arranging	LaRose	Main Salon	10th Chime to 11th Chime
Animal Affinities	Lafleur	3rd Floor	12th Chime to Swan Flight
Introductions	Lavande	Grand Foyer	13th Chime to 14th Chime
Tea		Evening Salon	Rainbow to First Blush
Dressing		Morning Glory Buttercup Suite	Heart Swans
Dinner		Dining Room	2nd Gong to Dismissal
Social Hour		3rd Floor	3rd Gong to 15th Chime
Bedtime		Morning Glory Buttercup Suite	

Attendance is mandatory unless excepted in writing by staff or administration. Tardiness will not be tolerated.

I had so many questions. How many chimes could there possibly be? What happened to the first gong? How in the heck did this obviously important paper end up under a box where I might never have found it? Why was one of the classes legit called Architecture? Why didn't anything, ANYTHING on the schedule sound magical? No potions. No spells. Nothing. Then, and maybe most importantly, what time was "Circling Swans" exactly?

It was 8:05, but apparently real time didn't matter at Belles Demoiselles, since normal times were nowhere on the schedule. I raced onto the balcony and breathed a huge sigh. The swans were swimming in a perfect circle like a carousel. I had time. I grabbed a towel and stuff and ran out into the hallway looking for the bathroom, but every door looked like somebody's room. I had used the bathroom in LaToya's room, but LaToya had made it pretty clear she didn't want to be seen with me and, anyway, she didn't answer when I knocked. She was probably already downstairs. At that point, I decided a baby wipe out of my makeup stuff would have to do.

The baby wipe couldn't do anything about the tea in my hair, but it smelled kind of minty, like fancy shampoo. So I just tugged on my shoes, grabbed the pencil case and matching notebook my mom had sent, did one last check for sleep crust or drool marks, and headed for the dining room. I didn't need a bathroom, anyway. I could hold it.

As I closed the door, I caught one last glimpse of myself in the mirror. My hair was amazing. My outfit was supercute. If I could have started a witch-stagram right then and there, I would have; that's how much I looked the part. Even the flowers over my door agreed. They were fresh and open and holding their heads high. I took that as a good sign as I went downstairs.

I forgot all about the bathroom the second I walked in. Everyone stared at me, but I didn't mind. There was a small cloud of butterflies and a bird or two swooping overhead. Definitely a Cinderella-type entrance and I was digging it. A couple of the teachers even put their glasses on to get a better look. I could still feel the magic tingling my scalp. It felt good.

I was the last one in the dining room, but I didn't mind that, either. There was one empty seat left and it was at Angelique's end of the table. Celeste and Desirée were there, too, but it was definitely Angelique's end of the table.

I sat down in front of a fancy place setting with a napkin ring and everything.

"What can I get you, Miss?" a woman in a gray uniform said.

There wasn't a menu. I hadn't eaten anything the night before, and I suddenly realized how hungry I was. I looked around the table to see what everyone else was eating. There was half of a croissant on Celeste's plate and a few bites of scrambled egg on Desirée's, but it was hard to tell exactly what they got, because they all looked like they were finished. Then three more women in gray uniforms started picking up plates from the table. They were definitely all finished. I started to panic, wondering how cool I could make scarfing down a plate of eggs look. LaToya took a sip from a teacup, and I thought of something. Something I had been waiting to say for a long time.

"I'll just have coffee," I said. The words came out exactly as grown-up as they sounded in my head, which, let's be honest, is not how that usually works.

The waitress smiled and nodded and came back a few seconds later with a silver coffee pot, pouring the coffee I ordered into a cup with a matching saucer. The coffee was black. I blinked at it.

"I didn't think you'd make it, Hasani," Angelique said.

I noticed again how perfect her hair was. Every single kink flowed into perfect springs that cascaded down her shoulders like bouncy waterfalls. She took a sip from her cup. I smiled and picked mine up, too.

"The schedule was hard to read." *Especially under a box*, I thought in Celeste's direction. "But I figured it out."

Celeste looked like she wanted to say something, but Angelique checked her with a look. I tried not to smile at that and took a sip of my coffee, magic humming in my fingertips. The coffee was not as bitter as LaToya's tea, but that didn't mean it was good. I wanted to spit it out, but teachers were staring at me. Angelique was staring at me. I caught eyes with Dee, but she only mimed putting her napkin in her lap. I swallowed.

I thought I might have to keep choking it down like that, but then I spotted a tiny pitcher of cream and a sugar bowl with tongs. I'm not sure if I was more excited about the sugar cubes or the fact that I was sitting next to Angelique and she was actually smiling at me. I put in about ten cubes of sugar and some cream, then whirled my spoon around to stir it all in.

Dee was still gesturing at me. I put the stupid napkin in my lap. She calmed down.

"Y'all match," Desirée said, looking between me and Angelique. Her locks perfectly framed her smile.

Angelique smiled again.

"I love purple," Celeste added. Her smile was nervous. She *did* hide my schedule under that box, then. There was nothing else to be nervous about.

I took a sip of my coffee. It was so good that I drank the rest in one gulp. I mean, the cup was small. There wasn't that much in there. But still.

"Sweet," Angelique said.

I couldn't tell if it was a question or not, so I nodded. "I only like coffee sweet," I said. I mean, who likes coffee bitter? I expected Angelique to agree with me. She didn't.

"You would," she said, her voice cool. "Do you drown everything you consume in sugar, or just the coffee?"

"What's wrong with sugar?" I mean, seriously. Why would they put it on the table if they didn't want us to use it?

"I can't believe they let you in here," Celeste burst out. Her voice was quiet, but it was trembling like I had done her something. "It's obvious you're a wildseed. Everything about you is just dripping with new. But I didn't know you were ignorant, too."

"Celeste," Angelique said. "She doesn't know."

"I know. But isn't that what ignorant means? No, sorry, Angelique. You're right," Celeste said. "I shouldn't have said ignorant. I'm talking about Hasani, after all. I should have said 'ignant' instead, right?"

I'd heard lots of people say ignorant that way. It was always mean, but when Celeste said it in her soft, polished voice, it was double mean. My mouth opened, but no words came out.

Desirée stifled a giggle. Angelique was looking across the room as if nothing happening at this table interested her in the slightest. Celeste, on the other hand, was looking right at me.

"And this sad attempt to copy Angelique's hair? How desperate could you be? It doesn't make you a witch. It just makes you a Pinterest fail."

There were gasps. Celeste wasn't being loud, but other people must have been listening. The girl sitting next to me inched her chair away like I was measles and her parents were anti-vax.

"I'm sorry to be shocking, but it's true. She has the nerve to sit down next to us when she's obviously been squeezing her magic like a circus freak. It's so cringe."

"I di—"

"Don't bother lying about it. That ridiculous weed on your head is still growing."

I looked down at my shoulder. I'd felt something there, but I thought it was just my new hair. It wasn't. The cute headband vine had grown way longer than my hair. When I left my room it only had three flowers. Now there were at least a dozen, and the vine was half-way down my arm.

"Celeste," Angelique said gently. "You're letting yourself get worked up."

For one glorious second, I thought Angelique was going to check her. I mean, not *check* her check her. Angelique was too refined for that. But put her in her place a little bit. Remind her how uncool it was to be so uncool to people. Luz did that for me sometimes and I did it for her, too. That's what friends do.

Well, maybe Angelique was Celeste's friend, but she definitely wasn't mine. The next thing I knew, Angelique looked right at me and said, "Celeste, she's not worth it."

A chime tinkled, carried through the room on a gentle breeze. The teachers at the far end of the table stood up, and all the other girls followed suit. I just sat there like an idiot, my notebook and pencil case biting into the skin where I had shoved them under my thigh. There was nowhere else to put them. They didn't belong at the table.

The lady in the gray uniform picked up my coffee cup. "Order a café au lait next time," she said with a wink.

I know she was trying to be nice, but it didn't make me feel any better.

"Hasani?" a warm voice said from behind me.

It was Miss LaRose, her long locks twisted into a beautiful bun, her skin glowing. She didn't even need powder.

"May I speak with you a moment? In private?" she added sharply.

A bolt of fear shot through me. No offense to anybody else, but I was one of the good kids. I was not used to teachers using that kind of voice with me and, for real, it had me shook.

Dee, who was standing at the far end of the room, gave me a "Sorry, I tried" shrug and tacked herself onto the crowd of girls leaving. That's when I knew that, officially, I was in trouble.

"Yes, ma'am," I said.

"Miss," she corrected. "We usually allow girls to choose their own places at breakfast and luncheon and I'm sure you would prefer to sit with your friends." *What friends?* "However, I will be holding a place at luncheon for you to sit next to me. You need more support. The clink of your spoon was absolutely deafening."

"Yes, ma'am," I said.

"Miss," she corrected again. "And, while I applaud your efforts to blend in with the school's decor, a rapidly growing vine is not . . . how should I put it? Fitting."

Somewhere in the next room, someone snickered.

So much for being alone.

CHAPTER NINE

CHARM AND MAGIC

"I shooed the flies," Dee said, rolling her eyes at a staircase I hadn't seen before. There was no one on it, but I could still hear giggling. "Come on. I'll help you pull the vine out of your hair."

Dee opened a door under the stairs, and I almost cried. Again. It was a bathroom. The tiny kind my grandmother would have called a powder room. It had a mirror and a sink and, thank goodness, a toilet. I can hold it for a really long time, but even I had my limits.

"Hold on a second," I said, shoving my little notebook and pen into Dee's hands before dashing in and closing the door.

Sweet relief. I didn't even realize how bad it was until everything was all good.

"Dang," Dee's voice came through the door. "Sounded like you were holding it since last night."

I was looking around for regular soap. All the ones I could see were shaped like little fleurs-de-lis.

"I was," I said, deciding to just use one of the fancy soaps. It looked like solid gold but melted into a soft lather the instant it touched water.

When I came out, Dee's eyes were still open like *WOW*.

"I couldn't find a bathroom."

"If you don't like the one in your room, there's a ton of these little ones all over. I can show you where they are."

"There's a bathroom in my room?"

"Dag. You didn't know that? Yeah. There's a bathroom in all the rooms and a spa on the main floor, but you have to make an appointment."

"Yeah. I guess I missed the grand tour, among many other things." Miss Lafleur had told my mom and I not to be late. I just wished I knew that I'd be late even if we were on time. How did everybody else seem to know so much? "That includes the part when they explained how to not look like an idiot."

I had already ripped the vine out of the front. Dee was gently teasing the rest of it out of the parts I couldn't see.

"You don't look like an idiot," she said. "You just look a little—"

"Wild?" I supplied. LaToya had called me that. A wildseed.

"Green. I was going to say green. I did try to warn you."

She did. I still didn't know what was so wrong about me. Everybody at Belles Demoiselles could do magic. Did it really make a difference if I didn't have curtains or put sugar in my coffee or whatever? It didn't make sense for there to be little groups inside this little group.

"You did a good job, though. It came out really thick and even. You're lucky."

Dee was talking about my hair. "Thick and even" was not how people usually described it. I looked at myself in the mirror again. The front was a little paillé from tearing out the vine. I smoothed it down with some water. It looked better with the flowers, but it still looked good.

"Maybe I'll start a hair channel," I winked. I was joking, but it wasn't a bad idea. Hair channels are huge.

Dee rolled her eyes.

"Bonjou, Miss YouTuber." It was the waitress lady from earlier, smiling at me like she was my auntie. Believe me, at that point I needed the love. "I thought you might want this." She held out a tray with a pastry that looked like a rose, if roses were made out of perfectly browned dough. I ate it in one bite. Strawberry and ginger and rose? That last was a surprise, but I was digging it. It was like a Pop-Tart, but with a celebrity glow up. There were probably crumbs falling all everywhere, but I honestly did not care. That pastry was heaven.

"So good," I said.

The waitress lady beamed. Definite auntie smile. "I didn't want you to go hungry. You make it down on time tomorrow."

"Yes, ma'am. Uh . . . miss," I corrected myself.

She waved my correction away. "Don't worry about all that, sha. I'm just glad I caught you."

"Mèsi, Manmzèl Camille," Dee said.

Miss Camille nodded and left us outside the bathroom.

"Come on, Miss YouTube. Let's get to the Grand Foyer before you're late. Again."

I was all set up to repeat "grand foyer" in my imitation of Dee's perfect French accent as a comeback to her jibe, but I let it slide. It felt good to have someone who'd want to tease me again. It felt like ages since I'd talked to Luz. Longest. Day. Ever.

"Where is everybody?" I expected us to be the last ones again, but either we were first or in the wrong room.

"They're probably still primping upstairs, but we don't need to because we already look good," Dee grinned, running a hand across the tapered part of her cut like that proved the point.

I laughed and flicked a coil of hair across my shoulder. "At least we're on time."

Dee did look, cute, though. Her bow tie was on point, but I was especially digging her flower-print combat boots. On brand, but still on theme. Very cool.

Miss LaRose greeted us warmly, which, let's be honest, is not what I expected after getting pulled on the side after breakfast. "Welcome, Demi-Rose and Hasani. You're both looking lively and lovely. Please make yourselves comfortable," she said, gesturing toward a smaller room off the Grand Foyer.

"Demi-Rose? That's a cool name."

She shrugged. "I like Dee. Let's sit over here."

There were a bunch of desks. They were like regular school desks but made of fancy wood with fancy cushioned chairs and a white vase where the pencil holder should have been. It didn't matter where we sat. It wasn't like there was a front row or anything. The desks were in a circle. So I followed Dee to the other side of the room and sat at a desk next to the one she picked.

The girl who sat beside me at breakfast came in next. She smiled nervously in our direction and chose a seat on the opposite side of the circle. The next three girls did the same. Celeste, Desirée, and Angelique chose desks together next to a girl with a honey-brown Afro. When LaToya came in, she pretended not to see me, which got more obvious when she ended up sitting two desks away.

"Don't sweat it," Dee whispered when she saw me staring in Angelique's direction. I think she thought I was mad or something. I wasn't. That's the sad part. Even though Angelique had made it very clear that she basically hated everything about me, I still wanted to be her friend. Or, at least, I wanted her to want to be my friend. Something about her was just so cool that I didn't even care that she was mean. I just didn't want her to be mean to me. Sad, right?

The desks filled just before the 2nd chimes rang. They were different than the ones at breakfast. Those sounded like someone clinking a spoon on a glass. The 2nd chimes were more like music. They rang through you. So did Miss LaRose's voice as she swept into the center of the room. It was like she was a whole different person from the one who was basically yelling at me earlier. I liked this Miss LaRose better.

"Greetings vary greatly by culture," Miss LaRose said, "but contrary to what you may believe, the first step of an effective greeting in any culture isn't knowing the appropriate welcoming words or gestures. We'll learn those eventually, but the most important thing in any greeting is to know who you are. For instance, I am Miss LaRose. I am a mother and a daughter and a travel enthusiast, and I pride myself on being a first-rate scholar. I did not say any of these things when I greeted you. I didn't have to. I know them. I know who I am, and it comes across before I say a word. Therefore, when I speak, what I say is a confirmation, not an initiation. That is what makes my greeting so effective. So before you can hope to greet people effectively, you must first know who you are. You have to feel the truth of yourself in your bones and let it radiate out from you."

Miss LaRose swept her hands in the air when she said "radiate." It would have been funny, except I could feel it radiating, warm and soft and making me feel important. Like Miss LaRose knew me or at least wanted to know me. Basically, the opposite of how she talked to me after breakfast. Miss LaRose was wearing a white suit, but the way she walked, you would have thought there was a cape flowing behind her. She smiled, turning to look at each of us. When she looked at me, my heart beat faster. Magic. Miss LaRose was using magic. I felt it tingling on my skin, flowing in from the outside, and breathed a sigh of relief. Finally. This was what I had come for.

I sat up straighter, not wanting to miss a thing in the lesson about greetings. There had to be a way to use this on my channel. Wasn't I supposed to be letting my subscribers see the real me?

"Set the voice print at your desks. Then we'll begin."

The girl across from me put her hands on the vase and said, "Silver bells." A small bouquet of flowers grew into place. I watched until the flowers bloomed like their name, except the bell-shaped petals were white, not silver.

Other girls joined in quickly.

"Daisies."

"Louisiana irises."

"Hibiscus."

I put my hands on the vase and said, "Morning glory," hoping my voice would blend in. Instantly, morning glories spilled out of my vase and trailed onto the floor.

Miss LaRose waggled her fingers in front of them as she passed by and my vine shrank back, leaving three flowers peeking over the side of the vase. I was disappointed but felt better when I saw her adjusting other people's flowers. Some of the girls were having trouble getting their flowers to show up at all. LaToya must have said "sword lily" five times and her vase was still empty. But when she said "gladioli," it worked.

Miss LaRose floated around the circle, waggling her fingers here and there until the flowers in every vase were about the same size.

"Good," she said. "Now we'll begin. Take a deep breath and decide who you are."

That was it. The full instructions. I looked at Dee to see if Miss LaRose was serious. Was there a workbook or dry erase board or something with more info that I was missing? But Dee was staring at the tiny roses in her vase, looking like she was holding in a deep breath, so I did the same. I decided I was a daughter and an artist and a YouTuber, even though I hadn't been able to check on my subscribers for a whole day. When I heard everybody else letting out their breath, I did, too.

"Good." Miss LaRose seemed pleased. "I think everyone is ready for the next step. Say who you are in a calm clear voice. The computer will monitor your progress. I'll be here to assist."

It's one thing to think who you are in your head. It's another thing to say it out loud.

"I am a first-daughter's first daughter, and I am excellent."

I knew that was Angelique without looking. First of all, I knew her voice. Second of all, I could just feel her confidence. It radiated off her like . . . like magic!

Other people joined her at the same time I did, but I didn't pay attention to them. I got it. I understood. And magic was still buzzing in my fingertips like it had been all morning. I focused on the feeling, imagined it moving up my spine and into my head as I spoke.

"I'm a daughter and an artist and a YouTuber," I said. Angelique puffed a laugh. It might have been a coincidence. It might not have been a laugh at all. Everyone was talking by then, but Angelique was definitely looking in my direction. She caught Celeste's eye, then Celeste nudged Desirée and they laughed, too. So did the girl with the honey-brown Afro.

I ignored them. My magic was beautiful, and there was a trail of purple morning glories to prove it. I could barely feel theirs. It hardly moved their flowers at all.

Miss LaRose smiled encouragingly. She waved her fingers, my flowers shrank back, and I did it again. I felt who I was radiating out from me, making my skin shine like luminizer. The morning glory vine filled the pot again. It was shorter but fuller and the flowers were even more lush. There must have been twenty of them on a foot of vine, and every one of them was perfect.

Miss LaRose stopped in front of every desk. Sometimes she put on her glasses to watch one of the girls at work, sometimes she gave instructions. She kept telling Dee something about charm and magic. Honestly, the only time Miss LaRose seemed frustrated was when she was correcting Dee. Her smile with Dee was kind of fake. I tried not to notice, but I couldn't help but wonder what Dee was doing wrong. Every time Miss LaRose stopped in front of me, she smiled and reset my flowers. It felt great. My magic was getting stronger every time I said who I was. Well, maybe not stronger, but better, like when you ride enough that the front wheel stops wobbling on your bike. It got to where my flowers came out smooth every time.

I didn't realize the room was quiet until Dee sat down.

". . . and a YouTuber." My voiced echoed.

The problem with sitting in a circle is that everyone can see you. Even when you don't want them to. And the person you're sitting next to, who is probably the person most likely to give you a smile or a thumbs-up when everything is going wrong, is actually the hardest person to see. In the silence, my voice was way too loud, and when I tried to look at Dee to see why I was the last one standing, the person I actually saw was Angelique. That time, she really was laughing. The next thing I knew, Angelique was shrieking and covered in vines.

CHAPTER TEN

DEEPER AND DEEPER

"**I** didn't mean to!"

I tried to apologize. The way Angelique was shrieking you would have thought I threw poisonous snakes on her, not flowers. OK, vines. Vines with little vine claws. But her friends and Miss LaRose had most of them ripped off before I even figured out what was happening. The only reason I knew I was the one who did it was the morning glory petals being thrown on the floor.

"You're OK, Angelique. You're OK," Miss LaRose said, but her voice sounded more like she hoped it was true than she knew it was true.

Angelique *was* OK, though. It's not like the vines were slicing into her flesh. None of them had even gotten in her hair. It was still perfect. But you definitely would not have known that from the tears streaming down Angelique's face.

"That must have been a frightening experience. Would you like to freshen up in your room?" Miss LaRose turned to the rest of us. "Can someone escort Angelique upstairs? Who is her roommate?"

"Angelique doesn't have a roommate." Celeste made it sound like that made Angelique royalty or something.

"That's right," Miss LaRose said, looking more worried for a second. But only for a second. She smoothed out to magazine perfect before I could blink.

"I'll take her," Celeste and Desirée said at the same time.

"That's fine." Miss LaRose nodded and waved her hand.

The three of them left together, Celeste and Desirée holding Angelique up like they were human crutches, Angelique covering her face and sobbing like she had just been mauled by a bear. The girl with the honey-brown Afro scrambled after them, too.

"Monique?" Miss LaRose said.

I thought Miss LaRose was going to stop honey-brown Afro girl, who was apparently named Monique, from going with them. They clearly had enough people.

"Ask Miss Camille to send up some lemonade on your way."

Monique nodded and ran off just before the chimes. The chimes were different again, but I didn't get a chance to think too much about them, because Dee grabbed me by the arm and pulled me out of the room ahead of the rest of the girls. I was kind of relieved. The other girls had been ignoring me, but after Angelique made her dramatic exit, they were all staring me down like I had tried to murder her.

"Thanks," I said. "I don't know what happened. I was trying to make my flowers grow and I guess I just slipped?"

"Wait. You were trying to make your flowers grow? Bold choice." Dee raised her eyebrows, impressed. "I thought I was being a rebel wearing pants. You, my friend, are a master."

Miss Lafleur fluttered by like a magazine picture, just like Miss LaRose, only instead of wearing white, Miss Lafleur was all browns and pinks with a fragrance to match. She looked different, but it took me a second to figure out why. Then I caught the difference. Her hair wasn't tied up in a bun like it had been at my house. It was flowing long and free. I stared. Dee nudged me.

"How are you enjoying Belles Demoiselles so far?" Miss Lafleur said, her smile indicating that she clearly did not know I had just flower-mauled another student. "It looks like you're making friends."

Friend. Singular.

"It's great!" I said brightly. I don't even think I was lying, at least not all the way. Some of it was great. I mean, I had only sort of barely made one friend, people were always laughing at me, my room was decorated with random stuff my mom grabbed from WalMart at the last minute, and I had just accidentally tied up the coolest girl here with vines, but, honestly, even with all that, it wasn't all bad. I had made a potion, my hair looked amazing, I could pretty much make flowers grow on command at that point, and everywhere I went it felt like a unicorn was about to come around the corner. Seriously next-level. I only wished I could film it. This place would make a killer vlog.

Miss Lafleur smiled her Glinda smile. "I knew you would do well. I can't wait to see you in class. Keep up the good work!"

I literally gave her a thumbs-up. No. Not just a thumbs-up—two thumbs-up. Somehow the second thumb quadruples the corny. It didn't dim Miss Lafleur's smile, though. She floated out toward the front door and left me and Dee to make our way to the next class.

I barely remember Art and Architecture. Miss LeBrun talked the whole time. There were slides, I can tell you that much. I started taking notes, but I must have zombied my way through the lecture because the next thing I knew, Dee and I were heading outside for Fragrance. Chimes still tinkled through the air as the rest of the girls joined us around a fountain in the garden. I say "joined us," but there was at least a five-foot gap around me and Dee at all times while Miss Lafleur gave us a tour of the garden. There was also pointing and eye-rolling and whispering, but only while Miss Lafleur was caught up explaining which parts of which flowers made which kinds of scents.

"Ignore them," Dee said.

I wished they would go back to ignoring me.

Angelique and her crew didn't appear before the next chimes. Those I recognized. They sounded like the wooden ones my mom hung on our porch. I was just about to tell that to Dee while, at the same time, wondering if Angelique would be at lunch, when I noticed the woman in uniform from breakfast waiting at the edge of the garden. She was holding a silver tray.

"Oh, no." Dee sighed.

There were two envelopes on the tray. Dee took one, mumbling, "Mèsi, Manmzèl Camille."

The other one had my name written on it in sparkling blue ink. "Thank you," I said, taking mine off the tray.

Miss Camille nodded sympathetically and went back inside.

I opened my envelope. It was another copy of my schedule. "I already have this," I said. Then I saw that, besides being written in blue instead of purple, one other thing had changed. Lunch was no longer in the dining room. It was now in Room One.

"Where's Room One?" I asked.

"The principal's office. I have to go, too," Dee said. "Let's go get this over with."

𝒶 few minutes later, we were standing in front of a closed door on the second floor. There were no flowers on it, but it did have Office de la Directrice painted on it in shiny gold letters.

"Do we knock?" I asked. My hands were trembling. I'd never been sent to the principal's office before. I didn't know the protocol.

"No. We do this," Dee said, placing one hand on a gold plate on the door. I did the same.

"Ki cé ça?" an electronic voice asked.

"Demi-Rose LeBlanc," Dee said.

Dee raised her eyebrows at me.

"Hasani Marie Schexnayder-Jones," I said. Warm rays of light swept across me as I spoke. They started at my feet and head, criss-crossing my throat as I said my last name. I would have called it a body scan, but that felt more like it was scanning my soul.

"Parti. Entre. Voice key accepted. You may enter," the electronic voice said. The door swung open. Miss Villere was typing away at a computer. She barely looked up when we walked in.

"Asi," she said.

Dee sat, so I did, too. There was a table next to the desk that looked like it had been set for dinner.

When Miss Villere finally looked up from whatever she was typing, she narrowed her eyes at Dee, then reamed her out in a string of syllables that I couldn't understand. But I didn't need to understand them to know that Dee was in trouble. Dee hung her head and nodded, and when she did talk all she said was "wé," and "mo shagrin."

Then Dee got up and left me there without looking back.

Miss Villere turned to me.

"Why have you come to Belles Demoiselles?" she asked. Her accent was thick, but I could understand what she was saying when I concentrated, thank goodness.

"To do magic?" I said.

"To do magic?" she scoffed. "Charm? Yes. Magic? No."

"Magic, no?"

It is possible that I copied her accent a little bit. Not on purpose or anything. I was confused. But still. She didn't seem to notice, so I kept going, hoping she wouldn't.

"But this is a witch school. Aren't we supposed to learn magic?"

Miss Villere's rose glasses were hanging around her neck. She put them on and stared at me like she was trying to decide if I was telling the truth or not.

"This is Belles Demoiselles: Pensionnat des Sorcières. Magic is for hooligans. Belles demoiselles use charm. That's what you're supposed to learn at a finishing school. Charm and restraint. Not vulgar magic. New witches like you blaze hot. You burn off all the power you have quick, then you wilt like a rose left in the sun. Burning up magic like it's nothing is well and fine when a witch is your age, or even nineteen or twenty, but what about when you're thirty or forty?"

I stared at her.

Miss Villere laughed. "I know you can't think that far ahead, but if you're lucky, it'll come. What if you use your magic up on foolishness before you get old? Throwing magic around will only make it burn off faster. You'll be depleted. And trust me, there's nothing sadder than a depleted witch wishing she could make the world go her way again. If you want your power to last, you have to learn restraint. Drip it out little by little or not at all. That's the real strength. You understand?"

I nodded my head, but it didn't make sense. Why have magic and then not use it?

"I spoke with Angelique's family. They are very upset that their daughter was attacked on school grounds."

"I didn't attack her," I blurted.

"You didn't mean to attack her, but you did. That is what makes new witches like you dangerous. They get mad and—boom—flowers everywhere. And for what? That is why I did not try to stop the board from offering you a place here. You're a danger as you are. Who knows what you'll do without even meaning to. It's not your fault. With no family to teach you, it's no wonder. I thought being around the other girls would show you a better way so you won't be out in the world giving women like us a bad name, growing flowers everywhere you go."

A Danger? Me? My eyebrows were up so high I couldn't even blink. That's when I realized what was happening. Miss Villere thought I was one of the bad kids.

I had never, ever in my life been mistaken for a bad kid.

I didn't even know what to think. I just knew she didn't understand.

"I didn't do it on purpose," I said again. "I'd never hurt anyone on purpose."

"That is what I told Angelique's parents. They know you're a wild-seed. Pardon my language, but it's true. I had to tell them so they would know that you don't know any better. They've agreed that you can stay if you apologize. I've called you here to find out if that's what you want to do."

"I have a choice?" That seemed weird.

"Of course. Belles Demoiselles is not a prison; it is a place of honor. Of history. Ask the other girls how many of their sisters and cousins were not invited to attend when they made thirteen. Any one of those girls would gladly take your place. If you want to go home now, I will call your mother and we will make the arrangements."

My mom! What would she say if she got a call from the "fancy school" saying I was some kind of hooligan who attacked a girl?

"I'll apologize," I said. "I really didn't mean to attack Angelique. I was just trying to make my flowers grow and it slipped and . . ."

"You were trying to make flowers grow?" Miss Villere sighed.

I nodded.

"Oh, non. Non. Pòv bèt."

Miss Villere turned all the way to face me. She looked me up and down, like she was trying to decide for herself who I was. All I was was confused.

When she talked, her voice was gentle, like she was talking to a toddler. It wasn't the first time someone at Belles Demoiselles had talked to me like I was stupid, but I had to take it. Maybe I was stupid. "The flowers are not your magic, shè."

My eyebrows shot up again. That was news to me. I mean, growing flowers is a pretty useless magical power unless you want to be some kind of super-florist, but, I mean, you work with what you've got, right?

"Flowers are what happens when you don't know what you're doing and you use more magic than you should. Like pouring out a bucket to fill a thimble. You might fill the thimble, but mostly you just end up pouring a lot of good water on the ground."

I blinked. That's what Dee was talking about when she said I was being a rebel. I wasn't. I was just being stupid. Duh. Now it all made sense, including Miss LaRose shrinking my flowers back into their container. She wasn't giving me a chance to grow them again; she was trying to help me not look like such an idiot.

"I am not your teacher, but let me offer you this one lesson. You are a witch. You don't have to try so hard to be what you already are. No amount of showing out is going to change that, anyway. Angelique is what comes from generations of proper education. With time, you can get there, too, if you are diligent in your studies and careful of the company you keep. We can give you the tools, but only you can decide who you are."

Why was everybody at Belles Demoiselles always asking me who I was?

"Smart girl like you? What do you want to be? A doctor? A politician?"

"A YouTuber," I said, then I felt embarrassed. My mom always rolled her eyes and said stuff about "my potential" when I talked about my YouTube channel. My dad wasn't much better before he met Sandy.

But Miss Villere didn't laugh. She didn't smirk or tilt her head sideways or anything. She just nodded.

"A number of belles demoiselles do very well on YouTube. A charming witch can succeed at anything, particularly where technology is involved. Don't get me wrong. Wildseeds go viral all the time, but two weeks later no one remembers who they are. People have moved on to the next funny dance."

It was strange to hear Miss Villere, who was like a grandma with an old-fashioned accent, talking about "technology" and pantomiming the moves to the zipper dance. I didn't mean to, but I probably grinned. I don't have a good poker face.

"You think it's funny? It's true. Belles demoiselles don't just go viral, they become influencers. Magic is for the moment. Charm is for life. With us, you can learn to be a charming witch, a good witch. What you do with it after is up to you, but while you are here, you have to try your hardest to be good, you hear?"

I nodded, but I'm sure confusion was all over my face like I had written it with a marker. Was Miss Villere telling me I needed to be good because she still thought I wasn't good?

"Good girls, belles demoiselles, don't use potions." Miss Villere let her glasses slide to the tip of her nose. If they were anything like the ones Miss Lafleur had let me use the day before, she could see the magic glowing lavender all around my body. The feeling wasn't as strong as it had been that morning, but it was still there, humming all over. Or maybe it was just as strong, but I was just getting used to it.

"Have you ever heard the phrase 'Don't gild the lily'?" Miss Villere asked.

I shook my head.

"It means when you take something beautiful and perfect and ruin it trying to make it better. It's something like being 'extra,' though that's not quite it."

It was so wrong to hear Miss Villere saying "extra" like that.

"Taking potions is gilding the lily. Your magic is already powerful. Any girl invited to Belles Demoiselles has no need of such nonsense and I would highly advise you to discontinue it."

"But I—"

Miss Villere put a hand up. "There is no point in denying you took a chevelure potion. I can see the excess magic dripping from you even without my glasses. Don't worry. I know you're not the one who prepared that potion. Was Demi-Rose the one who helped you?"

I shook my head no. Dee didn't do anything and LaToya hadn't done anything I hadn't asked her to. Even good girls don't rat people out unless they really have to.

I changed the subject, hoping Miss Villere wouldn't press me. "Did you already tell my mom about Angelique?"

"I would never do that, shè. It is up to you to tell her. Only you can tell your story. But I would not worry about it too much. We all make mistakes and we all must learn to forgive. Your maman will understand."

Yeah. But would Angelique?

CHAPTER ELEVEN

GOOD AND BAD

*L*unch with Miss LaRose was not fun. Let's just say she was way thornier outside of class. She spent the whole time telling me I was stirring my tea wrong. Apparently it's "Up down, not round and round like a tornado." Before we started, I had planned to ask her about "charm and magic." She had said it to Dee about a thousand times, but even if she hadn't been looking at me like I smelled like fertilizer, Miss LaRose was too busy correcting my posture and my elbows for me to get a word in edgewise. Then the chimes rang for us to go to The Art of Arranging and, even though Miss LaRose was teaching that class, too, at that point I figured that the less I talked to her, the better.

Dee didn't motion me over, but she also didn't stop me from sitting with her, which was a step up from everyone else in the room, including LaToya, who I guess didn't know she should be grateful that

I hadn't just told Miss Villere that she was the one who gave me the chevelure potion.

Miss LaRose started The Art of Arranging talking about the "energy of all things." That sounded magical, but it didn't take long for me to realize that she was literally talking about how to arrange furniture in a room. Not magic. I know Miss Villere said we were supposed to be saving our magic, or whatever, but furniture arranging? Seriously?

By the time she split us up to work in pairs with miniature replicas of New York apartments and Bywater doubles, Miss LaRose had called on Dee three times. Dee was different now. More like the other girls. She still had super-short hair and combat boots, but it wasn't until then that I noticed how much she was trying to fit in. She was sitting up straighter. She was wearing only one pair of earrings. Her chin was perfectly parallel to the floor. Dee, but not Dee. And when she answered Miss LaRose's questions, her voice had a strange lilt to it that was more like Angelique's or Desirée's. It was kind of sad. Still, Miss LaRose picked apart every one of Dee's answers so much that, when Miss LaRose paired us up, I knew I had to say something.

"Miss LaRose is the worst," I whispered.

Dee nodded her head, starting to agree with me, then changed her mind and shook it instead, mumbling something that sounded like "play the game 'til you know the game." When I asked her to say it again, she didn't.

"I don't want to make her any madder. It's bad enough as it is. Let's just do this," she said.

Arranging stuff in little dollhouses was harder than I thought it would be. And I was wrong. It did have to do with magic. Apparently there is energy everywhere and the way it flows makes it easier for your power to just waft through a room even if you don't do anything, like finding a good spot for one of those plug-in air fresheners. That actually seemed like it might be useful. Maybe if I set up the stuff in my studio just right, I could get more likes on my videos without having to cry and rant. Where you put the mirrors makes a big difference. I moved the mirrors in our little dollhouse so that they were angled to reflect light off each other, kind of like Miss LeBrun's slide about the Hall of Mirrors in Versailles. I guess I was paying more attention in Art and Architecture than I thought.

Unfortunately, my mirrors were all wrong. Apparently the French dudes who built Versailles didn't know what they were doing where energy flow was concerned. Even more unfortunately, Miss LaRose corrected Dee, even after I said I was the one who did the mirrors.

It wasn't fair. Why was she out to get Dee like that? My skin buzzed with the injustice.

Miss LaRose looked at me through her rose-colored glasses. I was probably so purple with magic I looked like Thanos.

"Demi-Rose comes from a long, distinguished line of witches. She should know better," Miss LaRose said, as if that explained it.

"Dee," Dee mumbled after Miss LaRose had swished away in her too-white suit. Then she put the mirror back where I had it.

Desirée, Celeste, and Monique appeared after 10th chime. I wished they hadn't. I mean, I knew I was going to have to face Angelique and apologize eventually, but Angelique wasn't even with them. All they did was ruin the relief I felt leaving Miss LaRose to go to the one class I had been looking forward to: Animal Affinities.

My schedule said Animal Affinities was on the third floor, the same as our dorm rooms. I hadn't seen a classroom on the third floor. Then again, I hadn't seen a bathroom on the third floor, either. Maybe one of the rooms I thought was a dorm room was really a library or something.

When we made it to the top of the stairs, Miss Lafleur was standing right in the hallway holding a huge basket. I felt relieved, and, weirdly, like I was seeing my mom. Maybe because I had seen my mom hold a basket of laundry like that a bunch of times. I don't know.

But right then, the only thing I could think of was that I wished Miss Lafleur was the one "taking time" with me instead of Miss LaRose, who had informed me at lunch that I needed to sit with her at meals and tea times until my elbows were "under control."

"Belles demoiselles, please open your doors," Miss Lafleur said.

We all went to our room doors. I mumbled, "Morning glories," and opened my side a crack. Celeste flung her side wide and stood right in front of it. I was a little embarrassed to stand under my half of the doorway. After what happened in Greetings, ev-er-y-one knew my flower was the morning glory, but the flowers looked wrinkled and sad like they were as embarrassed of me as I was of them.

"A good witch uses charm, not magic," Miss Lafleur began when we were all standing in front of the correct door.

There it was again. Charm, not magic. But there had to be at least a little magic in getting the swans to do that heart neck thing, right?

"Magic is a part of us and nothing to be ashamed of, but, just like you learned to use the bathroom and groom yourselves in private, the same is true for your magic."

For some reason, Desirée, Monique, and Celeste had to hold back giggles when Miss Lafleur said "bathroom."

"Some animals can make this particularly difficult," Miss Lafleur continued. "Let's start with something straightforward. How many of us have pet cats at home?"

A bunch of girls raised their hands.

"How many of us have had cats who are not our pets come close enough for us to touch them? Perhaps at a friend's home or even on the street?"

I had to think about that for a second, but then I remembered how the stray cat Luz's family feeds—the one we call Sir Drools-a-lot—is always trying to rub his head on my leg. I raised my hand. So had everyone else.

Miss Lafleur nodded like she already knew we'd all have our hands up. "Cats and witches have a natural affinity. A witch can call even the most reluctant cat with a t-t." She double kissed her teeth and double snapped her fingers at the same time. "This is not a very useful skill. There are very few occasions in life when one needs to call a stray cat, and, if one is not careful, it is possible to end up surrounded by an unreasonable number of them. Given the chance, cats will bask in the font of a witch's magic like mermaids in moonlight. The real power is to stop them. So, for this activity, we'll practice just that. Each of you will create a stream of power and then close it off as quickly as you can. Now, I know some of you may feel uncomfortable wielding your magic openly in public. That is why I've chosen this hallway for our first lesson. Feel free to slip into your rooms for some privacy if you like. We'll start with ten minutes and work our way down from there. Ready?"

Miss Lafleur adjusted her rose-colored glasses, then lowered the basket to the ground. Kittens, y'all. The basket was filled with kittens. They were so adorable and fluffy that I was literally naming them in my mind. Zufi. Snowball. Mr. Whiskers. I couldn't help it.

"Begin," Miss Lafleur said.

Letting magic build up was easy. I didn't have to "let" it at all. It was waves hitting the shore. Already there, just waiting for me to use it. And finally, finally, I was supposed to use it.

I know Miss Lafleur said that using magic was like going to the bathroom or whatever, but score one for not having a witch for a mom. My mom had never made me feel weird about it, so I didn't run into my room. Dee and I were the only ones who stayed.

Dee lifted her chin at me and I gave a nod back. Then she took a deep breath and, no joke, I saw Dee's magic. Like, in real time. No glasses. It was red and faint and if I hadn't known better, I might have thought she was blushing, but I did know better. There was no mistaking the glow.

If Dee's magic was an ember, mine was a flame. No wonder Miss Lafleur had made such a big deal about it on that video. Compared to Dee's, mine was huge.

The kittens were roaming all over the hallway, running in and out of rooms, rubbing their adorable little chins on whichever ankles were closest. Some of the girls had obviously picked them up. I could hear cooing coming from several of the rooms. Stuff like, "Who's a pretty kitty?" and "Hello, Mr. Fuzzypants" in tiny baby voices. I was no better. They were so stinking cute, they made me want to go in my room, but not to hide. I wanted to see if my mom had packed any ribbons. The fluffy orange one I had named Othello definitely needed a ribbon. Blue would have been perfect, but purple would have been cool, too. Just being near him made the magic prick up my skin with goose bumps. It was heavenly.

I peeked in our room. Celeste was on her bed. She petted the gray kitten politely, then got up and walked back into the hallway, a smug look on her face. The gray kitten looked after Celeste for a second, but she didn't follow. She came over to me, and she wasn't the only one. A tiny tabby came next. Then a Russian blue. Then the one I had named Snowball, who was all the way on the other end of the hallway.

"Remember, mesdemoiselles. Charm, not magic."

Oh, right! I was supposed to stop the magic after I started it. I had no idea how. Everyone else did, though. They all cut their kittens off, and I went from four kittens to fourteen in a matter of seconds.

"Charm, Hasani, charm," Miss Lafleur giggled nervously.

I knew that meant I wasn't supposed to be using my magic, but I swear I wasn't trying to.

Stop.

Off.

Cancel.

Remove.

Unsubscribe!

Nothing worked. The hallway breeze didn't stop little beads of sweat from forming on my forehead or shoo the kittens away. They just loved me and, even though I knew I wasn't supposed to, I loved them back.

Miss Lafleur kissed her teeth and the kittens went back to their place in the basket.

"OK, then. That was a good first try. Everyone please return to the hallway. I know it can be hard to control one's magic, especially when one is nervous and inexperienced. But that is why we are here. To learn." Miss Lafleur smiled. Her speech was clearly meant for me. "So let's learn from each other, shall we? Some of you already had excellent techniques. Celeste, would you mind sharing yours?"

Celeste brightened. "I just did what my mother always says. 'Swish and swipe.'" There were matching hand motions. Cute ones.

"Good!" Miss Lafleur smiled. "I usually say, sip, dab, dab, but I like your mother's phrase, too. I'll have to add it to my list. OK, then. Let's try it again. If you feel a little surplus of magic welling up, just dab it away like tea from the corners of the mouth. Sip, dab, dab. The kittens will be happy to receive it, and you must show them not to expect more. Sip, dab, dab. Just swish and swipe." Miss Lafleur gave

Celeste a quick look. Celeste smiled. She wasn't exactly gloating, but she wasn't exactly trying not to, either.

Miss Lafleur put the kittens down again. Almost everybody went into their rooms. A few of the kittens followed them. Dee stayed outside again, and this time, so did Celeste. None of the kittens went near her. Not one. Celeste was standing not two feet away from me, but all the kittens ignored her like she wasn't even there and came straight for me.

For real, part of me was glad they did. Hadn't Miss Lafleur said kittens like to bask in fountains of magic, or whatever? Didn't all of the kittens coming to me just prove that I was more magic than anyone else? Every part of me wanted to let my magic flow free, even if it drew all the kittens in Vacherie. Then I saw the worried look on Miss Lafleur's face and remembered that I was supposed to be keeping the kittens away. It was so stupid.

Dee was at the far end of the hallway. Most of the girls had come out of their rooms. Dee had to walk past all of them to get to me. She got between me and Celeste and pressed something into my hand.

Miss Lafleur looked away.

"For luck," Dee said, pressing a little fish medallion into my hand. The metal was cold but it got warm, almost hot, the moment it touched my skin. My magic was flowing so quickly that my hand felt numb, and there was way more where that came from.

121

"That's enough, Dee," Miss Lafleur said.

Dee nodded and slipped the charm out of my hand and into her pocket.

Somebody down the hall chuckled. LaToya was right across from me, looking guilty, like it was her fault.

I thought about ignoring everyone else, even Miss Lafleur. The kittens and I understood each other. Only Celeste's smirk stopped me. This was a test, and I was failing.

What had they said? Sip, wipe, dab?

The sipping part made no sense, but dabbing and wiping I could do. I started petting the kittens, letting the magic in my fingertips pour out onto them. The kittens purred, but they didn't move away.

Chuckles turned to giggles.

"She can't help it," Dee said. "She's new."

That didn't stop them from laughing. The only thing that did was Miss Lafleur delicately clearing her throat.

"Let's try again, mesdemoiselles," she said.

Miss Lafleur kissed her teeth and we started again. It didn't get any better. If anything, it got worse. By the end of the period, everyone else was able to keep the kittens away with a single pet. A few, like Celeste, could do it with just a look.

"You using too much," Dee hissed before the last round. "Just a little. Then wipe the extra on the kitten."

"I am. They like it," I whispered back too loud. It kicked off a new round of laughter.

Miss Lafleur had to pull a few of the kittens off me, including Othello, who had gotten his little kitten claws tangled in my hair.

Miss Lafleur dismissed us early so we could freshen up before our next class.

"Our next class is Introductions? Didn't we already have that?" *And why would it be last? Shouldn't it be first?*

"Nah," Dee said. "That was Greetings. It's different. Greetings is about you. Introductions is about other people."

Somebody sniggered. Dee motioned with her head for me to follow her downstairs, which was fine with me. No part of me wanted to have to face Celeste in our room, though Othello was giving me sad kitten eyes as we walked away from Miss Lafleur and her basket. I missed him already.

"It's so hard," I said. I was talking about leaving Othello. Dee clearly did not know that.

"It's that potion," Dee said. "Potions amp up your magic. That's why you're having so much trouble. It's just gushing out of you."

"Good girls, belles demoiselles, don't use potions." Miss Villere's words came easy, like I had been saying them my whole life.

"Yeah, right. I bet most of these little princesses use potions," Dee said. She made princess sound like a curse word. "They just knew better than to take one right before school."

"You said potions are bad," I said.

"I said they were a bad idea," Dee corrected. "I never said they were bad. My grandmother always says there's a time and a place for everything. Come on. Let's get a good spot."

We had made it to the Grand Foyer. Dee pulled me over to a spot by a three-tiered fountain with different flowers floating on each level. I thought it was so we'd have a better view of the teacher, but it turned out it was that the edge of the fountain was the only place you could sit. When other people came in, they kind of glared at us for taking the good spots but then stood in little clumps nearby. Dee nudged me. She was holding back a grin. I couldn't help smiling, too. The edge of that fountain was more comfortable than it looked.

I was just starting to feel better when Angelique drifted in, her cloud of attendants right behind her.

Pain gripped my stomach. I knew that feeling. It was guilt. As much as I wished it weren't true, Miss Villere was right. I had basically attacked Angelique with flowers. Angelique had never been nice to me, but maybe she had been trying to keep me away because maybe she was a good enough witch to know that I might hurt her. And guess what? I had. Even if she wasn't hurt, I was wrong.

"Sorry," I said.

Angelique pretended not to see or hear me. I didn't blame her. I sounded fake to me, too. Maybe the best apology I could give her was to just stay out of her way. And Celeste's. Maybe Dee's roommate would trade places with me. That might make it better for everyone.

Miss Lavande swept into the Grand Foyer in her lavender suit. My ears were buzzing. I could barely hear her. From what I caught, she was saying the same lesson Miss LaRose had given us that morning. Something about knowing who you are or deciding who you are or something else that didn't seem to matter. The next thing I knew, everyone was pairing up. Someone was coming toward me. I looked up, expecting to see Dee. It was Angelique. Her brown skin glowing like a doll, every shiny kink of her hair in place. She put her hand on my shoulder, and I felt like I knew her. I could feel her mother and her grandmother standing behind her, proud of who she was, proud of her being excellent.

Angelique and I were standing in front of another pair of girls. Thuy, who was wearing a passionflower barrette, and Celeste.

"This is Hasani," Angelique said, her voice warm and clear. "She's a wildseed from the ghetto part of New Orleans who doesn't know how to comb her hair and hasn't taken a shower since she got here."

"Pleased to meet you," Thuy said before she caught herself. She wasn't pleased to meet me. No one was. No one should be.

I wanted to cry.

I wanted my mom.

I wanted Othello.

I wanted to be right.

I wanted Angelique to be wrong. She wasn't.

The next thing I knew, the Grand Foyer was covered with morning glories. Banisters, arches, ceilings, floors. They were everywhere except on Angelique.

Everyone pulled the vines off, some laughing, some looking horrified. Miss Lavande dismissed us. I let everyone leave the room without me, even Dee.

Miss Camille was waiting by the door with another envelope. I didn't have to look at the green ink. I already knew it had my name on it.

I read the letter.

"A picture of you in an identifiable area of our campus was posted on the Internet. It has been removed. The posting was a clear violation of your contract and has been noted in your record. Report to the Grand Foyer at First Blush."

What picture? I thought. Then I let it go. Did it matter? Maybe Celeste had taken a picture of me when I wasn't paying attention. I didn't remember seeing her with a phone, but I was sure she could have done it. Maybe while I was sleeping or something. I wouldn't put it past her.

The letter was folded in with a new copy of my schedule. I knew I was in trouble, but I was actually relieved when I saw that my Rainbow to First Blush class had been replaced by Remediation. I was pretty sure "remediation" was the Belles Demoiselles word for "detention," but that didn't matter. I wanted the day to be over.

Be careful what you wish for.

Miss Villere met me in the Grand Foyer at Rainbow. All she said was, "Your flowers do not belong here. Take them out and don't disturb anything else."

Then she left.

There was a ladder and an enormous gray trash can on wheels in the middle of the floor, the kind the custodians at my school had. It was clearly put there for me to use, so I got to work. The vines on the floor were pretty easy to pull up. There weren't any other flowers there. The ones on the walls were a different story. I had to go in and pick out the little vine claws one by one. It got dark. I missed dinner. I was hungry and trying not to cry. I remembered the snacks that my mom packed. That made me feel better until I was pulling vines so far up the wall that there were moths and butterflies flying out every two seconds. That's cute when you're standing a few feet away. It's not cute at all when they keep flying in your face. Plus Miss Villere said not to disturb anything. I was as careful as I could be, but every time something flew up, I cringed. That was bad enough, but the darker it got, the more I realized that there weren't just birds and butterflies in the house. There were bats.

Yes, technically bats are pollinators, but I'm willing to bet money that nobody is thinking about pollination when a bat comes flying at them in the dark. I shrieked. Then I thought of Othello's little claws and how much worse they would be attached to a bat and how easy it would be for said bat to get tangled in my hair, and I shrieked some more.

Nobody came to rescue me, but I guess nobody needed to. The bats actually weren't, like, attacking me or anything. It's just that after I saw them, I couldn't stop seeing them, and every one seemed to be close to a morning glory vine.

By the time I was done, the third-floor hallway was pitch-black. I was sure I was the only one left awake until I saw Dee. I wasn't sure it was her at first. It was dark and I was tired. But besides being vaguely Dee-shaped, whoever was sneaking up to the fourth floor was carrying combat boots as she tiptoed up the stairs. Teachers stayed on the fourth floor. I didn't know what Dee was up to, but I wasn't about to call out to her. I just hoped she didn't get in trouble. All I wanted to do was check my phone and go to bed.

Celeste was sleeping in her little yellow sleep mask. My phone was still where I left it, thank goodness. I settled on my bed and clicked it on, hoping there would be enough signal to send my mom a message. There was a little green check mark next to the good morning message I sent her, so that one went through. The one I sent to Luz had a check, too. But now, no bars. No service. I wanted to call my mom so badly. At least I had a message from her. I expected it to be all: *Did you eat salad?* so I had to blink to be sure I was reading it right.

Check your YouTube, honey. It's blowing up.

I laughed in spite of everything. I could exactly hear my mom saying "blowing up" like a parent and I missed her so much.

I had two messages from Luz, too. One with her and Miguel dipping marshmallows in a ridiculously big chocolate fountain and another that was a screenshot of Sandy's IG.

She such a poser! She not even from New Orleans and she's already rocking the fleur-de-lis jewelry? Can we hate her now?

No messages from my dad, but now I knew why. He was obviously too busy with Sandy to even shoot me an "OK." He didn't even have to type it out. Two letters. He couldn't even do that.

I went back to the screenshot of Sandy's IG. The pic was of her planting flowers in my mom's garden. Well, it was my dad's garden, but he had bought it for my mom and that was what mattered. To make it worse, the electric charging port on the convertible was in the shot, which was crazy because it was on the driver's side and the garden was on the passenger side. Did my dad back the car in just so she could get this #green shot? I swiped off the screenshot, but not before I saw #greencar #greengoddess #blackgirlgreenthumb #blackgirlmagic.

My dad wasn't in the shot, but he didn't need to be. It was his house and he had probably taken the picture. They may as well have been hugged up posing together.

My phone was dying. I tapped the flashlight app to find the cord, but that only made the battery turn red and I still couldn't find it. That's when I freaked out. Not badly. No flowers. Just tears.

Celeste got up and walked to a door next to her bed that I thought was a part of her closet but turned out to be a bathroom. She pushed back the shower curtain, unhooked my charger from the showerhead, and handed it to me.

"Angelique put it there," she said. "It was a joke." Then she got back in her bed and pulled down her sleep mask like nothing happened.

Yeah, maybe Angelique hid it, but you let her, I thought. I didn't say that, though. I may not have known what was going on with magic and stuff, but I wasn't stupid. Celeste didn't have to give me my cord, and I knew more than anything that I needed a friend, or maybe just one less enemy. If nothing else, at least I had found the bathroom.

CHAPTER TWELVE

MASKS AND DARKNESS

Of course Celeste was already up and in the shower before my alarm rang. I might have hit snooze if I hadn't had the urge to check my phone. Nothing from my dad. Nothing from anybody, for that matter. It was like my phone just didn't work at Belles Demoiselles. If I couldn't figure that out soon, it was going to be a problem. I only had one more scheduled post.

"I never have signal," I said, texting my mom the same thing. When I pressed Send, the progress bar didn't even pretend to fill up.

"Maybe you should get a better phone," Celeste said, coming out of the bathroom. I resisted the urge to tell her that I wasn't talking to her. I mean, I was talking, I didn't stop when she came out of the bathroom, but I wasn't talking to her. More like talking in general and she happened to be there. So much for us being friends. Luckily, she was already dressed, so all she did was slide on her little yellow flats, smooth out her flowered dress, and leave.

That's when I got out of bed. There were a few vines wrapped around my wrist, but nothing too bad. The extra magic from the chevelure potion was dying down. I just pulled the vines off and kept it moving. The shower was calling my name.

My mom always yelled at me about getting my hair wet, but my mom wasn't here and I had a ton of new hair to play with. I'm not gonna lie. Dunking my head under the shower spray was amazing. My coils were all bouncy and springy and stretched down my back when the water got in there really good. I felt just like one of the shampoo girls on commercials. Of course I forgot we hadn't packed any hair stuff until I had completely drenched my head. I didn't have a wide-tooth comb or a wet brush or anything, so I ran my fingers through it a few times and smoothed down the front with my palms in the bathroom mirror.

"I don't know what Mom is always so worried about. This looks good," I said, deciding I just might wet my new hair like that every day.

Satisfied, I threw on some clothes. Celeste was wearing a dress. All I had left were jean shorts, but a quick look in the mirror said my hair more than made up for it. A new copy of my schedule was waiting for me—on my desk this time. I grabbed it and headed out, hoping to make it downstairs early enough to actually eat breakfast this time. LaToya was waiting for me outside my door.

"Took you long enough," she said. "Here. Drink this."

My eyebrows popped up. I don't know if it was from the shock of LaToya acknowledging me or the fact that she thought I would drink another one of her potions right before class.

"No, thank you," I said, trying to make it sound as unthankful as I could.

"It's coffee," she said.

I looked at the cup. It did look like coffee and cream, but I didn't take it.

"It's not poison."

"Is it a potion?"

"Yes," LaToya said, looking at me like she still expected me to drink it.

I stared, surprised she came right out and said it.

"Coffee is a potion. Coffee and chicory is a different potion. So is mint tea, rose water, golden milk. Practically everything is a potion if you know how to use it," LaToya said. "They have coffee and chicory downstairs, but you need the chicory right now more than the coffee, so I made you a special blend. My mom says the old New Orleanians always put chicory in their coffee because it keeps your magic in check."

Side-eye.

"Look, I'm just trying to help you. I feel bad about yesterday. I didn't know you were gonna drink straight coffee at breakfast. That probably made it worse. Coffee and chicory make it better. Kind of like an antidote. Your magic is still oozing." LaToya waggled a finger at a vine growing on my shoulder.

I yanked the vine out but didn't reach for the cup. Fool me once and all that.

LaToya rolled her eyes, took a dramatic sip, then handed me the cup. It smelled like coffee. I took a sip. Tasted like coffee, too. Really, really good coffee that slid down smooth like ice cream. With every swallow, the buzzing in my fingertips got a little softer. I had sort of forgotten it was there until it started to disappear. I downed the rest of it in a giant swallow. The waves of magic had been crashing inside of me, but all of a sudden, they got quiet. Not disappeared or anything. More like when you're walking on the edge of the water at the beach. The water pulls back, but when it reaches out to touch you again, it's soft and in a rhythm. You know when it's coming, and you know that when it does, it'll feel good.

LaToya grinned. "It's good, right? I put sugar in it. Don't tell anybody. Want to go to breakfast?"

Oh, so now you're willing to be seen with me? The thought flashed through my head, but of course I didn't say that. What I really said was, "Sure," and, "Why is everybody against sugar, anyway? Is it a diet thing?"

"No. It's the whole forcing people into chattel slavery so other people can eat cake, thing."

My eyebrows shot up so high, I didn't have to say anything. *Whaaaat??* was written all over my forehead.

"Oh, yeah. You didn't know? Belles Demoiselles was built by people who were being forced to work the sugar plantations before they learned how to work their magic. Not eating sugar here is kind of like a tribute to them."

"Seriously? It's not about, like, diabetes?"

"Nope. Slavery."

"So why do they even serve sugar, then?" I said, thinking of all the cubes of sugar I had put into my coffee. "I mean, they put it out at every meal."

"Choice. You can eat sugar if you want to. It's more symbolic than anything, now. I mean, how long has it been since sugar was grown by people forced into slavery?" LaToya laughed.

Not that long, actually?

I didn't know what to do. Say it was weird she was laughing about slavery? Laugh, too?

In the end I went with, "I'll skip the sugar."

That seemed easiest.

LaToya nodded and we made our way into the dining room. I expected her to ditch me when we got downstairs, but to my surprise, she almost sat with me. I mean, she didn't, but that wasn't really her fault. I had to sit with Miss LaRose, and I couldn't blame her for sitting with Thuy and Kalani instead when she found out. I didn't want to spend my breakfast being corrected, either, but I didn't have a choice. At least I got to eat. It's crazy how much better I felt after scrambled eggs, strawberries, and a second cup of coffee and chicory—cream, no sugar.

At the end of breakfast, Dee was waiting for me outside the dining room.

"My bad," she said.

"For what?"

"For not stopping you from taking that potion. I thought you were playing. I wasn't thinking about you being the only witch in your family and everything. That's tough, man. But my mama says you're from Vacherie."

Seriously, how was I the only person with no phone signal? I wanted to talk to my mom, too.

I nodded.

"Cool. Check under your pillow tonight," Dee grinned. "Oh! And it's only for Vacherie people, so don't tell anybody. I don't want anybody to get in their feelings."

Obviously I had questions, including if I actually qualified as a Vacherie person since I was from New Orleans, but by then we were walking into Greetings. Miss LaRose seemed thrilled to see me, even though she had scowled at me all through breakfast and I'm pretty sure she expected me to coat the place in morning glories again. I didn't do as badly as I had before, though. To be fair, I probably couldn't do any worse than I had done on the first day, but still, there was progress. We did the thing again where we had to say who we are. After the first round, Miss LaRose told Angelique and Tyra that they could move to thinking it instead of saying it. She was not about to say that to me. My flowers still grew every time, even if I only put in the tiniest bit of magic. Just a little bit. Eventually Miss LaRose stopped having to shrink them back. But still. I was struggling.

Miss LaRose kept smiling and pausing at my desk. She said, "Well done, Hasani," so many times you would have thought I was actually doing it right. I wasn't, but no one got tied up with morning glory vines, either, so at least there was that.

In Art and Architecture, Miss LeBrun talked about Senegalese builders and Creole architecture, and how it was thanks to them that La Maison des Belles Demoiselles had a permanent, perfect breeze flowing through it without fans, even when you only opened a few windows. Miss LeBrun didn't mention that the Senegalese builders were enslaved. Everyone seemed to know that already, including me for once, thank goodness. Who knew my parents' history lectures would be useful someday?

In Fragrance, Miss Lafleur had us find our signature flowers in the garden blindfolded, using only our "magnetic energy." Apparently, magic and flowers were opposites, so if you could "quiet your magic" to just the right level and "listen," you'd walk right up to your signature flowers without even trying, like the needle on a compass. I got turned around a few times. I kept pointing toward the house when everyone else was being led somewhere in the garden, and I couldn't make my magic quiet, whatever that meant. The waves of it weren't crashing as strong as right after I took the chevelure potion, but it sure wasn't quiet, either. Still, I managed to feel my way to the morning glories in the garden eventually. A little vine had grown in my hair from the effort, but luckily Dee and LaToya motioned at me until I realized, so I pulled it out and chucked it onto the topiary before Miss Lafleur noticed. The only thing that stopped me from being the last one to finish was that Danielle's flower, the Louisiana iris, was planted in the middle of a pond and Danielle didn't want to get her shoes wet.

Lunch was OK. Miss LaRose had her nose wrinkled up like I wasn't wearing deodorant and corrected me the whole way through, but, honestly, it wasn't that bad. I mean, I wish I could have been basically anywhere else, but I made it through. The trick was smiling and nodding. When I stopped asking questions and figured out what she was talking about when she said "tipping the soup spoon," she mainly talked to Kalani and left me to eat my soup in peace.

Art of Arranging was right after lunch. So, basically another double period of Miss LaRose. Not something to look forward to, but it turned out not to be as bad as I thought. No one else grew any flowers, of course, even though Miss LaRose corrected all their furniture placements way more than she corrected mine. She was definitely going easy on me, which I guess should have been cool but somehow only highlighted my failure. Like everybody else could read but she was just happy I knew the letter B.

When 12th chime rang, everyone headed out to the front of the building to Animal Affinities. Apparently class today was at Swan Lake. I hadn't read my schedule. I'd just stuck it into a notebook in case I got separated from the herd, but if classes were going to keep switching locations, it made sense that they kept giving us new ones.

Swan Lake was heart-shaped. It should have been cheesy, except it couldn't be because it was so awesome. From my balcony it looked more like a teardrop, but that had to be the angle, because up close it was definitely a heart with swans drifting back and forth like they were dancing to music.

Miss Lafleur stood next to me. I thought she was doing the cool TV teacher move where you stand next to the weirdo to show the other kids they're not so bad. That is not what was happening.

Miss Lafleur cleared her throat. "Schedules are personalized, Hasani. Please refer to yours for the correct location at 12th chime so that the rest of the class can begin our Day 2 lesson."

She wasn't mean about it or anything, but I thought she would go ahead and start the lesson. Give me a chance to slip out while no one was looking. She didn't. She stood there and looked at me until I pulled my schedule out of my notebook and read it. Sure enough, I wasn't supposed to be at Swan Lake. I was supposed to be at the last Japanese magnolia with Miss Villere.

This was awful. First of all, everyone was staring. Again. Second of all, I wasn't going to get to learn whatever everyone else was going to learn at Swan Lake and, unlike all of our other lessons, it seemed like whatever was happening at Swan Lake was going to be cool. Third of all—do people say third of all? Third of all, a class taught by the principal is never good news. The only consolation was that when I made my way over there, Angelique was there, too. A corner of her schedule peeked out of her bag along with a glimpse of lip gloss and a tiny perfume bottle. It looked like she had laid it out for an Instagram pic. She closed her bag when she saw me looking, but I had already seen "Japanese magnolia" in purple ink when Miss Villere gestured us over to a little pen of kittens.

Othello scrabbled up, trying to get to me. If his little claws had been able to sink into the slick sides, he would have.

"Neither of you mastered lesson one. Excellence is a ladder, not a hopscotch. No skipping steps. Don't let it happen again."

I thought Angelique would say the reason she hadn't mastered the lesson was that she had missed the lesson because of me, or at least remind Miss Villere that it wasn't her fault, but all she said was, "Wé, mamzelle."

I nodded and tried to look as humble as Angelique did.

"All right, nah. Let's get to work. Watch me."

I could still barely understand Miss Villere when she was talking, but it was the exact opposite when it came to seeing what she was doing. As soon as she climbed into the pen, I could see her collecting magic in her hands and flicking it like drops of water from her fingertips to the eager mass of kittens. She hadn't given us rose-colored glasses, but I could see her magic, anyway. The kittens drank it up, but instead of giving them more and more, Miss Villere made them wait for it, like Luz's dad made their puppy wait for a treat when they were training him. I thought that was mean at first, but Luz's dad said, "All dogs are hopeful, but dogs that live with people need to see us as pack leaders. They can hope, but you can't let them demand." Miss Villere was doing the same thing, but with cats and magic instead of dogs and bacon, and I could actually see it. It was dope. And once I saw it, I got it. It only took me two tries to get all the kittens, including Othello, to stop coming toward me. It's not that they were avoiding me or hating me or anything. They were waiting, hoping for me to give them a drop of magic.

"Byin bon, Hasani. Va jwènn lézòt," Miss Villere said, nodding toward Swan Lake. I didn't know the exact words she was saying, but I knew she was telling me I could go back to the rest of the class. Before Angelique. I tried not to gloat. I mean, it was only Angelique's first time doing the lesson and it was my second. I had no idea you could make your magic visible like that, but Miss Villere had, and with her literally showing us what to do, it was . . . easy? What was hard was not smiling and giving my hair a little flip when I walked away. OK. A big flip. It was a lot of hair.

Miss Lafleur was still talking to the whole group when I made it back to Swan Lake.

"Not just any insects. It's important to draw the right kind. Butterflies. Beautiful moths. Ladybugs. The occasional beetle. Insectivores are fine as long as they are widely considered pollinators. Nothing too fierce. However, dragonflies are the exception to that rule. They're bloodthirsty hunters, but their delicate wings more than make up for it. So, draw three and have the rest leave you be," Miss Lafleur grinned like she had said something funny. "And remember, demoiselles. Charm, not magic."

Miss Lafleur let her grin fade to a shy smile, and less than a second later, three butterflies fluttered in her direction, then landed one at a time, two on her hair, one on her shoulder. She looked less Glinda, more Mary Poppins. It was awesome.

"And release," she said. The butterflies flew away as delicately as they had landed. I couldn't see her magic like I could see Miss Villere's, but I knew they were doing the same thing.

"Charm, not magic, demoiselles. You have until the last swan flies. Begin."

I knew what to do, but it was harder than I thought it would be. Insects were so little and they hardly stayed still. It took me a while to figure out that instead of flicking magic, I had to pool it and lure them where I wanted them to land like my magic was nectar or an aphid. Unfortunately, what drew moths also drew gnats, and what drew dragonflies also drew mosquitoes. It was frustrating, but as soon as I felt my magic welling up too much, I thought of Angelique, still over with the kittens and Miss Villere. That was enough to stop me from letting it overflow. I didn't want to go back over there.

Angelique made it to the lake about halfway through the lesson, but by then I had already gotten a dragonfly to land on the back of my hand and a butterfly to land in my hair like a barrette. I wasn't the first one to finish, though. That was Casey with three Gulf fritillaries on the palm of her hand. She was telling everyone how lucky she was, for once, that her signature flower was a butterfly attractor.

Thuy was second, with a dragonfly, a blue-green bumblebee, and blue morpho butterfly. I finished third, but I may as well have been first, it felt so good to not be last. And when Miss Lafleur said, "Good job, Hasani," it didn't feel like a weird pat on the head for the wild-seed. It actually felt like she meant I did a good job. Weird, right? It was everything I could do to not flip my hair again.

And, as if that wasn't enough amazing for one afternoon, when Miss LeBrun told us to pair up for introductions in Introductions, Celeste chose me. I was scared at first. I mean, who knew what she would say. But it turned out to be perfectly normal. Cool, even. Celeste introduced me to Thuy.

"This is Hasani. She's a green witch who's getting a really big following on YouTube. Her channel, MakeupontheCheapCheap, has over 10,000 subscribers."

First of all, 10,000? My mom wasn't kidding about my channel blowing up. I really needed to get my phone working.

Second of all, how did Celeste know that? Was she lowkey stalking me this whole time, but, like, in a good way? And how was she getting signal on her phone?

Third of all, that was so nice! I didn't know what a green witch was—turns out it's just the polite way to say a witch who doesn't have a witch mother—but I knew it wasn't mean. It felt too good when she said it. Maybe we were going to be friends, after all.

At the end of class, I tried to keep the thing with Celeste going by saying, "I wonder what kind of scones they'll serve at tea" in a British accent. The accent was perfect in my head, but when I said it out loud, I sounded more Lafayette than London, so it was for the best that Celeste was too caught up with Skylar and Casey to hear me. I would have sat with them, but Miss LaRose insisted that I sit at her table at tea time, too, to practice knees and saucers. And when Miss Lafleur saw me heading upstairs with everybody after tea time, she pulled me on the side and made me read my schedule in front of her.

"Green, Hasani?" Miss Lafleur said when I pulled the schedule out. "That is dangerously close to gold."

She said "gold" with a little wrinkle on her forehead like gold was a bad thing, but I didn't ask her why because I was too busy trying not to cry again at what my schedule said. Morning glories. I was supposed to be cleaning up morning glories from now until bedtime. Again. All the progress I made melted away.

"I cleaned them up yesterday," I said.

"If you had finished, we would not be having this discussion."

"But . . . there are bats," I said. Saying it out loud made tears actually well up. I tried to blink them back in.

"The pollinators are just doing their jobs. If you'd rather not share their space with them, I'd suggest you get done before dark." Then she sighed and put a hand on my shoulder. "I'm sure you've learned something that can help you. You'll get it, Hasani."

Would I, though?

I wasn't done before dark. There weren't morning glories everywhere, but that was worse, because it made them much harder to find. I didn't realize that Miss Lafleur had been trying to give me a hint until the bats were already flying around. Actually, they kind of helped me. There I was wishing someone would teach me some kind of magic echolocation to find flowers in the dark, when *click*. I should have smacked myself on the forehead because . . . duh! Someone had.

You've had the power the whole time, young Padawan. Use what you have learned. My mind said it in Yoda's voice, or maybe it was Miss Piggy with a cold because that's totally not how Yoda talks.

Honestly, I don't know what took me so long. I could do this. I concentrated on quieting my magic enough to feel the pull of the flowers. I had to pull it all the way back to ripples on a pond before I felt the first morning glory, but it went faster and faster after that. Good thing Miss Lafleur had made us find our flowers blindfolded, because by the time I found the last one, it was pitch-black.

For a second, I thought it must still be "social hour," because the light was still on in the third floor hallway, but the hallway was empty and everyone had their doors closed like it was bedtime. I opened my door, prepared to tiptoe in quietly in case Celeste was sleeping, but I forgot all about Celeste the moment I opened the door. There was a kitten on my bed.

If Othello could have flown to me, I think he would have. As it was, he was ridiculously, adorably trying to get his little kitten courage up to jump off the bed. Forget about dripping magic as a treat. I poured it into him and he soaked it up, climbing all up my shoulder to poke his little head out and mew from behind my ear. I thought I would die from the cuteness. I was probably giggling for five minutes before I realized Celeste was sitting on her bed staring at me.

She had a kitten, too. The Russian blue I had been calling Anastasia was quietly curled up on her bed.

"I'm so excited! I can't believe we got kittens. Is it a test? Do we get to keep them?" I said, picking up my phone so Othello and I could take a selfie. Thankfully my phone was charged. And I had messages. And 402 notifications on YouTube. 402!

Celeste didn't seem as excited. "We finished lesson one," she said, like it was no big deal. Maybe it wasn't to her. Or maybe she was just tired. She was already ready for bed, her sleep mask propped up on her head like a headband.

I didn't take the hint.

"What did you name yours? Mine is Othello."

"Smokey," she said.

Anastasia was a way better name for her. Everyone named gray cats Smokey, but I didn't tell her that.

"Cute! I wonder if we're allowed to bring them to class and stuff." How much better would The Art of Arranging be with kittens running around looking like giants about to storm the tiny houses?

"There's food over there." Celeste motioned to my desk. "Demi-Rose brought it. She said it's from Miss Camille, but . . ." Celeste gave a little shrug.

There was a little tray with cheese and crackers and grapes. I was so hungry it looked like full-blown dinner. It was cool of Celeste to mention it. I might not have seen it otherwise.

"Do you want some?" I said, jumping up to get it.

"Just don't leave food in here. I don't want to get roaches."

"Fair," I said, making a note not to mention the snacks my mom packed. "You sure you don't want any?"

Celeste didn't say anything. She just sort of closed her eyes and pulled her sleep mask down.

"See you at breakfast," I said as she settled under the covers.

Celeste popped up on one elbow and yanked her mask back up.

"Look," she said, "we're not going to be friends."

"What?" I blinked.

"It seems like you're thinking that we might be friends, and I'm just letting you know that we're not."

"Why?"

"I just don't like you." She said it flat, not yelling or anything. I think I might have liked yelling better. Flat made it feel like I legit did not matter at all.

I just sat there opening and closing my mouth like an idiot. Why was she saying this?

"I never did anything to you."

"Why does that matter? I just don't like you. Sometimes you don't like people. This isn't a cartoon. We're not all going to be best friends and run off to Ponyland together. Let's just be fine and leave it at that."

"Did you post a picture of me?" I asked.

"What?"

"I got in trouble yesterday for posting something that had Belles Demoiselles in it, but I didn't post anything. I didn't even have signal. Did you take a picture of me and post it?"

"Are you serious right now? Just because I don't like you doesn't mean I'm trying to sabotage you. It's not even worth my time."

Celeste pulled her sleep mask back down, and I left it there. I didn't exactly believe her, but it didn't matter. Othello was purring.

I scooped up Othello, my phone, and cord, threw some stuff into a little purple basket of shower things my mom had gotten me, and walked into the bathroom. It was nice. White tile. Huge mirror. Perfect light. I turned the shower on, but that was only a cover so Celeste wouldn't hear me. I needed to do something that would calm me down and, at that point, only one thing would.

I set up some rolls of towels on the edge of the counter and plopped Othello inside. I didn't think the towels would actually stop him from falling off the edge of the counter, but I thought they might slow him down. He was ridiculously cute jumping around like he did, especially when he noticed the equally adorable kitten in the mirror. I pooled a little magic on the counter and watched Othello roll in it. Something about the bright blue of his eyes next to his orange fur made me want to copy it. I was sure I could, so I splashed some water on my face, patted it dry, and got to work.

People laugh at the dollar store eye shadow, but that's only because they don't know how to use it. The expensive stuff is for people who want someone to make beautiful colors for them. The dollar store stuff is for people who want to make beautiful colors themselves.

I pulled out a palette of reds and pinks and my trusty glitter palette. The one on there that they called "gold" was the best yellow I had ever seen. It was filled with glitter but still blended perfectly with other textures. It was exactly what I needed to change the reds and pinks to a color that matched Othello's fur. I didn't even think to record what I was doing until after I had mixed the first shade of orange. It looked dreamy on the back of my hand, so I dove in with a heavy coat from the center of my eyelid out. I mixed some lighter shades and darker ones, using them to soften the edges and create the idea of Othello's stripes. I put blue at the corners. A bright blue that I only tipped with a touch of gray. I was nervous that where the blues and oranges touched it would turn a mucky green, but it didn't. It was a perfect shadowy brown. I finished with liquid liner. Cat eye because, I mean, come on. It was a kitten makeover. It looked amazing, but it was even cuter when I held Othello up so his little face was next to mine for a closing shot. I sped the video up, put some music behind it, and scheduled it to upload with the title: Kitten Makeover + Meet Othello. I had no signal, of course, so absolutely nothing happened when I clicked Upload, but I felt better, anyway. And even though it had been running for goodness knows how long, when I finally got into the shower, the water was still hot.

I didn't see the mask until Othello and I were done recording and had climbed into bed. It was under my pillow right on top of my list. I pulled it out by accident, thinking that my sheets had gotten tangled up or something, but no sheet I've ever owned was that soft and smooth. As soon as I could see what it was, I knew it was special. Important. It just had that feeling, you know?

One side of the mask was midnight blue with a scene of the full moon over a forest clearing. My name was stitched into the stars. The words "L'Invitation a Cirque des Sorcières de Vacherie" were sewn in small letters like a beam of moonlight. I ran my fingers across the stitches, wondering how anyone could make them so small and perfect, even with magic. The other side of the mask was perfectly smooth and shimmered with flecks of gold.

That's when I remembered what Dee said. "Invitation" and "witch" were easy enough to understand, even in French. I didn't know what I was being invited to or where to find it, but I knew I was going.

CHAPTER THIRTEEN

BLUE AND GREEN

I tried not to let it, but even with the mask tucked back under my pillow, the thing with Celeste really bugged me. I mean, I'm a nice person. Who just decides they don't like you when they've never really even talked to you?

Othello helped. When I petted him, it was like the worst of my worries just melted into his crazy-soft fur. After Celeste left that morning, Othello and Anastasia—I could not call Celeste's kitten Smokey—curled up together in a little beam of sunlight on my bed. I almost snapped a pic of it to show Celeste how cute they were, and possibly also to show her how happy Anastasia was on my side of the room, but I didn't. Instead I dripped a little magic into Othello to apologize for leaving him all day. The way he drank the magic up, I was sure he was going to be miserable without me. Then Anastasia looked at me so hopefully. I couldn't just leave her out. Celeste had barely touched Anastasia at all that morning, so when Anastasia meowed at me with her huge green eyes, I ran two fingers across the top of her head. It was barely any magic at all. Just a dribble. Celeste would probably be mad at me for doing it, but I honestly didn't care. If she was going to be rude, I could be rude right back.

The mask was still under my pillow. Granted, I didn't speak French or Creole or whatever language was written on the mask, so I had no idea what it said, but that wasn't really a problem. To have an invitation that cool, I knew whatever it was, it was dope. I'd just ask Dee to expound on its dopeness right after breakfast.

Dee gave me a nod when I got down to the dining room, but she always sat as far away from Miss LaRose as she could. I didn't blame her. Everything I did made Miss LaRose cringe, but somehow whenever Dee was around, she ended up correcting her even more. That morning, Miss LaRose made me pick up my cup and put it down on the saucer literally thousands of times until the cup made zero clinking sound. I could do it if I was really careful and concentrating really hard, but every time I thought I'd gotten the hang of it and tried to start talking at the same time, the stupid cup would clank again.

I was staring at my cup, imagining my arm was slow and steady like the crane in those toy-grabby games at Chuck E. Cheese, so I missed the moment when Angelique entered the room. I knew something big was happening. Nothing gets that quiet unless something big is happening. But by the time I looked up, everyone was talking again and Angelique was sitting at the head of the table, her hair swooped and pinned up into a perfectly coily crown on top of her head.

Then I noticed her fleur-de-lis charm. It was pretty, but not pretty enough for all the other girls to be staring at it the way they were. We were in Louisiana. Fleur-de-lis stuff was everywhere. That did not stop the other girls from staring and fawning over her even more than usual, which I would not have thought was possible.

"She got her charm," Dee said on the way to Greetings. "Don't worry about it. Everybody will get one."

The way everybody was acting, the charm either came from Mr. Beast or AnyaDo0dle herself. Or, like that charm was the east and Angelique was the sun.

Angelique ate it up. She held court all day. Even the teachers treated her differently. In Greetings, Miss LaRose let her just say simple things like, "Welcome," and "Good morning," while the rest of us were still forced to mentally recite our whole life histories before we could say one word. And in Animal Affinities, when Angelique made three Gulf fritillaries land on her head in three seconds flat, Miss Lafleur pulled her on the side for a private lesson with the swans.

But Dee was right, though. I don't know how I hadn't noticed it before, but all the teachers were wearing fleur-de-lis charms just like Angelique's on thin silver necklaces.

Between classes, Dee and I were the only ones who weren't practically shoving people out of the way to walk next to her. I mean, I wanted to, but with thirteen other girls trying for the same spot and Angelique hating me and everything, I figured I didn't have much of a chance.

Then in Introductions, Angelique was allowed to introduce herself by just saying her name, and I swear that when she did, I felt like I knew her a little better. Like I could trust her. Like we were friends.

Meanwhile, I wasn't the only one who wasn't on Angelique's level, but I was the last one who was still accidentally growing flowers when I said my name. Small ones, but still.

Dee was trying to make me feel better on the way to tea time.

"It's just your clothes. You need better clothes," Dee said, which was not helpful since I didn't bring any better clothes. Everybody at Belles Demoiselles had custom wardrobes of clothes and accessories designed around their signature flower. Even Dee had her flowery combat boots. I'd already worn the purple outfit that my mom grabbed at WalMart. Everything else I had was basically shorts and T-shirts. Cute shorts. Cute T-shirts. But still shorts and T-shirts. My mom was right. I should have brought a few more fancy things, but I didn't need Dee to remind me that I still didn't fit in.

LaToya interrupted us, saying, "Might I join you ladies for tea?" in a pretty good British accent.

"You're not going to freshen up?" I said, trying to do the accent back. Mine came out more like Kentucky.

"I'd rather hang out with y'all," LaToya said.

That was surprising. LaToya had been glued to Angelique's crowd, which, to be fair, at this point was pretty much everyone else in the school.

Dee nodded. I was going to go upstairs—to play with Othello, not change my clothes—but I nodded, too, and the three of us sat down together around a low table that was set for tea.

LaToya talked first, pouring tea for us at the same time, like stopping the china from clinking was not hard at all.

"Everyone is saying that's the fastest anyone's ever gotten it," LaToya said, offering me the sugar dish. I shook my head. "Obviously, we can't check the records, but it makes sense. Three days. Can you believe she got it in three days? I was just hoping to get it before the last week of classes. And did you see her do the thing with the dragonflies? You couldn't even tell it was her. It looked so natural. I bet Miss Lafleur chooses her as a protégé. I can't wait until I get my Belles Demoiselles charm."

Dee nodded but already seemed over it.

I wasn't. "Protégé?" I laughed. "I mean, yeah, Miss Lafleur was showing her some stuff with the swans today"—stuff I really wanted to know about, but that wasn't the point—"but saying that makes her Miss Lafleur's protégé is a little dramatic, right?"

LaToya's eyes perked up the way they did whenever she knew something other people didn't know. "You know about the protégé program, right?"

She barely waited for me to shake my head.

"So, when you pass the test to become an official belle demoiselle—"

Blank stare. Luckily Dee explained.

"All the teachers vote. It usually doesn't happen until the last week, but . . ." Dee shrugged.

LaToya jumped back in. "Anyway, when you pass the test to become an official belle demoiselle, you get an official Belles Demoiselles charm and, once you have it, one of the teachers can offer to mentor you, which is huge because they'll basically teach you everything they know and they might tell you their real name and everything."

"Wait. Those aren't the teachers' real names??" I asked.

"Nah. Privacy," Dee said. At the same, LaToya said, "It's a tradition."

Then they both shrugged and said, "Both."

"OK...," I said. This was a lot. "So why do they wait until you have a charm to teach you for real? Shouldn't they be teaching us now? Isn't that why we're here?"

"They are teaching us, but this is special, right?" LaToya said, her face glowing. "Like, beyond. The stuff we can do now is babyish compared to what we'll be able to do once we've earned our charms. That's why there's a whole week after classes end before we officially go home for the summer. It's time for the teachers to work with their protégés, if they pick any. They don't have to."

Dang. I didn't have to say it. It was written all over my face.

"I know, right? I'm hoping Miss LeBrun chooses me, but how cool would it be if Miss LeBrun chose me, taught me everything she knows, then, like, a famous belles demoiselles like Serena Williams shows up at the closing ceremony and chooses me, too?"

"Serena Williams is a belle demoiselle?" I said.

LaToya shrugged. "I don't know. Maybe. But that would be so cool, right? My dad would flip."

Maybe AnyaDo0dle was a belle demoiselle, too. I mean, maybe not. But maybe. I needed one of those charms.

Then it dawned on me. "Wait a minute. Is that fleur-de-lis necklace what's making Angelique so good?"

To be honest, I was kind of relieved. It sucked that as soon as I was getting kind of good at something, out of the blue Angelique could just show up and be way better. If the fleur-de-lis necklace was the reason, that was better somehow.

"It's a charm," LaToya corrected. "And the Belles Demoiselles charm doesn't make you good. You get the charm when you are good. You have to have really good control of your power before they'll let you store it, and the Belles Demoiselles charms are the best charms on the planet. That's why everybody wants to come here so bad. Supposedly a Belles Demoiselles charm can store like ten years' worth of magic. Even a kismet could do something cool with that. If she could get in. Which she couldn't. But still. I don't know what Angelique did to get her charm so fast, and she won't tell me. Believe me. I asked."

"What? I thought y'all were getting all buddy-buddy," Dee said.

"I mean, that was the plan," LaToya said, not embarrassed at all. "I knew it wouldn't be easy. Her family is pretty established. Eight generations of witches. They're crazy rich and they didn't even have to underpay people to do it. If I had gotten my charm first, I think I would have had a real chance. It's probably not going to happen now, and Angelique will probably make sure nobody else will hang out with me, either." We were alone, but LaToya dramatically lowered her voice, anyway. "Angelique knows about my family business."

"What business?" I asked.

They both looked at me.

"Funerals," Dee said, like it was obvious.

"Oh. I didn't know," I said. "I don't know LaToya's family."

"I don't know them either," Dee said, "but her signature is the gladiolus, so . . ."

"Sword Lily," LaToya corrected.

"Either way, it's a dead giveaway."

LaToya rolled her eyes, but she didn't seem too mad. "I've never heard that one before. Har dee har-har. Very clever."

Dee shrugged.

"And, for your information, gladioluses are not the only flowers used at funerals," LaToya said. Dee gave me a look like *See?* "So just because my signature flower happens to be a sword lily doesn't automatically mean that I come from a long line of morticians. I mean, I do, but that's not the point. My grandmother is a fourth-generation funeral director and her flower is a pink orchid. It's just a coincidence. But Angelique must have looked my family up on the Internet and told everybody what we do. Now the only time any of them say anything to me, it's a funeral pun."

"You think Angelique told everybody to do that?"

"She doesn't have to," LaToya said.

She didn't need to say anything else. We all knew it was true. There was nothing I could do to make LaToya feel better except join in her misery.

"Angelique is mean, but I think Celeste might be worse," I said.

I expected them to join in. After all, the three of us were the only ones not in Angelique's entourage. But no. What I got was both of them saying, "Celeste's really nice" and "I like Celeste," at the same time.

I told them what she said in our room about not really caring one way or another if I lived or died. They were unimpressed.

"That's not mean," Dee said.

"You're right. It's meaner than mean. Celeste basically said that I don't matter. That's cold. Way colder than Angelique."

"Sorry, Hasani," LaToya said. "I'm with Celeste on this one. I mean, you can't expect her to want to be your best friend after you took her sister's spot. I'd be salty if you took my sister's spot, and I don't even have a sister, let alone a twin."

Celeste was a twin? That was news to me.

"Hasani didn't take her spot," Dee said. "Celeste's sister is a kis-met. She didn't get a spot. She didn't even get on the waiting list."

"That's not what Celeste said. Celeste said her sister was all set to come, but at the last minute they said they were using that spot for a wildseed charity case even though Celeste's family had paid good money for both of their girls to come. No offense, Hasani. I mean, you obviously have a lot of magic. You probably need to be here more than Celeste's sister, even though you can't pay. I mean, even with the chicory you can barely control yourself. That's a lot of magic."

LaToya was smiling at me like that was supposed to be some kind of compliment, but I could only sort of smile back. It hurt, and it wouldn't have if it hadn't been true. To be honest, I had no idea if my family could have afforded Belles Demoiselles without a scholarship. I didn't think we were poor, but I also didn't have all the stuff everybody else had, so maybe we were.

But that wasn't even the part that hurt. The part that hurt was LaToya being too polite to come right out and say I was the worst one there. The only reason I had friends at all was because a better girl, a girl who deserved to be there, didn't want them. And I wasn't even sure Dee and LaToya and I counted as friends. We were more like a collection of rejects.

LaToya pulled out her phone and started scrolling pictures.

"You have signal?" I said. I hadn't even bothered to bring mine.

"I don't. I saved it. Look," she said, showing me a pic of two Celestes, one in red, one in yellow. Dang. She *was* a twin.

"Great," I said. Because what I exactly wanted at that moment was to stare into the face of the girl whose life I stole.

"Drop it, LaToya. Hasani didn't take her spot."

"If you say so," LaToya sang. She obviously disagreed.

People were starting to come in, including a couple of teachers. "Let's save it for social hour, ladies," Miss LeBrun said, glancing pointedly at LaToya's cell phone.

LaToya put her phone away, but that pretty much squashed our conversation.

*A*s the sky began to turn pink and everyone headed upstairs, Dee held me back.

"See you tonight?" she said.

I raised my eyebrows. Then I remembered. With all the Angelique fleur-de-lis stuff, I hadn't gotten to ask Dee about the mask.

"Oh, right! It's in French, though, so I don't know what it says yet."

"Don't worry about it. I'll walk you over," Dee said.

"You sure it's OK for me to go? I'm from New Orleans."

"Grandmé Annette says different. I went to see her the other night to put in a good word for you, but she said you were already on her list."

"I was?"

Dee shrugged.

"Back garden after lights out?"

I nodded. Dee turned to walk away.

"Wait," I said. "I don't have detention tonight."

Dee gave me a thumbs-up. "Cool?"

"I mean, I don't have detention tonight, so I'll be at social hour. It's my first time. Will you help me survive?"

Dee shrugged, but she couldn't hide the smile from her eyes. Maybe we weren't just a couple of misfits. Maybe we were friends.

Turns out, social hour is the one time of day there's actually signal, so everybody hangs out in each other's rooms sending memes and links to funny things on the Internet and checking their social media. When I say "everybody," I mean everybody except me and LaToya and Dee. And when I say "each other's rooms," really I just mean Angelique's room. LaToya, Dee, and I ended up in my room with Othello and LaToya's kitten, Laveau, and, for the first time in what felt like months, I was able to check my YouTube account.

HOLY. CRAP.

142,008 views.

13,287 subscribers.

1,212 likes.

833 comments.

Zero downvotes. None. They loved me. They *loved* me!

I jumped up and ran in front of the bathroom door and hit Record.

"Sorry to be away, you guys. I'm out here learning tons of stuff to make our channel better. Just tell me what you'd like to see in the comments below. Oh! And say hello to Othello!! Isn't he so, so cute? I recorded an Othello-inspired get ready with me the day I adopted him. I'll link it in the description box. See you soon, but until then, I hope your day is magic." Waves of magic crashed against my fingertips as I typed up the links and description. I was all set to pour the overflow into Othello, but none spilled out. I grinned. I was actually controlling my magic. It felt amazing.

Instead of doing a finger kiss peace sign like AnyaDo0dle, I closed out with double finger kiss, heart. It just felt right. Then I tacked on my opening, chopped out the part where I ran to the bathroom, and hit Upload.

"Can I be in your next one?"

I looked up from uploading the kitten update.

LaToya was smiling. Dee was smiling, too, but more like she had just seen me pick my nose than she wanted to be in a video.

"Sure," I said. "I was thinking about doing a whole kitten-inspired makeover series. Want to be my first?"

"OK!" she said. "Let me just finish sending this message to my mom, and then I'll get Laveau. I need her to soften up my dad about Laveau before I talk to him."

I nodded and started scrolling through the comments on my rant video. Everyone was so supportive. I was clicking through their profiles so I could subscribe to their channels. That was another one of AnyaDo0dle's tips that I'm glad I followed because that's how I realized that some of the people who had left nice comments were girls from Belles Demoiselles. Tanvi, whose screenname was AR0sebyany0thername, had said, "I feel you, girl." Thuy, aka SilverbellsandCockleShells, said, "Parents are the worst. Hang in there." Tyra, Monique, Kalani, and Valerie had all left hearts or smiley faces or comments that said, "Notification gang!" on my eyeliner tutorial. And _AnnieOaky_, my first ever commenter, had left another comment thanking me for giving her a shout-out. I hearted it and said, "You know it, girlie! Us NewTubers have to stick together. <3"

I tried to at least like all the comments, but there were so many of them that it was taking me a while to get through.

Two comments in a row said something about AnyaDo0dle. I felt a flash of panic and clicked over to her channel and gasped.

"What's wrong?" Dee asked.

"I missed two new videos from AnyaDo0dle!"

"OK," Dee said. "Just watch them now. The Internet is forever."

I shook my head. She didn't understand. I had never missed a new upload from AnyaDo0dle before. Never. I was always in her first thousand likes, sometimes in her first hundred. And I commented. I always commented. Now I was late.

I clicked Play on the first one.

AnyaDo0dle sang out, "Hello, Lovelies," like she always did. "You know I like to support my subscribers however I can. I love you guys. So since so many of you have liked and commented on my tips for YouTubers series, I'm guessing a lot of you guys want to be YouTubers and that's so, so, so, so cool. So guess what? I'm going to pick one of you to do a collaboration with. To be eligible, you have to be a subscriber with a YouTube channel. That's it. So, if you're a NewTuber and want to do a collab with me, comment below. I'll announce the winner in my LiveStream on Thursday. If you're new here, remember to like, comment, and subscribe and click that little notification bell. Love you! Bye!" That's how AnyaDo0dle signed off on all her videos, but for once I didn't feel the love. I had missed it. It was Thursday. I'd missed it. I'd missed my chance.

Dee and LaToya looked just as horrified as the next video auto-played.

"Hello, Lovelies!"

I shut it off. I couldn't do it. I couldn't listen to AnyaDo0dle announce somebody else's name.

"That sucks," Dee said.

You think? But I didn't say it. She was just trying to be helpful. She didn't know that the whole reason I wanted to learn about magic was to grow my YouTube channel, and here was my chance and, even with magic, I had somehow missed it.

I wanted to text Luz. Luz would know what to say. She'd send me something funny with a dog and hat and a taco and I'd laugh and not feel so bad, but as soon as I opened up my message app, there was a chime and my signal went dead.

"I know you can't upload it today because it's past chimes, but do you want to record the makeover anyway? It might make you feel better. We could do it in my bathroom so you don't keep Celeste up," LaToya said.

Dee shook her head.

I knew she was shaking it because we were supposed to be going to the mask invitation thing, but LaToya thought Dee was shaking her head at a copy of my schedule on my desk. She picked it up.

"You're already on green?" LaToya said just as Celeste entered the room. Celeste smiled and nodded at Dee and LaToya, then went into the bathroom. LaToya kept talking. "Yeah, you'd better get to bed on time. You get too many more of these and you won't have to worry about getting a charm."

Question mark face.

"You're almost on gold," LaToya said.

Double question mark face.

"That's bad," she said. "Very bad."

"How is gold ever a bad thing?"

"It's reverse rainbow. We all start off on purple. When you get a demerit, you move back to blue, then green, then gold."

"Gold? Seriously? Why not yellow? Why gold?"

"To catch your attention. That's the last stop before Troublesville. If you get orange, a full committee of belles demoiselles has to review your case and decide whether or not you can still earn a Belles Demoiselles charm. If you get on red, forget about it. You don't get a charm AND they delete you."

"From the planet?"

"From the Internet."

That sounded worse.

"They can't do that. How can they do that?"

"There's magic woven into all the Belles Demoiselles tech. They can definitely do that. Get some sleep. We can record my video tomorrow, Greenie," LaToya said with a wink.

I didn't think her comment was that funny.

Dee hung back as LaToya closed the door to her own room.

"You still coming, right?" Dee whispered.

I hesitated. I was already on green. I had missed the collaboration with AnyaDo0dle. All I really wanted was to climb in bed and cry over that. Maybe let Othello rub his little face against my face. I didn't want to do anything that might get me in trouble. Without winning that collaboration, magic was the only hope I had to grow my channel big enough that AnyaDo0dle might collaborate with me anyway someday. No, not magic. Charm.

I shook my head.

"My channel," I said. "I know it sounds stupid, but I really want to grow it big. Like, me and AnyaDo0dle are friends, big. I can't get kicked out. At least not before I know how to use charm to do that."

"This'll help. I promise," Dee said.

Something about the way she said it. I nodded. And after Celeste had put on her sleep mask and turned out her light, I put on my fancy embroidered mask and met Dee in the moonlight.

CHAPTER FOURTEEN

CIRCLES AND MOONLIGHT

"It's sort of secret, but not really," Dee said.

We were cutting across the garden, goddess statues casting moon shadows on the walkways.

"That makes no sense."

"Well, most belles demoiselles don't want people to know they're witches. Grandmé and the others don't care who thinks they know what." Dee said "Grandmé" with an accent, like she was one of the Vacherie cousins I could barely understand. "So when Grandmé Annette invites the Vacherie people from Belles Demoiselles, we masquerade. It's not sneaking out. Well, not exactly. I mean, we're allowed to come and go. It's not illegal or anything and, technically it's not against the rules, but . . ."

"It's frowned upon," I finished.

I was trying to be funny. I'd heard that in a commercial once. "Frowned upon in this establishment . . . !"

But Dee said, "Exactly."

"How do you keep this stupid mask on?" I said, tugging at it and yanking a chunk of my hair in the process.

"I don't know. I've never worn one before. Honestly, I didn't know if I would get one until I got it. Grandmé Annette was pretty mad when I decided to go to Belles Demoiselles," Dee said.

A step later, we were off the Belles Demoiselles grounds. I know because out of nowhere the air was thick and hot and my hair was sticking to my back like a wool cape in June. What am I saying? My hair basically *was* a wool cape, and it was definitely June. By the time we got to a little house with the back porch light on, I was dripping with sweat and would have given my left kidney for a scrunchie.

There was an old woman standing on the porch waiting for us. Grandmé Annette.

"Vyin isi. Donne mò gaddé to."

Grandmé Annette's skin was brown like mine. Her hair was long, too, but I could tell from the way her braids shone in the porch light that her hair was probably more curly than coily. Still, I felt like we were more alike than different. She held my face in her hands and smiled at me, saying more words I couldn't understand.

"Vyin wa," she said.

"She only speaks English, Grandmé Annette," Dee said.

"Egal." Grandmé Annette waved Dee's words away. "You come dan bon lalinn."

Both of us looked at Dee. "A good moon."

"The right moon," Grandmé Annette corrected with a wink. "This girl don't hardly speak Creole, either, and she born here. At least you have an excuse. Come. They all gon' be waitin' for us before long. Let's go get you ready and you can tell me what you doing with all that hair. Demi-Rose must give you hers, too, hunh?" Grandmé laughed.

Dee rolled her eyes, but Grandmé Annette wasn't through with her.

"Since when do you wear fancy shoes, shè?"

Dee looked embarrassed. "You know I have to wear them to do it their way."

"Well, their way is not our way."

"I know," Dee said, leaning down to unlace her flowered boots. "I'm taking them off."

"Well, at least they taught you something at that fancy school. I see you can keep the mosquitoes off you. Both of you."

I had forgotten about mosquitoes. There weren't very many out during the day on the Belles Demoiselles grounds, but out here at night there should have been millions of them. I guess I was keeping them off me. I just didn't notice until Grandmé Annette pointed it out.

"Now, show me what else you can do," Grandmé Annette said, raising her eyebrows at me.

"Like, with magic?" I asked. What could I do? Nothing useful, that's for sure. "I thought we weren't supposed to use our magic because it makes us burn out or something."

"The good comes with the bad. That's life. But never you mind. We'll see soon enough. Come inside and get ready for the moon."

Apparently getting ready for the moon meant eating. Grandmé Annette showed me a trick to tie my hair up without a scrunchie so I wouldn't "catch a heatstroke," but after that it was all food. I wasn't hungry, but the way Dee shook her head when I started to say that made me know the only acceptable answer was yes. Grandmé Annette fed us okra and tomatoes with shrimp and sausage and tall glasses of icy cold water, and when she thought we had eaten enough she brought out a special jug from "the icebox," which Dee assured me was just a refrigerator.

Grandmé Annette poured a little into my glass and nodded for me to drink it.

"What is it?"

"A potion," she said. "Wild mint, cane juice, and lemon. Give it a little sour to balance the sweet."

"Cane juice? Isn't that just sugar? I thought witches don't eat sugar because of . . . you know . . . bad stuff."

"Sugarcane was just grass until it was shaped by our magic. It has power in it, especially right after it's cut. Just because somebody did evil with a thing doesn't make the thing evil. If you not evil, you can use it just fine. You not evil, are you?"

I shook my head.

"Good. Then you can have some if you want it. I grew that cane myself." She flicked her fingers and a clump of sugarcane taller than we were appeared right next to us in a flash of green. Right in the middle of the kitchen floor.

I blinked.

"I can see your magic," I said.

"That's 'cause you kin to me. If you were my granddaughter, you'd see it even stronger, but a second cousin will do. So what took you so long to come home, hunh? Why you stay away?"

"I don't know. I didn't know I was supposed to come. I just got my magic."

Grandmé Annette laughed. "You don't get magic, you are magic. It's already in you. It's in all your family. That's the way."

"No," I said. "My family's not magic. I'm a wildseed."

"We all wildseeds," she said like that explained everything. "Here. Take this, City Girl, so no matter where you live, you remember Vacherie is your home, too."

Grandmé Annette held out a little silver charm like the one Angelique got from Belles Demoiselles, but instead of a fleur-de-lis, it was a dolphin.

"Are there dolphins in the swamp?" I asked, hoping it didn't sound too stupid. Maybe I should have said river?

Grandmé Annette smiled again. "The dolphin reminds us that we were all wildseeds at one time. You'll understand more when you're older."

Dee had a dolphin charm, too. I'd seen it before. She'd tried to help me with it once, I realized as she slipped it out of her pocket and tied it into a belt loop on her jeans. Grandmé Annette put mine on a thin chain around my neck, then she brought us out into the night.

It was full dark. The only light was the moon and a sprinkling of stars. Grandmé Annette led us through the cypress trees like she had a flashlight until we got to an open space. There was a fire in the middle. I'd never seen a campfire before. It was cool, but I was way more impressed by how many people were there. I don't know how many I thought there would be, but there were too many to count in the crackling light.

"Everyone helps everyone in the circle," Dee said as we got closer. "The more people, the better. You'll see."

Grandmé Annette stepped into the center and held her hands up. Everyone got quiet. She put her hands down and two girls poured water on the fire, so the only light left came from the sky. Smoke wafted up, scenting the air as beautifully as any flower in Miss Lafleur's garden.

In the moonlight, some of the people in the circle shimmered like they were coated in fairy dust. I thought they must be the strongest witches, but then I remembered what Grandmé Annette said about being able to see magic more the closer people were related to you. My mom was right. I did have a whole lot of family in Vacherie.

A woman stepped into the circle and sang something out in Creole.

"She's saying her problem," Dee whispered. "Now everybody will try to help."

The glistening people started first. Some spoke, others just waved their hands and bits of watery light floated away from them toward the woman in the center. She closed her eyes and inhaled, soaking it all in. Then more women started to step forward. Some of them jetted out streams of light so sparkling and bright that I had to blink so my eyes could adjust and, suddenly, the empty patch of swamp was filling with flowers. Those were the witches. The ones who came before them must have been kismets, sharing what magic they could. It was like watching a trickle next to a stream. I thought it must have been embarrassing to be the one with a few drops of power when there were people around you who looked like they were pouring out rivers, but none of the kismets looked embarrassed, and none of the witches moved the kismets out of the way. They all worked together. It was beautiful to see, but it was beautiful to feel, too.

It happened like that over and over again. Someone would call out a problem, and the others would send their magic to solve it. Sometimes flowers appeared, sprinkled in kismet for good measure. I wasn't sure if it was because the witches in the circle couldn't stop themselves from overflowing or because they didn't try. Whichever way it was, magic surrounded me like water in a swimming pool. I must have been related to almost everyone there, because there were only a few people whose magic I couldn't see. I could even see Dee's. I had seen it before in the hallway, before she pressed her dolphin charm into my hand during the kitten lesson. She was probably trying to show me how she was doing it, but I didn't understand. Once I knew what I was looking for, I could really see it. It was faint, but it was there.

Dee stepped into the circle. At that point, there were so many currents of sound and magic that I couldn't understand what she said even though she was right next to me. A stream of magic swirled into the pendant on her hip, then into her and she seemed . . . I don't know. Happy? Happier? I let my magic flow to her, too. It was easy to do after watching everybody else. And before I knew it, I was making my own requests. I started with AnyaDoOdle, but my mom and my dad and kept slipping in. So did Sandyandfree, even though I wished I could forget her. I didn't think I said anything out loud, but peo-ple answered me, anyway. Almost like voices on the wind. *Wildseed*. But when they said it, it didn't sound bad. It sounded like "free." Like something to be proud of. Their magic filled my pendant and pushed through to my fingertips, and suddenly I felt like myself again. I remembered who I was. A witch, yes. But a witch with a plan. And a YouTube channel. In my mind, I could already see the checklist form-ing. It was about to be on.

Eventually people started to slip away. No one lit the fire again. Everyone found their way by moonlight and went in all directions, even into a path in a sugarcane field. That's when I saw her. There were so many girls there in so many sizes and shades of brown that I hadn't noticed her before. She wasn't wearing her fleur-de-lis charm, but even with a mask on I knew it was her. There was no way anyone else had hair that coily, that perfect.

Angelique.

CHAPTER FIFTEEN

PLANS AND PROMISES

"Feel better?" Dee asked.

We had just crossed from hot and humid to cool and dry, so I was feeling pretty good, but I would have been, anyway.

"Yeah," I said. "I feel way better."

"Me, too," Dee said.

"You, too? What were you feeling bad about?"

"My mom," Dee said.

"Oh!" I laughed. "I thought you were about to say something about Miss LaRose. I was gonna say, 'Ignore her. She only has one vote.' That can't stop you from getting your charm, right? But your mom, that's different. What's happening with her?"

"One teacher *can* vote you out," Dee said. "It has to be unanimous."

"Oh."

"And that is the thing that's going on with my mom. My mom is Miss LaRose."

Dee kept talking. I had to blink back my shock. Her mom was Miss LaRose. I mean, LaRose—Demi-Rose. I guess it made sense. And I guess it also explained why Miss LaRose was so hard on her. She probably expected her to be perfect. But still, *wow*. I did not see that coming.

Dee had never talked this much, and I didn't want her to stop. She told me about how Grandmé Annette had stopped talking to her mom when her mom started working at the school. Dee never stopped visiting Grandmé Annette, though, and now she basically had to choose between them, but she didn't want to because she loved them both.

"That's rough," I said when Dee had been quiet a while.

Dee shrugged.

It was cool to have Dee talking to me for real, like about what was going on with her and stuff, like we were actual friends. So I let her talk the whole way back to school even though all I could really think about was how incredibly dope my YouTube channel was going to be and I would have liked nothing better than to spill my plan to Dee right then and there. I was cool, though. Dee and I stayed together until we got to the third-floor landing. The teachers lived on the fourth floor. That's where Dee was going the other night—to her room in her mom's apartment. Dee gave me a smile before she slipped up the next set of stairs. I smiled back, wondering if it would be a good or bad thing if my mother was a teacher at my school. There were so many ways that could go wrong. I felt sorry for Dee, but at least she knew where everything was. At least she didn't need anybody to tell her the rules.

Angelique must have walked back to campus just like Dee and I did, but there was no sign of her, even as I slipped back to my own room. But I had my own stuff to deal with. Now that I wasn't trying to listen to Dee, my brain was all about MakeupontheCheapCheap.

I plopped on my bed, pulled out my list from where I had shoved it under my pillow, and, with Othello curled up in my lap and my cell flashlight propped up next to me, I got to work making some serious lists. This time with magic.

Dee had put her dolphin charm back in her pocket, but I kept mine on. I liked the way it looked. I liked the way it felt against my skin and how it gave the tiniest little buzz when you pulled magic out or let it flow in. Like a notification, but on vibrate. I smoothed the list out with my hand. "Long hair" and "make friends" were still there where I had scribbled them at the bottom. This list was about my channel, and they didn't belong there. I probably should have scratched them out, but I couldn't bring myself to do it. I checked them off, instead, then opened up the Notes app on my phone to start a new list. My dolphin charm buzzed as the app flared to life. I'd never made a checklist on my phone, but this list wasn't going to be like any list I had ever made before. Magic and tech, right?

From that point on, pretty much everything went right.

The next morning at breakfast, every girl in the dining room smiled at me when I passed. Some of them even spoke.

"Hey, Hasani."

"Good morning, Hasani."

"Congrats, Hasani."

I stood up even straighter, making sure my new dolphin charm gleamed in the light. It was even cooler than I thought if people were actually making room for me to sit with them. Unfortunately, I still had to sit with Miss LaRose, who eyed my new charm but didn't actually say anything about it. Dee didn't wear hers on campus, but if there was no rule against it, I was wearing mine. The dolphin charm might not have had as much power as the Belles Demoiselles fleur-de-lis we were all supposed to be lusting after, but it worked. I had seen it in action. Witches had boosted each other the night before by filling their charms. It was like a battery pack. Why would all those witches be using a faulty battery pack? If the dolphin charm didn't work, all the Vacherie witches would have upgraded by now, so the fact that they hadn't meant that I was right and all the snooty belles demoiselles wannabes were wrong.

When I woke up that morning, none of the magic from the night before was left in my dolphin charm, but that was actually a good thing. It left room for my spare magic. So in class when I felt it bubbling up and threatening to spill out, I didn't have to hold it in or wish Othello was nearby to soak up the extra. All I needed was my charm.

In Greetings, my flowers stayed exactly the same size. In Art and Architecture, I let a little bit of magic dribble out of the charm to brighten my face and make it look like I was paying more attention. I think I might have actually been paying more attention, too, because I had never realized how interesting Black Madonnas throughout history could be. In Fragrance, I was the second person to find the right carrier oil for my signature scent, and in The Art of Arranging, Miss LaRose complimented me on my mirror placements and, legit, it actually sounded like a compliment.

It was all because of my plan. That's the thing I realized when I was with the Vacherie witches. I'm a planner. I always have been. I make lists about making lists so I can check "make list" off my list. But ever since those morning glories sprouted on the St. Claude bridge, I had been sort of winging it. Having a plan felt at least a thousand times better.

The day wasn't totally perfect, though. I got a new schedule. Gold. I had to remind myself that the beautiful metallic gold letters were not a good thing. Only at Belles Demoiselles would gold not be good. Anyway, the fancy gold writing told me to go to Miss Villere's office at tea time instead of the evening salon.

I should have freaked out. Gold is basically half a step from doom, but I wasn't worried, because of my plan.

The schedule doesn't tell you why you're in trouble, but I could guess. It had to be the dolphin charm. Miss Villere was probably going to come at me about it being unseemly or gaudy or unladylike. Or else she would say that it was cheating to have a charm because I hadn't earned the Belles Demoiselles charm yet. But if that was cheating, everyone else already was, because another thing I had figured out at Grandmé Annette's gathering was confirmed that morning in Greetings: You can channel magic into your clothes.

At first I thought some of the younger witches had charms, because magic was flowing in and out of their pockets and sleeves. After I watched people working their charms for a while, though, I knew that wasn't quite it. Storing magic in their clothes was the only thing that made sense, even though it sounded nuts, so I watched Dee. In Greetings, I stared at her out of the corner of my eye until—BAM! The tiny roses printed on Dee's combat boots grew.

The flow of Dee's magic was pretty faint, but I could make it out. She was basically using her boots like a charm. All the girls were. That was why everybody else was always wearing flowers and flowered prints, which is something that would have been very helpful to know when Mom and I were packing.

So by the time I got to Miss Villere's office, I had my argument all together. If the other girls could wear floral prints to soak up their extra magic, I could wear the dolphin charm. A charm is basically just clothes, right?

I gave my voice print and walked into Miss Villere's office, ready to say all that. Of course she threw me a curve ball.

"If you are going to be filming on school grounds, you have to be more careful about the glare," Miss Villere said. She barely had any accent this time—or maybe I really was getting used to it.

"The glare?"

"We encourage all our girls to pursue their interests, but there is no success in carelessness. You agreed to only share information about Belles Demoiselles with your immediate family members, yet here I am warning you for the second time about posting images of the school on the Internet."

"I didn't—" I started.

"The glare," Miss Villere repeated. Then she tapped her desk and an image appeared on the wall. My first-day-of-school-outfit selfie posted on my mom's Facebook page. Miss Villere tapped her desk again and the image zoomed in to a little corner of the pic where a little bit of Celeste's mirror showed and was reflecting a little bit of the balcony. Maybe you could catch a little glimpse of Swan Lake, but it was so small and blurry that it also might have been my imagination.

"I didn't post that. I sent it to my mom," I said. "And I didn't know my camera was that good. Wow. They say you need a fancy phone to take good pictures, but—"

"We have excellent image-enhancing strategies," Miss Villere said. "They are far better than existing technology, but we don't kid ourselves that the world will never catch up. The Internet is forever. Someday someone might find your post and do the same thing I did. We can't have that. And it doesn't matter that you didn't post it. You are responsible for it. And there is this one, too."

She pulled up the video I had posted with Othello the night before and paused and zoomed in on less than a second of a sliver of the balcony door that I must have not quite shaved off when I edited my double finger kiss, heart outro.

"How did you even see that?"

"Our algorithms are strong. The only thing you need to know is that we are always watching. The offending images have been edited. I need you to tell me that this won't happen again."

I straightened my back and put my chin at the angle Miss LaRose taught me. I let my magic go just a touch, most of it filling my charm with a buzz instead of my fingertips. Then I thought of who I was—a witch with a plan who was going to meet AnyaDo0dle someday—and said, "It won't happen again." Then I smiled.

Miss Villere smiled back.

"Bien, shè," she said. "Just be careful. I don't want to see you in here again."

"Yes, ma'am," I said.

"Miss," she corrected.

"Yes, miss."

She nodded and went back to work, and I left deciding that I would film in the bathroom with the door closed from then on.

But my plan was working. I had no idea how well until social hour.

My room wasn't flooded with people, but since I was only expecting Dee and LaToya, I was shocked when Thuy stopped by, too.

"I just wanted to say congrats, again, Hasani. That thing with AnyaDo0dle is so cool."

What thing? What thing with AnyaDo0dle??? My brain was shouting as I tapped and swiped my way to AnyaDo0dle's page and the video I didn't have the heart to watch the night before.

"Hello, Lovelies! If you're new here, remember to like, comment, and subscribe and click that little notification bell. This video's going to be short and sweet, but it's still going to be HUGE. I'm announcing the winner of my NewTuber collaboration contest. You guys were so passionate about her in the comments and she also happens to be one of my most dedicated subscribers and you know we are nothing but a lovefest here, so that's saying a lot. I'm not going to make you wait on the edge of your seats or anything, so I'll just tell you. The winner of the NewTuber collaboration contest is Makeuponic theCheapCheap. Girl, I love what you've done so far and I can't wait to work with you. Until then . . . Love you! Bye!"

My heart was pounding and I was smiling so big I could feel it in my ears. She picked me. AnyaDoOdle picked me.

"Oh my god. You didn't know, did you?" Thuy said.

I shook my head, staring at my phone. I couldn't believe it.

"Check your IG DMs! She probably messaged you," Thuy said.

"I can't. My mom made me disable my DMs."

"Well, post a response! All that happened ages ago. She's going to think you're not interested."

Thuy was right. I grabbed my phone clip and ran into the bathroom. Othello followed. So did LaToya and Thuy.

"Hey, y'all. I'm so excited to get to work with AnyadoOdle in an upcoming collaboration. You have no idea how close I am to crying right now. I mean, AnyaDoOdle has been my favorite YouTuber ever since I was little and to have her pick me is just . . . wow. Like, I really don't know what to say. Thank you. And I can't wait to share whatever we create with y'all. I know it's going to be amazing. And, in the meantime, I have some new videos coming up for y'all. While I'm at camp, I figured I'd bring you a camp makeover series using all my dollar store makeup finds and my friend here—"

"LaToya," LaToya said, poking her head into frame.

"LaToya is going to be the first one."

"And I'm her friend Thuy, aka SilverbellsandCockleShells, and I'll be up next," Thuy said, poking her head into frame.

I wasn't even mad. Like, literally, the more the merrier.

Thuy ended up hanging out with us that night. She was cool. She's from California, but a bunch of her cousins are from New Orleans and it turns out that I had gone to zoo camp with one of them in third grade.

'd like to say that after that, everyone instantly liked me, but it was a week before everyone said hi to me, and longer before most people talked-to-me talked to me. That was OK with me, though. I was pretty busy training Othello, keeping my mom and Luz up to date, ignoring my father (who had finally texted me eight days after I left—eight!), and making videos for my channel.

Thuy, Kalani, Tyra, Casey, Monique, and Valerie all let me do their makeup for my Kitten Makeover series, and between that, Othello training vlogs, and a few lip and eye tutorials I did in the bathroom mirror, I was able to keep my promise about daily posts to my subscribers and, at the same time, make some new friends. Witch friends. That made two items I could check off my new electronic list.

Celeste didn't like me any better, but it didn't matter as much since: 1. Anastasia kept coming to my side of the room whenever Celeste wasn't around and 2. I finally had other friends. Eventually, I even got to eat with them. I went to sit at my usual spot next to Miss LaRose, but before I actually sat down, she said, "You must be tired of sitting with the older people. Wouldn't you rather sit with your fellow demoiselles?"

"Oh, no, Miss LaRose. I love spending time with you. I always learn so much," I said. I didn't even have to think about it. The words just rolled right out even though they were half lie.

Miss LaRose kept her face neutral, but I knew she was impressed. She had to be.

"I insist," she said. "Go and sit with your friends. I'll see you at The Art of Arranging."

There were only ten days left if you didn't count the closing ceremony, but better late than never.

"Yes, miss," I said, putting a little charm into my smile as I turned away. Wild, right? But that wasn't even the weirdest part. The weirdest part was when I realized after I sat down next to Thuy and Dee that I must have "descended" instead of plopping, because Miss LaRose nodded at me before turning to talk to Miss LeBrun.

I was shocked. Not that I sat without plopping. I'd done that hundreds of times. In a row. With Miss LaRose watching. What was new was that I did it without thinking. Believe me, when you first have to keep your back straight and your chin parallel to the floor while slowly sinking into a chair, you feel like a weird Barbie doll or, as Miss LaRose said, "a cheap, plastic soldier." Not only had I gotten better but, apparently, I had even gotten used to it. Now back straight, shoulders back, arms relaxed, chin parallel to the floor, elbows in, knees and ankles together was just sitting. I felt like a new me. A charming me. And when LaToya and Kalani entered the dining room a few minutes later as the second and third girls to receive their fleur-de-lis charms, I couldn't have been happier for them. I felt like we had all won that day.

My bubble didn't burst until that night. It was social hour and I was finally caught up on my YouTube comments, had scheduled a collab session with AnyaDo0dle, who was supercool about how hard it would be for me to film at camp and agreed for us to record when I got back to my home studio, and was settling down to scroll through IG to see what the competition looked like for when we started Othello's page, when I got a text from my mom.

"Honey, I don't want you to be upset . . ."

Heads up: That is the perfect way to start a message if what you actually want is for the person to be upset.

"Honey, I don't want you to be upset, but there's something important that I need to tell you. I know you have limited phone time, but call me when you get a second."

That message popped up over my IG page. I should have texted my mom back or called her right away. Instead I swiped up to close the message and swiped up again to catch a glimpse of some super-cute kittens sleeping in high-heeled shoes. You know. Something to put me in a good mood before my mom told me whatever bad news she had.

What I saw instead was a giant hand rocking the biggest rock I've ever seen. I mean, we're talking mega-diamond. I thought it was a jewelry ad until I realized the giant hand in the foreground was obscuring a bikini top and a wisp of wavy hair in the background. It wasn't an ad. It was a post from Sandyandfree83. The caption? "He always keeps his promises. I. SAID. YESSSS!"

CHAPTER SIXTEEN

DARKNESS AND LIGHT

"Hasani, calm down."

That was Dee. I could barely hear her.

"She's a witch."

That was LaToya. No one else's voice was so high. I heard her loud and clear.

"You don't know that," Dee hissed at LaToya. LaToya was holding my phone. "You OK, Hasani? I'ma go get somebody."

"No. Don't. I'm OK."

I was shaking and the floor was covered in morning glories. Othello rubbed his head against my leg. The dolphin charm didn't stop my power from surging, but the worst of it drained into Othello. He loved it, though. He purred and insisted I pet him until the crashing waves were just a light buzz that I could control. Then he started rolling around in the morning glory vines like they were catnip. All I could see were vines and a blur of orange fur. I didn't realize I was crying until I had to blow my nose. LaToya came out of the bathroom and handed me a wad of tissues. I blew my nose and wiped my eyes and plopped back on my bed. Vines pulled and snapped when I did, but I didn't care. This couldn't be happening.

"Better?" Dee asked.

I nodded. My hands were still shaking.

"What did this witch do to you?" LaToya asked, and I started crying all over again. Honestly, I don't even know why. I mean, it's not like my dad was dead or something.

"Stop saying she's a witch," Dee said. "You don't know that."

"Fine. What happened?"

"My dad just got engaged to some woman from Instagram," I said. "He's so stupid. Why would he do this? All he's been talking about is how he wants to make it right with my mom and then he turns around and does this?"

"My grandpa married somebody he met online. He hadn't even met her in person beforehand. My mom wouldn't talk to him for ages," Thuy said sympathetically. It did not help to think that this stupidity might be universal. At least my dad knew Sandy in person?

"Let me see her again," LaToya said.

I tapped the phone open and flipped it around.

Thuy and LaToya exchanged looks, then started scrolling through Sandy's Instagram page. Thuy looked unimpressed.

"What?" I sniffed.

"Nothing," Thuy said. "I mean, she's wearing a fleur-de-lis charm in a bunch of her pics, but that doesn't mean anything. New Orleans people wear fleurs-de-lis all the time, right? It's kind of your thing, isn't it?"

I nodded.

"Right. That's what I thought. Anyway, if she was a witch, you'd know. I wouldn't worry about it. If you think your dad's making a mistake, fix it."

"How?" I asked.

"Break them up."

"How?" I said again.

Thuy and LaToya squinted and shook their heads at me, putting their hands up like: OK. You can stop being so stupid now.

When that didn't work, Thuy said, "Hasani, you're a witch."

"Magic?" I said. "I can't do magic on my dad. That would be . . . weird." I thought of myself dripping magic into my dad like I did Othello. It felt . . . I don't know . . . wrong.

"I'm not saying you should use magic on your dad directly." Thuy laughed. "But there are other ways you can use it. Miss

Sandyandfree83 is working her own kind of magic on this situation. Trust me. She shouldn't be the only one."

Thuy and LaToya exchanged looks again.

"I don't think you should do anything," Dee said. Dee was the only one cleaning up the morning glories I had exploded everywhere, pulling vines from Celeste's side of the room and draping them over the back of my desk chair. "It sucks, but I'm guessing your parents split up for a reason."

"You've never seen my parents together," I said. "They're happy. They're, like, a perfect couple. They balance each other out. Everything has been out of whack since they split up. For both of them."

"Again, maybe I'm missing something, but people don't split up because they're happy." Dee shrugged, then she started pulling up the morning glories from my side of the room.

"All I'm saying is what's the point of being a witch if things never go your way? You're good with animals. Charm some lovebugs into their path and tell them it's a sign. Oh! Or the heart swans. Bring them by the lake when they come to campus and do the heart swans. Huge sign. They'll stare at each other and bat their eyes and fall into each other's arms." Thuy swayed around the room, flinging her arms around her invisible partner, then leaned back like it was a movie dip and she was the dippee.

"Wait. Do they bat their eyes or do they stare? It's kind of hard to do both," Dee said.

Thuy rolled her eyes. "You know what I mean. The point is, if you don't like the way things are, change them. There's no point in complaining. Besides, if your dad is as flighty as you say, he'll probably break it off before too long. He's probably just trying to make your mom jealous."

"Thuy, you are a genius and I am so stupid," I said, smacking myself on the forehead. "That's it. You're right. He's always doing stuff to get my mom's attention. Thanks!"

"You're welc. Oh, shoot!" she said looking out the window. "The swans are about to fly. I told Skylar and Casey I'd meet up with them, too. I'll see you guys later. Good luck, Hasani. Sorry your dad's being stupid."

"Thanks," I said.

The minute Thuy closed the door, I mean, the very second, LaToya said, "The three of us should form a coven."

Dee stopped pulling up vines and stared.

"A coven?" I asked.

"You know. Like the one you and Dee went to that night? After you said you didn't want to stay up late so you wouldn't get into trouble, but then as soon I went to my room you snuck off without me? That one?"

LaToya blinked.

Dee and I looked at each other.

"We . . ." I began.

"I followed you. Well, I tracked you. Same difference. Anyway, I'm not mad, and it's not against school rules or anything. I checked. I'm sure the one y'all went to was all wildseeds, anyway." *Not all wildseeds*, I thought. *Angelique was there.* "But imagine how great it would be to have a coven of belles demoiselles. I mean, y'all haven't gotten your charms yet, but when you do we'll be amazing together."

"What about Thuy?" Dee said. "I thought y'all were tight."

"We are. But Thuy lives in California, and the three of us will all be in New Orleans after Dee transfers to NOCCA."

I looked at Dee. That was news to me. But LaToya didn't even stop for a breath.

"Plus, if we invited Thuy we'd be four. Three's a better number. I mean, thirteen is best, obviously, but I thought that would be too much to start out, so three. Us three. What do you say?"

"A coven?" I repeated. I was having a hard time wrapping my head around it. "I don't know. A coven sounds pretty . . . witchy."

They both gave me a look.

"Seriously?" Dee cocked her eyebrows at me.

"You know what I mean!" I protested. "I don't mean witchy-witchy. I mean, like, witchy in a bad way."

"No. I don't know what you mean," Dee said flatly.

"There's nothing scary about a coven, Hasani. We're witches. That's what witches do. Support each other. Even the best witches can't go it alone. Actually, the best witches don't even try. I know the coven you went to was just a bunch of wildseeds, but come on. Was it scary?"

Dee acted like she was busy picking up vines, but she was really just busy avoiding eye contact.

I almost said, "No, the Vacherie witches weren't scary," but I caught myself. If it were only me, I would have just answered. I mean, who cares? It's not like LaToya wanted to go hang out with "a bunch of wildseeds," anyway. But it wasn't just me. Dee didn't even wear her dolphin charm on school grounds. There must have been a reason she was holding that back. I didn't know what it was, but I didn't want to be the one who made her spill it.

"I don't know," I said. "I mean, what would we have to do?"

"Just promise to support each other and have each other's backs."

"No, like, blood oath or anything?"

"OK." Dee stopped pretending to be absorbed in vine cleanup long enough to say, "Now you just sound ignorant."

"Sorry!" I said. "But is there?"

"No," LaToya said.

"Sorry. Coven just sounds . . . bloody. Could we call it, like, a best friend squad?"

"That is from She-Ra, and no, we're not calling it that," Dee said.

"We don't have to call it anything," LaToya said, "as long as we're there for each other. Deal?"

"Deal," Dee said.

I was surprised Dee agreed, but the next thing I knew she was holding out a spray of her signature flowers and LaToya had put her hand out, too, entwining her sword lilies with Dee's miniature roses. That left me. I added my flowers to the mix. It was actually really pretty. I kind of wished I could film it.

Othello was the one who broke the mood. He and Anastasia started weaving in and out of my legs doing little kitten hops of glee from all the extra magic dripping off me.

"Great," LaToya said. "I think I should quiz the two of you for the Belles Demoiselles test. I mean, they could ask you anything, but it can't hurt to practice. We can't have the two of you leaving without Belles Demoiselles charms, especially not now that we're going to be supporting each other and everything. Oh, but first we have to do something about Miss Sandyandfree83!"

"Ugh," Dee said with a little smile. "You had to bring that up again? She just calmed down."

Dee was right. I had just calmed down. I forgot she could see my magic.

"Thuy was right," I said. "That's just my dad being my dad. I totally overreacted. It's nothing."

"It's not nothing. Witches have powerful instincts. If that Sandy person makes Hasani flip out that much from an IG pic, she must be dangerous. That's why we have to help. What's Hasani supposed to do? Avoid Instagram?"

"Block her?" Dee said.

"And block her dad, too? No. I didn't want to say anything in front of Thuy, because I don't know her that well, but I think she was on to something."

"That's what I just said."

"Not about your dad being flighty. Animal Affinities. You are really good at it, Hasani. What if you used that to give your dad a little nudge?"

"You mean the swan thing?" I asked, confused. Was she literally just repeating Thuy's idea, just without Thuy in the room?

"I mean, you could do that. But come on, this is not a cartoon. This is the real world. What are the chances that heart swans are going to magically get your dad to act right? I'm talking about something more direct."

More direct? I gave her a look. "Are you talking about using magic on my dad? Like . . . influencing him?"

"Just enough to get him to act like himself again."

Slow blink. I could not believe what I was hearing.

"What? That's what you want, isn't it?"

"Not like that," I said.

"None of your family are witches. No one would even see what you were doing."

"You can't influence people with magic like that," Dee said. "Not to straight up change what they think. People are too smart. Same for dolphins and octopuses and . . ."

"Octopuses?" I asked.

"Yeah. Octopuses are mad smart. There was this one—"

"Not can't, *shouldn't*"—LaToya cut in—"but I think you're missing the point. Hasani, your parents are really happy when they're together, right?"

"Yeah," I said. They were. They really were.

"And that changed when this Sandyandfree person showed up, right?"

I nodded.

"So basically, it's really likely that Sandyandfree83 is already using magic on Hasani's dad. If Hasani did influence him, she'd only be putting things back the way they were."

"*If* she's a witch . . ." Dee said the "if" real hard. "That still doesn't mean that Hasani should be using her power to influence a whole human being like that. Two wrongs don't make a right."

LaToya shrugged. "I was only trying to help. But you're right. We are good witches. We have to stick together and keep each other on track. Sorry for suggesting that, and sorry for suggesting you need help practicing for your Belles Demoiselles charms. We should all get them without help. It's the only way we'll know we deserve them."

I gave Dee a look. I never said I didn't want help on whatever the final exam was. But Dee didn't budge, and the next thing I knew LaToya was hugging both of us goodnight and saying she'd save us seats at breakfast.

"I never told her," Dee said when LaToya had left the room.

"Never told her what?"

"That I'm planning to move to New Orleans for eighth grade. There's this art school I want to go to, New Orleans Center for Creative Arts. NOCCA. But you have to be a New Orleans resident. My mom said I could move in with my dad if I became a belle demoiselle. That's why I'm here. But I never told anybody that."

"So how did she know?"

"The girl is good," Dee shrugged. "It's OK. I don't mind. I'm just glad she's on our side."

CHAPTER SEVENTEEN

OAK AND LAVENDER

The next day, three amazing things happened.

1. Miss Lafleur announced in Animal Affinities that "barring any inappropriate behavior" our kittens were allowed to go anywhere we went on school grounds. Anywhere, y'all. We're talking kittens in the dining room. It was amazing, especially when Othello was obviously the best one. He stayed on my lap purring unless I said his name, then he'd look up at me and do a short meow like, "Yes?" in response. Meanwhile, Angelique kept having to pull "Snowball" off the table, and Anastasia pretty much stayed at my feet no matter how much Celeste hissed "Smokie" at her. It was great.

2. Miss Lafleur let me make the swans fly away at the end of class. OK, with Angelique. But still!

And . . .

3. I talked to AnyaDo0dle! My mom still wouldn't let me open my DMs, so she set up a three-way call for me and AnyaDo0dle to work out the details of our collaboration while she listened in the background. I promise you I had tears streaming down my face the whole time. AnyaDo0dle was so nice and so cool and I honestly could have died right then and been satisfied. It was so amazing that it didn't matter that it happened at tea when no one had signal, so I had to take the call in Miss Villere's office while she stared me down, too. Totally worth it.

At social hour, LaToya asked me for help with her cat, Ra. I had barely finished explaining about pulsing tiny drops of magic for him to follow like a breadcrumb trail before LaToya just did it. She'd only had one protégé offer, but seeing how fast she learned, I was surprised. Dee was right. LaToya was good and I was glad to have her on our side.

She didn't act like she was mad, but she still didn't help us with our exam, even after we found out that Tanvi and Aarya were getting help from Kalani. I was actually starting to think LaToya was right that we should do it on our own, until the next day when Angelique processed into the dining room at breakfast in front of Celeste, Monique, and Desirée like a princess with her ladies-in-waiting. Every one of them had fleur-de-lis charms. Honestly, I wasn't upset. They had all watched their mothers do magic since they were babies, so it made sense that they'd all be among the first. Teachers would probably be tripping over themselves to take one of them under their wing.

Thuy and Skylar came down with theirs the next day at breakfast. Still cool. Then Valerie, Tyra, and Danielle all got theirs right before lunch, and I started to get nervous. Danielle was practically a green witch like me. She had a bunch of aunts who were witches, but they'd all gone away for college and ended up all over the country, so she had pretty much never seen anyone do magic before she came to Belles Demoiselles, and Tyra literally never had. Tyra was from Shreveport. Her parents were cardiologists. Her great-grandmother was a witch and a belle demoiselle, but she died way before Tyra was born and there hadn't been another witch in their family besides Tyra since. When Tyra got her charm, I officially had no excuse.

Tanvi and Aarya got theirs the next day. They were best friends and cared way more about the fact that they got theirs at the same time than that they were almost last. My only consolation was that Dee hadn't gotten hers yet, either. Then Dee got hers before dinner on the last day of classes, and I was officially the last one.

"See? Your mom can't stop you," I said. I know I sounded smooth, but Dee could see right through me.

"You're gonna get it," Dee said.

"What if I don't?"

LaToya answered. "You'll go home. Belles Demoiselles only after tonight."

"You're gonna get it," Dee repeated.

"Wait. Why are we even talking about me right now? You just got your charm!!! Congratulations!!! Did anybody ask you to be their—" I stopped short. Asking somebody if they had been picked as a protégé was like asking a YouTuber if they've hit a million subscribers yet. If they have, believe me, they'll tell you. Otherwise, it might be kind of a sore spot.

Dee was cool about it.

"Miss Villere," she said.

"I didn't know Miss Villere was an option!" LaToya squeaked.

Dee shrugged, but she was smiling, too. I was happy for her.

"I might have held out if I had known Miss Villere made offers," LaToya said. "It's probably because your mom's a teacher. Not that I'm not happy with Miss Lavande. She's perfect for me, really. No one is better at weaving their intentions. Once she sets her mind to something, she makes it happen. Without her, this place would basically fall apart. Plus she's the chair of the board, you know."

We knew. LaToya had said it eleventy-billion times.

Angelique stood up before the end of dinner. Her hair was gorgeous in six big plaits wound together like a bouquet of flowers. She was officially one of Miss LeBrun's protégés, although, naturally, every teacher had made her an offer. She raised her glass. "To all the charmed girls and their charms," she said. Then she added, "no matter what shape," and I swear she looked right at me.

I wanted to say, "You should know. You have a dolphin-shaped charm just like mine," but I swear Dee could read my mind and kicked me under the table before I did, so I just smiled and raised my glass like everyone else.

I'm glad I didn't say anything. Turned out it was a tradition for the first girl to get her Belles Demoiselles charm to give a toast on the last day of classes. Normally by then everyone had either gotten their charm or been sent home. My comment would have sounded more like salty haterade than witty comeback. Everyone smiled and clinked their glasses and afterward they gave me sad little looks and asked me about what I was planning with AnyaDo0dle.

But even talking about my call with AnyaDo0dle didn't make me feel better. I may not have started out as a very promising belle demoiselle, but by that point in the summer I was good. Good at etiquette. Good at class. Good at everything. Miss LeBrun liked my comment about sugarcane not being evil because of the acts of men. Miss Lafleur let me fly the swans. I was a good witch, even without years of watching other people do magic while they smiled and pretended they weren't.

I tried to tell myself I didn't need the fleur-de-lis. I already had the wildseed charm and it was amazing. How long had Grandmé Annette been doing magic with hers? She hadn't burned out. Her magic was beautiful. I liked dolphins better than fleurs-de-lis, anyway. They didn't use dolphins to brand people they were trying to keep as slaves, they used the fleur-de-lis, even if Miss LeBrun said that it was "reclaiming a symbol." I didn't even want the stupid fleur-de-lis charm, except I couldn't really convince myself that I didn't because I needed it. Getting the Belles Demoiselles charm was part of my plan. If I didn't get it, that was it. Mr. Paul would just drive me home, and everything would be like it was before. Crappy.

That night, I sneaked down to the evening salon during social hour. I just wanted to be alone. I spent a little while answering comments on my YouTube channel. There was another one from _AnnieOaky_. She was always so sweet. Apparently she had done another video where she followed one of my tutorials, and I felt a little pang of guilt when I realized that I still hadn't watched any of her videos. So much for loving your subscribers.

I clicked over to her channel and tapped a video where she was doing one of my eye shadow tutorials. She was doing the tutorial on herself and a doll, which I thought was a little weird—but hey . . . do your thing—until I realized that she had MADE THE DOLL. As in carved it herself from a lump of wood. Annie OAKy. Duh. Then she mixed dollar store eye shadow with clear acrylic paint and the doll's makeup came out amazing. She was better at doing the doll's than doing her own, but it really didn't matter because the doll's makeup was so cool and they looked so cute together in the closing side-by-side that I couldn't understand why the video only had 87 views and one downvote. I liked it to even her up and was about to start watching all her other videos when Miss Camille cleared her throat.

I looked up. Miss Camille was holding a tray with an envelope that had my name on it in orange. Not red, but it may as well have been. No way had I gotten another demerit and somehow also been invited to take the test.

"Good luck, miss," Miss Camille said.

I thanked her and opened the envelope to read where I was supposed to be. The solarium. Fifth floor.

I didn't know there was a fifth floor, but I sprinted up the stairs like I had been there a thousand times before. On the second to last step, I stopped to catch my breath and wipe the sheen of sweat from my forehead. Othello groomed himself while I tried to fluff out my hair. It was a little matted, so I smoothed the top instead before walking to the only pair of doors. The doors slid open and we stepped inside a huge room with a long table and a glass ceiling. No wonder there were no windows. Who needs windows when you have a glass ceiling?

The door slid closed behind me. Miss Villere and all the teachers were sitting behind the table. Miss Lafleur smiled encouragingly. I couldn't get a read on anyone else. That wasn't good.

I expected Miss Villere to be the one to talk, but Miss Le-Brun started.

"Good evening, Hasani."

"Good evening," I said, remembering who I was. That's the trick to introductions. You have to remember who you are—the best parts of yourself—and you really have to believe it.

Miss Lafleur smiled again, but then Miss LaRose started talking.

"You have come a long way, Hasani, but we question whether you have come far enough. We understand that you were not informed of the usefulness of floral fabrics prior to your arrival. That was an error on our parts that we will rectify if and when we choose to invite more green witches into our program in the future. However, properly containing one's power is a basic function that you should have been able to master in your time with us, with or without flower designs on your clothing. We learned that you recently had another magical outburst despite a containment item provided by the school and your own accessories."

Miss LaRose practically glared at my dolphin charm.

"Did Celeste tell you that?" I said it calmly, but it was full whine in my mind. How could they expect me to be literally perfect, especially with that jealous little fiend as a roommate? I didn't care what anyone said. Celeste was a hater. "I understand your concern, but it was only one time and I've had it under control ever since."

"No, Celeste has never mentioned you at all," Miss LaRose said. Ouch. "But your saying that does bring up another important point. We like to think of the belles demoiselles as a sisterhood. After all, behind every great woman there is a group of great women. Belles demoiselles support one another, which includes supporting a fellow demoiselle's anonymity if she wants it, and certainly does not include throwing another demoiselle under the bus as you just tried to do with Celeste. I'm going to be forthright with you. As it stands at this moment, I would not vote for you to join our sisterhood. That's nothing against you personally. I just don't think you're ready. And since the vote among teachers needs to be unanimous, if we voted right now, you would fail."

They couldn't have expelled me in a letter? They had to do it in a formal gathering of teachers to tell me I wasn't good enough? Fine. I kept my shoulders back, chin parallel to the floor.

"One more infraction and we would not have given you this chance. However, since you are a special case, instead of sending you home, we've decided to give you the option of convening a Conseil des Demoiselles. The council is made up of one hundred randomly selected belles demoiselles from around the world. You will not know who they are, they will not confer, and, if you agree to let them judge you, their decision will be final."

"Before you accept these terms," Miss Lafleur cut in, "you should understand that sometimes a witch's greatest strength is her anonymity. Right now, the only people who know about your powers are the ones in this room, your family, and other young witches who have as much to lose as you do. If you succeed, we will do what we can to protect you, but a hundred witches is a lot to control. We can put out fires, but we may not be able to stop the fires from starting in the first place. Do you understand?"

I nodded. AnyaDo0dle and I were recording our collaboration so soon. If any of the witches watching decided to out me, it didn't matter. I didn't need anonymity. I was about to be famous.

"Hasani, do you understand?" Miss Lafleur repeated.

"Yes, miss," I said with the suggestion of a curtsy. Miss LaRose taught me that.

"Bon." Miss Villere waved her hand and what I thought was a wall of fancy tiles turned from white to a dull, glowing blue. "We will ask you five questions. The one hundred members of this Conseil des Demoiselles will watch you give your answers through the monitors.

They can vote at any time after we begin. A violet flower is yes. A white flower is no. You need ninety yeses. If there are eleven white flowers at any time, you will have to leave this place."

"We need to be clear, Hasani," Miss Lafleur said, "that there are certain consequences of leaving that may be unpleasant. You'll still have access to the Internet, but your social media reach will be limited. Views would be limited to your closest friends and immediate family only. We don't think you would intentionally expose Belles Demoiselles, but it's a precaution we would have to take."

I nodded. On the inside I was on the verge of tears. LaToya said they might delete you from the Internet. It sounded bad when she said it. Now it sounded like a fate worse than death. All I could think about was my collaboration with AnyaDo0dle. If it only got twelve views, that would be worse than if it never happened at all. AnyaDo0dle would hate me for tanking her stats.

"Komprenn?" Miss Villere asked.

"Wé, manmzèl," I said. What else was I supposed to say? It was either do this or basically disappear.

"Bon," Miss Villere said. "Let's begin."

Miss LeBrun leaned forward, letting the rose-colored glasses slide down just enough for her to readjust them and draw attention to how her brown highlights sparkled against the bronze in her dress.

"Hasani, I'm impressed by how knowledgeable you've become in history. Would you please tell us, in your own words, why it is so important to study those who came before us?"

"Thank you for that question, Miss LeBrun." I was stalling, but I immediately realized that I didn't have to. I knew the answer. I'd learned it from YouTube. "Everything we do stands on the shoulders of the people who came before us. If we don't watch them and learn from them, we could spend our whole lives making things that have already been made before but never realizing it. When we study the people who came before us, we can avoid their mistakes and build on their successes to create something new and help humanity keep moving forward."

Miss LeBrun nodded. "Thank you, Hasani."

I smiled. I'm not gonna lie, I was pretty impressed with myself. That answer was really good. Run-for-office good. So why didn't I have any upvotes?

That's when I saw what was really happening. While I was talking, Miss Villere had been sliding magic under the table, building a shimmering fence of her magic between me and Othello. The lines were blurry and faint like mist, but I could see them well enough in the dim evening light. What I couldn't figure out was why she was doing it—until Othello took a step away from me and Miss LaRose made a face somewhere between smug and disappointed.

That was it. That was the test. They were going to try to take Othello away from me. No. Worse. They were trying to get Othello to leave me, and, if I'm being honest, the whole thing made me really mad. Why would they drag Othello into this? He was just a little cat. He loved me and I loved him and he would never leave me, so why were they trying to make it seem like he would? What kind of monsters were they to sit there smiling or just plain pretending like nothing was happening at all while they did this?

I swear I felt myself hulking up and almost laughed, because I had answered my own question. This was why they were messing with Othello. They wanted to get me riled up. They wanted to see me explode. Well, I wouldn't. I just wouldn't. There was too much at stake.

"Hasani," Miss Lavande began, "how would you create a signature scent that highlights positive attention while severely limiting negative attention?"

"I'd start with rose and ginger, but add chicory to the base."

Othello took another step, then another. I couldn't snap for him or kiss my teeth. A witch would only do that if she were desperate, and I wasn't desperate. I was a witch with a plan. A plan I made right that second, but it was still a plan.

I dropped a puddle of magic at my right foot, the kind I thought of as sticky sweet. People say cats don't like sweet, but those people have not met Othello. He leapt for it, slipping over Miss Villere's barrier and skipping the drops of her magic she had put down to lead him to her. I could only imagine that all the other teachers were trying to lure Othello away from me, too, and I just couldn't see it. I swirled my right finger, leaving a little spiral of magic for Othello to follow on the floor. He loved following drops of magic on the ground, especially if they led back to me. It was literally Othello's favorite game, like an obstacle course. We had done it jillions of times with Othello making his way through trails of LaToya's magic or Dee's to find the one that brought him back to me again. This was no different. So what if the other magic came from teachers?

I pulled from my dolphin charm to make streams of magic that flowed like tiny rivers. Othello loved it. He leaped and pounced, pausing to lick a paw and pretend he wasn't stalking before jumping back into action again. It was adorable, like he was fighting an invisible yet equally adorable foe. In the end, he walked around my right leg and curled up between my feet.

Othello had come back to me, but still no upvotes. What was I missing?

My dolphin charm was empty, but Othello rubbed his head against my foot, refilling my magic without me having to ask him.

Miss Villere made another wall of magic, thicker and easier to see than the first one. It surrounded Othello in one move, looping around him perfectly to cut him off from me. It would have, too, if I hadn't poured out another puddle in time. A trickle of my magic passed Miss Villere's. It wasn't much, but it was enough to keep Othello in place.

Were they just going to keep trying to take Othello over and over again to see how long it would take me to freak out in front of the witches on the council? Maybe old me would have freaked out, but new me was good. The one thing I had a lot of practice with was getting people to like me. 27,804 likes, by last count, and no downvotes. I didn't plan to break my streak.

That's when it hit me. The questions were a distraction. Othello was a distraction. And I had let myself be distracted.

I stared up at the monitors on the wall. They were the audience. I couldn't see the witches on the other side of the squares, but I didn't need to. Every video I had made this summer was practice. The goal was upvotes and I knew how to get them. It was my time to shine.

Miss LaRose asked her question. "Why do you think you should be a belle demoiselle?"

I smiled, filling it to the brim with charm just like I did in my intros. "First of all, Miss LaRose, thank you so much for the opportunity to come here and learn. I know it was a difficult decision, but everyone has made me feel so welcome."

That was at least fifty percent lie, but it didn't matter what I was saying. I needed a chance to talk. I needed a chance to charm them.

There were too many monitors for me to charm them all in one smile. As far as I could tell, this council of witches didn't have a chat I could slip into. That was the challenge—maybe if I knew how the monitors worked, I could weave some charm into them. Magic and tech, right?

That's when everything clicked. I didn't need to know how it worked. I didn't know how my cell phone worked, either, but that didn't stop it from sending texts . . . at least not when there was signal. But that didn't matter. These monitors did have signal.

I let what was left of my magic pool in my fingertips and imagined that all of these screens were subscribers and I was just loving them in the comments like AnyaDo0dle had said. A lavender flower appeared on one screen. I held my smile, turning to look around the room as naturally as I could, my charm a thin stream.

"But to answer your question, Miss LaRose, the truth is it's not up to me. If the people in this sisterhood see something in me that's good enough, I'll be thrilled, but whatever they decide, I couldn't be prouder to have been a part of this little family, even if only for a short time."

Violet flowers began to dot the screens.

"No matter what the outcome is, I will always cherish the friend-ships I have made here."

More flowers popped up on more screens. All of them violet.

Othello moved closer to Miss Villere. I sent a wider stream through Miss Villere's wall. A little cat door for Othello to walk through.

"And I have learned more than I ever thought possible."

Holding Othello in place was using a lot of power. The flow of my magic was getting weaker. A burst of emotion would have filled me back up again, but that was wrong, too. They would see it. They would know. They would call me wild. My dolphin charm was empty, but I wouldn't need to keep going if I got to ninety. All I had to do was get to ninety.

"So thank you." I beamed. "Thank you for finding me and giving me a chance to learn more about myself than I ever thought I could."

There was a flood of lavender flowers. I caught a flicker of white light out of the corner of my eye but silenced it with more magic in my smile. The screen went black along with a few others. I shut them out and let my mind fill with the sea of purple that overwhelmed them. I froze for a moment, not wanting to look at the dark screens but knowing that Miss LaRose and all the rest were waiting for them to vote. My smile felt stapled on, but I tried to make it look soft and natural and pretend that I wasn't every bit as focused on the black screens as they were. No white flowers appeared and, after what felt like an eternity, Miss Lafleur breathed a sigh of relief, Miss LaRose nodded politely, and Miss Villere said, "Ninety-seven. Bon. Bokou bon, ma belle demoiselle."

CHAPTER EIGHTEEN

FREEDOM AND PAGEANTRY

I'm not gonna lie. That fleur-de-lis charm felt good when Miss Lafleur fastened it around my neck. I loved my dolphin charm, but it took only a hot second for me to realize that a Belles Demoiselles fleur-de-lis was the business. It was like a signal booster, extra storage, and a charger all in one. I never thought about taking my dolphin off, though. Maybe because, right there in that high-tech solarium, after she had put my fleur-de-lis in place, Miss Lafleur beamed at me and said, "Perfect. Now you're double-charmed."

The other teachers smiled. Though it would be going a little far to say Miss LaRose smiled. She didn't look at me like something smelled bad, which I'm sure took effort, but everybody else smiled and congratulated me like they had been looking out for me the whole time. Miss Lafleur was the only one who walked me to the stairs, though.

"I'm sure that by now you're aware of our protégé program," she said. "I'd like to offer you a place as mine."

"Seriously?" I asked. Heart swans? I mean, you had me at hello.

"Seriously," she said. "But take tonight to think it over. I'm sure you'll have several more offers before morning."

I seriously doubted that, but she wasn't wrong. Miss LeBrun met me on the third-floor landing.

"How did you get down here before me?" I said, looking around me. Could the teachers apparate? Had they seriously been apparating and disapparating the whole time?

"The elevator, dear," Miss LeBrun said. "I normally take the stairs, but I wanted to be sure to catch you before you went to bed. Are you too tired to take a walk?"

Apparently the building did have a secret spa. Miss LeBrun pushed something that opened a bookcase and there it was, plain as day. She walked right through it, though, past a steamy room with a pool bubbling from a waterfall to a cozy little library with a large desk and two enormous chairs. A laptop was the only thing that stopped it from looking old-timey.

"I hope it's not too humid for you in here," Miss LeBrun said, gesturing for me to sit. "The waterfall sound is so soothing, though, that it makes it worth the trouble."

"I don't mind," I said.

"I asked you to come because I wanted to offer you a place as my protégé," she said.

I know it's weird at this point, but I was legitimately shocked.

"It's perfectly OK for you to say no. I'm sure Miss Lafleur has a special place in your heart, especially since she was the one who got to deliver your acceptance message, not that I didn't fight her for it," Miss LeBrun laughed.

Double shocked. They had fought over me?

"But I would kick myself if I didn't at least offer you a place. Influencing the decolonization of history may not sound exciting at first, but believe me, it is. The travel alone makes it all worthwhile. So, what do you say? Are you interested in learning to use your magic to correct the record and turn the tide of history?"

"Thank you so much for your offer," I began.

Miss LeBrun waved my words away. "No need for formal apologies. Miss Lafleur is a dear friend. She'll take good care of you. And if you're ever in Senegal, send a text. I'd love to show you around Dakar if you have time."

"Thank you," I said, standing to leave. I had always thought Miss LeBrun was cool, but Miss LeBrun was *mad* cool. I pulled out my phone. "What's your number?"

Miss LeBrun looked puzzled.

"What number should I text if I'm ever in Senegal?"

"Oh," Miss LeBrun laughed again. "Any number you like. Just send a text and I'll send a car over for you. No obligation, of course. Consider it an open invitation."

When I got back to the third floor, I expected everyone to be sleeping, but it was seriously like a party up there. Every door was open, Tanvi and Aarya had music blasting from their room, and Celeste was carrying a box out of ours.

"Surprise!" LaToya said when I walked in. Only my side of the door worked.

"What's going on?"

Dee was sitting on Celeste's bed. Correction. Dee was sitting on a bare mattress. Any trace of Celeste in the room, including Celeste herself, was gone.

"We heard the good news!" Dee said. "Congratulations!"

"Yes! Congratulations! Congratulations! Congratulations!" LaToya didn't just say it three different times; she said it in three different accents.

"Celeste is moving out?"

"Just to my room," LaToya said brightly. "Since you're staying now—I always knew you would—but since you're staying now I figured you could use a little space from . . ." LaToya pointed at her room and wrinkled her nose.

"We can do that?"

"Of course we can do that. We're all belles demoiselles now. Students follow rules. Belles demoiselles make them. Plus I cleared it with Miss Lavande. My room's plenty big. We're all set."

"Thanks, LaToya. That was very cool of you."

"Anything for my coven. Now let me go make sure Celeste isn't doing anything crazy over there." Then she flitted off, leaving me and Dee alone.

Dee rubbed a hand over her hair. "I was thinking—" she started. I didn't let her finish.

"That you should move into this room immediately? Because if you weren't, I'm begging you to. Please???" I stretched it out with my cheesiest grin.

Dee laughed. "Cool," she said.

It became clear very quickly that being a belle demoiselle was the dopest thing on the planet. First of all, there weren't any chimes. It was like every hour was social hour and, blessedly, there was plenty of phone signal to go with it. There was just kind of always food in the dining room and, if it wasn't food you wanted, you could order more from a menu. Like a restaurant, except you didn't have to pay. The dress code was way better, too. I guess technically there never was a dress code, but now people were really coming with the flavor. Celeste still looked the same, but Dee came rocking with a new bow tie and hair color for every day of the week, Kalani killed the grunge look, complete with nose ring and perfectly ripped fishnets, and even Angelique had more of an egirl/school girl/anime girl look.

It didn't hurt that the teachers didn't walk around wearing rose-colored glasses. In fact, we hardly saw them at all, and when we did, I barely recognized them. Only Miss LaRose stuck to her white suit. Everyone else had switched it up, especially Miss Lafleur. She was wearing jeans and her hair was in two French braids. From far away, I thought she was one of the kids.

"I'm so glad you accepted my invitation," she said when I met her at the lake on that glorious, first day of freedom.

"Are you kidding? I basically just called my mom and then came right over. Animal Affinities is the best class here. I can't believe I get to work with you all day. That thing you do with the swans is super-sweet. Will you show me?"

Miss Lafleur smiled. "It's just a bit of pageantry. It's for fun. Like your glitter kitty eye shadow."

"You've watched my videos?"

"Of course. Hasn't everyone?" she said with a wink.

I smiled.

"Now, as for the swans, it takes quite a bit of influence, as you can probably tell. I only have them work like that for summer term."

"Why? Is it too hard on you?"

"Not on me. On them. Swans may not be what we think of as intelligent, but they do have a certain amount of free will, wouldn't you say?"

"Don't they basically just go by their instincts?" I said.

"Don't we all? That doesn't mean we don't have free will. But an argument can be made that the less free will a creature has, the more cruel it is to take it away. No, these swans only put on a show when the students are around. The rest of the year they are free to be who they want, where they want. I flatter myself to think that we must be giving them an otherwise ideal life since they don't fly away, but still."

"So, you think it's wrong?" I said.

"Oh, there's a time and a place for everything. I think it would be wrong to do it longer than I have to, but a short time won't hurt, long-term."

"How would you know if you were hurting them?" I asked.

"Besides them flying away. I mean, what if they were so influenced that they wouldn't fly away, even if they were hurt?"

Miss Lafleur clasped her hands together excitedly. "Such a smart girl," she said. "That's it exactly. You've brought me right into our first lesson: Recognizing the Signs of Over-Influence."

Easily excitable. Exaggerated actions. Mood swings. Withdrawal. She basically described my dad. My first thought was to tell my mom. But what was she going to do? That night, I told LaToya and Dee instead.

"Sandy's a witch," LaToya said. "I told you. Now what should we do about it?"

"Nothing," Dee said. "We should just let that man live his life. We all have enough stuff to do. Hasani, don't you have eleven billion videos left to edit?"

"Seven," I said. It was my Countdown to Collab series to get ready for my collaboration with AnyaDo0dle. It was all set to happen the day after the closing ceremony.

"What does Miss Lafleur say you should do?" LaToya said pointedly.

"Nothing," Dee said again.

"Dee's kind of right," I said. "Miss Lafleur says that most of the time it fixes itself if the creature goes without being under the influence for three days."

"So you just need a plan to keep your dad away from your future step-monster for three days," LaToya said.

"Or she could finish editing her seven billion videos and learn her part for the closing ceremony," Dee said.

They were both right. Why not do both?

#Witchlife

CHAPTER NINETEEN

FLOWERS AND RAINBOWS

The last week with our mentors may have been chill, but the closing ceremony was all Belles Demoiselles. Dresses had to be approved. So did earrings. Shoes. Hairstyles. Dee and LaToya tried to help me with my hair, but it was so tangled underneath that I just ended up smoothing it down on top like I had been doing. I was actually hype about the idea of dressing up and being elegant when my parents came. I told Miss Lafleur and she brought me the perfect dress: solid purple with a little hint of pink blush. It was exactly like a morning glory.

"Thank you!" I said.

"You're quite welcome, Hasani. And here." She pulled out a tiny container that was obviously makeup. "Biodegradable glitter. I know you like to sparkle, and this way our sea creature friends won't be suffocated by our plastics waste."

What? I thought. *Never mind. I'll look that up later.*

The next morning, the sky was filled with rainbows, chairs were set up on the lawn, and I couldn't wait to see my parents for breakfast. Breakfast wasn't in the dining room like it usually was. In honor of our accomplishments, each of us got to choose a special place on campus to eat with our parents. Thuy and I both chose Swan Lake, so my mom, Othello, and I walked there with Thuy and her parents.

I was lowkey annoyed when I realized Thuy had picked the same place. I mean, yes, it was her suggestion, but why had she suggested it if she was going to do it, too? The whole point was to set a mood. Having other people around would ruin it. But I didn't have to worry. When we got to the lake, Miss Camille directed us into two different areas and I watched Thuy and her parents slip behind an almost invisible curtain before my mom and I went into the tent that was waiting for us.

Inside the tent was even better than what I hoped. You could see through the one side of the tent like there was nothing there. The view of the lake was perfect. Perfectly romantic. My mom hugged me, and I looked around for my dad. He wasn't there yet.

"Is Dad still parking?" I asked. I hadn't asked about my dad on the way to the lake. I'd just assumed he had to park far away and dropped my mom off right in front like he always did when that happened. Did he have to park in the next town, though?

"Othello is even cuter in person," my mom said, very much not answering the question. "And look at you! You look so grown up! And all this hair. Is it real? Who did it for you?"

"No one. It's a long story. Where's Dad?" I asked again, hoping she'd say, "In the bathroom. He has diarrhea," or something good like that.

"I'm sure he's on his way."

What? No! "Y'all came together, right?"

My mom shook her head. "I drove myself. I left him a message. Your father—"

"Somebody talking about me?"

My dad stepped into the tent. I threw my arms around him and he swept me up in a big hug like he did when I was little. It felt so good. I didn't realize how much I had missed him, and now that he was here, everything would be OK. It was fine if they didn't drive up together. We didn't really need that part of the plan for the rest to work. A few minutes in front of the lake while they waited for the ceremony would be just as good, especially if Othello and I slipped away a few minutes early to give them some time alone, and I doubled up the heart swans on my way out.

Then Sandy walked in.

Family. Only. How did she even get in here? Old me would have sprouted flowers. New me felt my dolphin charm buzzing against my skin. New me felt the power in my fleur-de-lis charm. Power I could tap into without even trying. It was comforting. It helped me think.

Sandy sat at the table next to my dad. A table I suddenly realized had been set for four the whole time. Miss Camille served us breakfast, holding the platters of food out in formal silence for us to serve ourselves, except for the coffee. Miss Camille put extra cream and sugar into my café au lait. I thanked her with a nod. I needed all the support I could get.

My dad complimented my "new hardware." My mom kept complimenting me on my manners. I couldn't appreciate either of them. My mind was on Sandy. What was she doing here?

After breakfast, my mom offered to come and help me pack.

"They made us do it yesterday," I said. I wasn't totally, totally done, but I didn't want my mom to come with me. For one thing, I didn't want her to leave my dad. For another, I didn't want her to see what I was going to do next. My mom had always been supportive of me going to witch school, but she was probably thinking Hogwarts, not coven, and I needed to gather mine.

*O*f course I couldn't. They were with their families like I should have been with mine, and Belles Demoiselles's campus was huge. No way I would find them. I pulled out my phone to text them but decided to text Sandy instead. Sandy kept checking her phone. She'd see it. I walked back to the lake, composing the message in my head. It was this whole thing about how much I missed my dad and how I needed to have him around and how, in a few years I'd go off to college and she could try to take him back, but I needed him for now because who doesn't need their dad even when they say they don't? Sandy had a dad. She must have. She'd understand.

I didn't have her number, so I opened IG and tapped Sandy's profile pic in my recents. It brought me to her page. The message bar was grayed out. Sandy's DMs were closed. Then I heard her laughing and saying how romantic this spot at the lake was and knew she was saying it to my dad right in front of my mom. I could just imagine the look on my mom's face and, before I thought about it too hard, I tapped the first pic on Sandy's grid and clicked the comment bubble instead. Then I typed out one word: *Homewrecker*. I don't remember clicking Send, but I do remember how much better I felt.

The rest of the day was kind of a blur. I gave the three of them a tour of the approved parts of the campus. Sandy and my mom both loved the garden. My mom was cool about it, but Sandy kept trying to take selfies and pouted when they didn't come out right. At the ceremony, Miss Villere gave a speech welcoming our families first in Creole, then in English. We were sitting in two rows on the veranda, like it was a graduation stage, except instead of having a curtain behind us, Miss Lavande had woven sheers that hung in front of us. It was kind of like the barrier that surrounded the campus, but thinner and easier for us to see through. All the families were seated on the lawn, sheers separating them like fancy box seats at the opera. They couldn't see us. They could only see Miss Villere. But we could all see them. My dad leaned over and said something to my mom. She smiled. They both smiled. They looked so good. Miss Villere said we were the result of the countless incantations and prayers said by our ancestors. That they wielded the power they had so we could wield ours.

My mom said something to my dad. Her eyes were smiling. He leaned toward her and said something back. They both laughed. Then my dad sat back up and put his hand on Sandy's knee. My mom stopped smiling. That's when I started the incantation. Just a small one. *There's no place like home*. It didn't work. My dad squeezed Sandy's knee and whispered something in her ear. Sandy giggled. I cringed.

Seriously, why would he do all that with so many people around? Maybe he didn't know I could see them? That ALL the belles demoiselles could see them? That he looked like an idiot?

My mom. My poor mom. She looked so uncomfortable. I couldn't stand it. I started saying the incantation faster. Miss LeBrun talked about how the school was founded in the sugarcane fields to make right from wrong. Miss Lefleur talked about the positive impact we could have on the planet. Miss LaRose talked about how empowering it was to be a graceful, cultured young lady. I repeated the incantation.

"Morning glory." Dee nudged me. There was a whole show going on for the parents. Rainbows. Birds. The whole nine yards. I was supposed to weave a morning glory blossom into the curtain that separated us at the same time as my flower's color appeared in the rainbow, then go into the Grand Foyer. I missed my cue. My dad was making googly-eyes at Sandy.

I flicked my fingers to throw my flower where it belonged, then scrambled into the Grand Foyer a little less gracefully than I should have, maybe because I was tossing a little of that magic in my dad's direction. I knew it wouldn't do anything—it barely even went past the curtain—but it made me feel better.

Chimes filled the air like raindrops. All of us were inside while our parents waited outside. This part of the ceremony wasn't for them. This part was for us, the charmed girls. The belles demoiselles.

One by one, we added our flowers to the Grand Foyer while Miss Villere said, "We do not need to smother one another. There is room for us all" in English and in Creole. The words were just a part of the ceremony, but they were true, too. There was, literally, room for us all. Phlox, daisies, peonies, lavender, roses, fleurs-de-lis, chrysanthemums, silver bells, passionflowers, buttercups, morning glories, orchids, hibiscus, sword lilies, and even Danielle's irises all found a place in the Grand Foyer along the walls and ceiling and, in Danielle's case, the fountain at the center. I had accidentally put my flowers here before, but now I would do it on purpose. Now they belonged and no one would tell me to take them down again.

Outside, the sky went overcast and just enough misty rain passed over to account for the rainbow that appeared to mark the end of the ceremony. It was beautiful. I wasn't thinking about it, though. I was thinking about Sandy.

When all our flowers were in place and the bees and butterflies were buzzing around them, Miss Lavande escorted the sworn guardians inside. The "sworn guardian," in my case, my mom, went with us upstairs to help us get our things. That was just another ritual. We had actually had to bring most of our stuff downstairs the night before so it could be ready for people to load into our parents' cars during the ceremony. The only things left in our rooms were a vase of our own flowers and the "discreet overnight bag" they'd let us hold on to. Mine

was a WalMart bag. I definitely could have carried that and the flowers by myself, but I was glad for the chance to talk to my mom.

"What do you think of her?"

I didn't need to say who "her" was. My mom sighed. "Honey. This
day is about you. We can talk about all of that later."

"It's embarrassing," I said. "She doesn't even belong here. What's
wrong with him?"

"I think your dad has been going through some things, but we all
go through things sometimes, and they're his things to go through,
Hasani. We have to respect his decision."

Do we?

I let it go, but facts are facts. My mom clearly thought my dad was
being stupid, she just didn't think we should stop him. For a second, I
thought maybe she was right.

Miss Lavande escorted my mom and the other sworn guardians
to the edge of campus. Another ritual. We watched them from the
third-floor balconies until they crossed through the gossamer curtain on the edge of campus, then we said our goodbyes to the teachers and followed them. Miss Lafleur looked less huggable in her pink
suit, but I hugged her, anyway.

"You're a good witch, Hasani," she said. "The world needs you."

I nodded. I didn't know about the world, but my parents did
for sure.

There were a bunch of families waiting on the other side of the curtain. I saw my dad first. He was standing with Sandy, but he was looking at my mom like he wished he could stand with her. Like he wished he could hold her hand instead of Sandy's. Like he just realized what a mistake he was making and wished he wasn't standing with a consolation prize. Like he had made a plan, but none of it was going right.

I suddenly felt really bad for him. The whole get-a-new-girlfriend-and-make-the-love-of-my-life-jealous thing was not going to work on my mom. Maybe that's the one part about Mom he didn't know. I wanted to save him before he went too far and ruined all our lives.

Tanvi and Aarya went up to Sandy to ask her if she was *the* Sandy-andfree83. Sandy smiled and looked embarrassed, but sure enough she signed autographs and took selfies with them. I wanted to barf until I realized that my dad had inched away and was standing with my mom instead. Then Mom said something and he leaned in close and I breathed a sigh of relief. They looked like a picture. I wanted to join them, to get in the picture with them, when it occurred to me that I should. It was a special day and I hadn't taken pictures with either of them.

I started to walk toward them. Sandy cut me off.

"Let's give them a minute," she said. "Seems like they have some things to work out. And I've been meaning to ask you: Does this handsome little guy have an Instagram?" Sandy cooed at Othello.

"No," I said flatly.

"Oh, come on. Don't be like that. Us ladies have to stick together. We should start him one," Sandy said with a wink. I felt it that time. The magic. It was clumsy. I couldn't believe she was a belle demoiselle and so obviously trying so hard.

"Sure," I said, wondering how in the world my mom could leave me stuck with this woman for so long. "I'll be right back. My friend," I said. Dee was close by, but she wasn't calling me.

"Your kitten is so well-behaved," Sandy said, like she hadn't heard me. "Does he do tricks?"

"What?" I said.

"Does he do tricks?" she repeated. "Like, can you make him sit?"

What kind of person asks if a cat can do tricks? I mean, yes, Othello could do tricks. Obviously. But cats don't do tricks. Everybody knows that. Then Sandy smiled, that clumsy smile brimming with pushy magic. I couldn't see it, but I knew it was there. No belle demoiselle would be so blatant unless she was trying to send a message. Sandy was definitely a witch, a belle demoiselle, and she wanted to make sure that I knew it, but that wasn't even the worst part.

No one else had been able to train their kittens the way I had trained Othello. There was only one way Sandy could have known to ask me that. She must have been one of the witches on the Conseil des Demoiselles. How else would she know what Othello could do? Sandy had been on the other side of one of those screens. She'd watched the teachers say all the things I had done wrong, watched me struggle to gain control. I bet hers was one of the screens that never lit up. Not a no vote, but not a yes, either.

A fleur-de-lis charm glinted in Sandy's hair. It was attached to a little pin stuck into her perfectly carefree bun. I wanted to snatch it out. I didn't. I smiled and made my eyes look extra wide and innocent and said, "Yes! He does. He's such a smart kitty."

Normally I squatted down a little and Othello hopped onto my hand, but I scooped him up off the ground and walked off toward my parents just in time to hear my father say, "Well, I don't know how y'all are gonna get home, then. I can't bring you. Sandy and I are driving straight from here to the beach."

"What?" I said.

"The car's only trickle charging, honey. I thought it would go faster, but we've only got about twenty miles. It looks like we're stuck."

"Dad can bring us home," I said.

"I can't, Hasani. Your mom doesn't want to have to leave her car here, anyway. It'll be a pain to get it again."

"OK. So you can just wait with us while the car charges."

Over my dad's shoulder, I could see Celeste and her sister and her mom and dad all getting into a car together. LaToya's mom and dad were talking with Skylar's mom and dad. Some families were leaving, some families were hanging back, but all the families were staying together. Why couldn't mine?

"I don't want to make Sandy wait that long, and we've got a long drive ahead of us."

"Dad, you're not going to leave us, are you?" I put my hand on his arm. *There's no place like home* floated through my head again. I swear I didn't mean to use any charm, but my dolphin hummed as I spoke. "You're supposed to help celebrate. My YouTube thing. Remember?"

Dee put her hand on my shoulder. "Hey, let's go look at your mom's car. Maybe we can fix it."

"We don't know anything about mechanics," I said, but I wished I knew all about tech so I could fix the car and my mom and I could leave my dad before he had a chance to leave us. Again.

"Come on," Dee said. "It's just tech. We can fix it."

The two of us went over to the car. I thought she was just trying to get me away from my dad, but Dee pulled the manual out of the glove compartment and, when I didn't answer her the first time, she made me get out of the driver's seat so she could press a button and the brake and the accelerator to do a reset and, voilà. My prayers were answered. The car battery read seventy-one miles to next required charge, and my mom and I could get out of there.

"Wait," Dee said.

I had my hand on the latch.

"LaToya says stuff."

I raised an eyebrow.

"LaToya says stuff, but she's just thinking out loud. She doesn't mean to do all that stuff, you know?"

She was not making herself any clearer.

"Just promise you won't try to, you know, influence your dad," Dee said. "No matter how mad you get."

"I won't."

Dee raised an eyebrow.

My dolphin charm was so hot that I thought it might burn my skin. That had happened sometimes with the dolphin charm when I wore it alone, but not once I got the fleur-de-lis. I had no idea how much magic I had to be throwing off for the fleur-de-lis to not manage it. Maybe Dee had a point.

"I won't," I said more calmly. I wanted to pull the dolphin off my skin, but I also didn't want Dee to know just how hot it had gotten, so I left it where it was. "I would never do that." Othello mewed outside the car door, but I got out instead of letting him in.

"All right. I know you weren't raised around all this, so you might not know how messed up it is to try to influence a person. Like, real messed up. But you said you won't, so—cool."

"Cool," I said.

I didn't say that I might have done it already. Honestly, I wasn't sure I had. Dee was right next to me. No way she would have been so calm if she saw me using magic to try to straight up make somebody do something, even if that somebody was my dad. Charm, not magic. And even if I had done it by magic, no way would I do it again, so . . . cool.

But once I got out of the car, I wasn't so sure anymore. I must have done something. My dad was acting like himself again.

Dee and I told my mom that the car had rapid charged after all, but my dad didn't throw up the deuces and leave. He stuck around and made a joke about forcing all of us to become mechanics. Stupid, I know, but I swear when he said it, it was funny. My mom laughed. I laughed. We all laughed—except Sandy. Then we talked a little more and my dad told Dee how close his house was to the school she wanted to go to in New Orleans, but he didn't say *his* house. He said *our* house, like our whole family lived there or something. I was confused until I realized what was happening. My dad was saying sorry, not just for being a jerk just then. He was saying sorry for everything. So when he actually apologized out loud and said he would bring us home, I wasn't surprised. It was weird, but maybe the incantation took a while to kick in. Whatever had happened, it was good. For me at least.

It was Sandy's turn to flip out.

"What?" she said. She wasn't loud with it at first, but she was obviously not happy.

To be honest, I had forgotten Sandy was there.

"I'm gonna go ahead and take them home. You understand, baby," he said, but my dad's voice wasn't ooey gooey. It was normal.

I blinked. The incantation worked. I had broken Sandy's spell.

"What?" Sandy repeated. She still wasn't loud, but by the fourth or fifth time she repeated it, she was.

Celeste's family had left, but of course Angelique's family was still there. Angelique's mother looked horrified, like she had somehow gotten caught up in an episode of *Real Housewives* and she hated that show.

Sandy made sure everyone out there heard her say, "Have fun with your family," as she slammed the door on the convertible and drove off.

My dad hugged me.

"Sorry about that," my dad said. "She's not usually like that. I don't know what was going on with her, but she'll come around."

I knew what was going on. Sandy wasn't the only belle demoiselle anymore and, apparently, she didn't like it.

Good.

CHAPTER TWENTY

CHANNELS AND CHANNELING

The ride home was like a scene from a movie. We sang Stevie Wonder songs and laughed and got strawberries from a guy selling them on the side of the road. And when my mom asked my dad if he had a rapid charging station at his house, he said, "I do, but I'd rather come Uptown if you don't mind. I miss hanging out with y'all."

I almost cried I was smiling so big, and I swear I wasn't doing any of it. Othello lapped up every extra little bit of magic that came up, so between that and the two charms, I know it wasn't me and, seriously, that's how my parents always are when they're together. I don't know why they ever broke up.

Scratch that. I was beginning to understand why they broke up, and she was rocking beach waves and a fleur-de-lis charm.

My dad stayed over that night. He slept on the sofa, but in the morning he and my mom got up early together and made breakfast for me. I heard them already talking when I woke up, and it felt so good that I just lay there for a minute listening to them. It had worked. Honestly, I didn't realize how much I needed it to work until it had. It was like I had been squeezing my shoulders the whole time, but I didn't notice until I finally relaxed.

So I picked up my phone and checked my notifications while my parents made pancakes and turkey sausage. My mom never ate stuff like that, but that's how chill she was. Sugar-and-meat-level chill. I figured I'd eat breakfast with them, shower, and get straight to work. I'd lost one day of shooting already. My channel was growing like crazy but, like Miss Lafleur said, magic can help, but it can't do the impossible. I still needed to put the work in and, crazy as it sounds, I was really looking forward to it, even the boring parts like editing video. I was looking forward to it all.

Of course, I didn't get anything done for my channel at all that first morning home. My mom cornered me with her detangling brush. The ordeal lasted until lunch time, my dad cracking jokes the whole time. The wad of shed hair looked like a nesting family of Furbies, but I suffered through it thinking that in my mom's hands, my hair would come out looking like Angelique's. Plus, my dad seemed super impressed that I had gotten my hair to grow so much at camp.

"What were they feeding you?" he laughed.

"All I know is that if Hasani is going to get her hair wet every day, the least Hasani could do is detangle it and use some leave-in conditioner. Right, Hasani?"

"Every day?" I asked. A dangerous question since she had managed to say my name three times, but both of them were in such a good mood that it was worth the risk.

"Every day you get it wet," my mom said.

That settled it. I got four French braids and promised to wear a shower cap.

The braids were cute. Not Angelique cute, but cute. People liked my braids in the comments, too, so it was all good. One thing was for sure: Having that much hair was a lot of work, and I did not have a hair channel. I had a makeup channel, and thanks to AnyaDo0dle, it was about to blow up.

It's not like I thought AnyaDo0dle and I were going to be best friends or anything, but I had talked to her on the phone again and, for the record, Anya is even cooler on the phone than she is in her videos, and I just really, really wanted to make a good impression, which meant I had to get to work making sure my backdrop was next-level no matter how cute my parents were being in the next room.

AnyaDo0dle's videos were always pretty simple, but it's actually harder to make something simple look so clean and polished than it is to do a bunch of fancy effects over shaky footage. I went with a wall of my signature flowers. Yes, that could have been a little over the top, but my camera and lights made them kind of a soft, shimmering blur in the background, so once I was in frame it looked really cool.

I was proud of it, so when LaToya texted me "WYD," I invited her over, even though I felt a little weird about it. The way LaToya talked, her house was some kind of mansion and mine definitely wasn't, but Luz was already coming over (she always came over; she lived two houses down) so I figured I'd just make it a little party, introduce the two of them and show them the videos I had been working on. Kind of a premiere party. I offered to Skype Dee in, but she said she was still getting ready for her big move, and she didn't want to give her mom any excuse to change her mind, so it was just the three of us.

Luz and LaToya both loved my backdrop. Each other? Not so much. My mom said I should just give them time, that it's hard sometimes to share a friend you've never really had to share before, but I didn't think that was it. Those two were like oil and water. The fancier LaToya talked, the more Luz played up her New Orleans accent, with random Spanish words thrown in, which, honestly, she did not usually do. I mean, sometimes she spoke Spanish, usually with her family. Sometimes she spoke English, usually with her friends. This throwing Spanish in on top of English was new, but it only happened when LaToya said stuff like how "quaint" it was to live so close to our neighbors and how much easier it must be to keep such a small house clean and stuff like that.

"She doesn't mean anything by it," I told Luz after LaToya's dad picked her up for her tennis lesson.

"Is that supposed to make it better?" Luz asked.

"Everybody at camp was kind of like that. You get used to it," I shrugged.

"Was it a camp for magical prissy pony princesses?" Luz laughed.

I laughed, too. I mean, what was I going to say? Because, let's be honest, the answer was pretty much yes.

The main thing meeting LaToya did was make Luz realize how much I had changed. Over the next few days, she started copying the way I walked and sat down and stuff. I think she thought I'd be embarrassed and go back to what I used to do, but I didn't. I liked being a belle demoiselle. I liked how adults smiled at me extra in stores and went out of their way to tell my parents what a little lady I was, and I loved how much easier it was to look good on camera. It was like the camera could see my magic, even when I wasn't doing magic. That is how I managed to not completely freak out and cry when, on the day of our collab, instead of doing a split screen video like we had planned, AnyaDo0dle showed up at my door.

My mom knew, of course, and my dad was there recording my reaction with his cell phone. I started to pull a little extra magic from my fleur-de-lis when I realized what was happening and that my dad was recording it along with the professional crew AnyaDo0dle brought with her. This was going to be great footage. I stopped myself, though. I didn't need it. Charm, not magic.

My tears of joy were perfect. AnyaDo0dle complimented my room and told me how professional my setup was. I'd upgraded a little bit. My dad ordered me a new camera and stuff, but the backdrop was all me. I thought I had done OK, but it felt really good to hear AnyaDo0dle say that. Really good. I did her full face with dollar store finds, she did mine with super high-end stuff and, in the end, she said that if she had my skills, she'd rock my dollar store finds every single day. Then she said, "So, all my lovelies on a budget, why haven't you followed Makeupon-theCheapCheap yet? Seriously. You need to pause this video and follow her right now if you haven't. And don't forget to click her notification bell. You do not want to miss whatever she has coming next."

Then SHE DID MY OUTRO. Double finger kiss, heart. I had no idea she was going to do that and I just about died.

I thought I'd have a ton of work to do getting my video to be as good as AnyaDo0dle's, but her production team did all the work, so two days later I got a notification from AnyaDo0dle's team that the video was scheduled to go live later that day. It was the same day Dee got to town, so she and Luz and LaToya all came over. Luz rolled her eyes when she saw LaToya, but her and Dee seemed to get along OK, which was good because, since my mom doesn't believe in fancy TVs, my mom, my dad, LaToya, Luz, Dee, and I all sat on my twin bed to watch the video on the computer in my room.

When I saw myself on the screen with AnyaDo0dle, it was like I was watching someone else. I couldn't even remember some of the stuff that happened, including the fact that we had said, "I hope your day is magic," in unison, before AnyaDo0dle did my kiss heart outro. It looked like we planned it. And AnyaDo0dle's production team had added a streak of glitter sparkles when we drew our hearts in the air. It was amazing.

So first we watched the video, and then we watched the views climb.

609

Refresh.

1,888

Refresh.

23,047

Refresh.

73,000!?

The count kept climbing and climbing. In less than an hour, we were already over 100,000 views.

"I'm not surprised. You were channeling some real movie star, Beyoncé vibes. I didn't know you had it in you," my dad said. "I'm proud of you, honey."

I wasn't channeling anybody else. I was being myself; he just hadn't been hanging around enough to recognize me. But I hugged him, anyway. It didn't matter. Maybe he didn't know me, but he was trying to know me. That's what mattered, and I loved him for it.

"Remember when your goal was 100 followers before the end of the summer? Ha! How about, 100 followers in less than a minute? Look at your subscriber count," Luz said. She was doing that little shoulder dance she does when she gets hype and refreshing my page on her phone at the same time. I was already at 40k, so I thought I'd hit 50k after the collaboration, but the way my subscriber count was jumping up on Luz's phone, I was heading straight for 100k. It was unreal.

Then my mom's phone rang. It was AnyaDo0dle.

Luz shrieked. Even Dee, who is always crazy chill, looked excited. My mom handed her phone to me to answer.

"Hello?"

"Congratulations, Lovely! Our collaboration has officially had a better start than any video I've ever launched."

"Really??"

"Really. My people love you even more than they love me. I've never hit a thousand likes without at least one downvote on any of my videos. You're a hit, girl!"

"Oh, I'm sorry!" I said. That was something I learned at Belles Demoiselles—saying something humble or apologetic, but then throwing a little charm in it—but I didn't throw any magic into it because the thing was, I really was sorry. I loved AnyaDo0dle. I was not trying to dull her shine. What if she thought I was? I think that was the moment I really got what Miss Villere was trying to tell us at our closing ceremony. AnyaDo0dle didn't need to be small for me to be big. There was room for all of us.

"Do not apologize, Lovely. Own your magic, girl. You are now an official member of the influencer's club."

"Is that a real thing?"

"It is now." I could hear AnyaDo0dle's smile through the phone. "Just remember me when your channel hits 100 million subscribers, OK? 'Cause that's where you're headed."

I probably thanked her a thousand times before we got off the phone. When I hung up, everybody was staring at me. My dad was smiling and my mother had a happy tear sliding down her face, but Luz was full-on crying, just waiting for me to get off the phone to hug me and start jumping up and down.

LaToya had to leave right after that, but Luz and Dee ended up spending the night. It was great. We just kept refreshing the video. It had hit a million views by the next morning, and my channel officially had 100,000 subscribers.

"Oh my god. You know what this means, right?" Luz said, shoulders wagging. "You're as big as AnyaDo0dle!"

"I am not as big as AnyaDo0dle," I said, grinning.

"Doesn't matter. You will be. What matters is what are we going to do for your 100k?"

The bag of dollar store makeup I had bought was fine for 50k, but not 100k. 100k was huge. I needed to do something big.

"Wait. I know," Luz said. "You should do what AnyaDo0dle did. You should do a collaboration with your biggest fan!"

"_AnnieOaky_!" I did not need to think about it. "She's been liking and commenting on my stuff since day one and she makes these adorable little dolls that do not get enough love," I said, pulling up her page.

"She made those? Those are dope," Dee said. "You think she goes to art school?"

"I don't know. I don't really know her, but the dolls are amazing, right? I told you they weren't getting enough love. Everybody's going to love her."

257

"I don't know about all that," Luz said. "Look."

AnnieOaky's videos had gotten some more attention since the last time I checked. All bad. I think the only likes she had were the ones I had given her. Luz put a like on one of them, but somebody must have unliked it at the same time, because the like count stayed at one. Dee felt so bad for her that she made an account just so she could throw some likes _AnnieOaky_'s way. Those stuck. Then we went into the living room to get my mom and dad to do the same thing, but before we could ask them, my mom said, "Why don't you come spend a little time with your dad before he leaves?"

What? Leave? He hadn't been here long enough for whatever Sandy did to him to be undone.

There's no place like home. There's no place like home.

"Oh," I said, trying to keep my voice casual, which is much harder than you think it is when you're also saying an incantation in your head. "Where are you going?"

There's no place like home. There's no place like home.

"I'm going home," my dad said. He got up and hugged my mom. Then he turned to hug me. "You can come with me. You know my house is your home, too."

"No!" I said a little too loudly.

Everybody stared at me. Dee especially.

I must have looked like a crazy person. Miss LaRose would have freaked if she saw me like that, and, weirdly, the thought of Miss LaRose watching me freak out was enough to stop me from freaking out.

I pulled myself together. It was easy. Like zipping up a jacket.

"I can't go to your house. Luz and Dee are here."

I let the incantation go, but when I did, I let him hug me. And when I went to hug him back, I let the tiniest bit of magic drip through. No more than I'd give Othello. Less, really. I didn't think about it. I just did it.

"You should stay," I said, holding that drop of magic so that it wouldn't sink too far into him, but it soaked in so easily that I might have done the opposite.

I could feel my mom giving me a look, but I kept my eyes on my dad.

"Nah. I shouldn't stay. You've got your friends and everything."

"That's why we came to talk to you," I said. "We need your help with a collab!"

He was caving. I could feel it. I hugged him again and let a little more magic pass through. That time it was on purpose. But it was just a little. Barely enough to influence a butterfly.

Luz and Dee looked at me like, *hunh?*

I was buzzing. This idea was brilliant.

"There's this girl named _AnnieOaky_—"

"Her name is Annie Oakley?" my dad said in his cartoon voice.

Sometimes it was hard to tell if my dad was being corny or for real. This was one of those times.

"No. Annie Oaky. Dad. Just let me explain. So this girl has a YouTube channel and it's amazing, but people are basically bullying her about it."

"That's awful," my mom said. "I wonder if we could get in touch with her mother . . ."

"No. Mom. That's why we're going to do a collab. My subscribers are so amazing. I've literally never gotten a single downvote and the comments in my comment section are so sweet—"

"That's impressive, baby girl," my dad said. I smiled. "Even Sandy gets downvotes."

Blank stare. Moving on . . .

"Anyway, I was thinking that if I do a collab video, my followers would start to follow her and then—"

"She'd get the nice comments," my mom finished for me. "That's wonderful, Hasani."

"It'll be even better if Dad does it with me," I said. I put a little charm in it, sure, but not a lot. "But, only if you want to," I said.

"I'm in!" my dad said.

Boom. And that, my friends, is how you kill two birds with one stone.

CHAPTER TWENTY-ONE

COMMENTS AND COMMITTMENTS

Dee made a perfect miniature version of my backdrop. I couldn't have done that with or without magic. Skillz. Luz convinced her brother to let me use one of his Ken dolls, which also took skillz. Her brother loved those things.

My idea was that I would do makeup on a doll like _AnnieOaky_ did but, since I had never done makeup on a doll before, mine would come out so-so at best. Then we'd cut to footage of _AnnieOaky_'s stuff, which would be way better than mine and show how awesome she is, and, at the same time, show the reason for the collaboration. After _AnnieOaky_'s footage, we'd cut back to me and my doll, which we would crossfade so it would be like the little plastic doll had transformed into a big one: i.e., my dad.

I'd never done makeup on an adult before, let alone an adult with a mustache. Facial hair is a definite complication for foundation, but it was fun and we laughed a lot, and in the end the split screen of my dad's makeover and one of the ones _AnnieOaky_ did had the same effect, even with the mustache. It was perfect. But when we went to post a teaser comment on Annie's latest video, her comments were disabled.

"We seriously can't send her a message?" I said.

Dee shook her head. She was at the computer. "Nah. _AnnieOaky_ hasn't posted for days. Not here or anywhere. She ghosted."

"Why would she do that? I mean, I know she had a few down-votes, but—"

"A few? This video has 187 downvotes and 2 likes. That's gotta hurt. I would have quit, too," Luz said.

Those two likes were from me and Dee. I remembered when we did them. I couldn't believe she didn't have any others. Her stuff was so good. She had to have gotten other likes. It didn't make sense that mine and Dee's were the only ones that stuck. Did people even go back and take their likes off videos like that?

I shook my head. "Dang. I wish we knew her IRL."

"We do," Luz said.

"We do?"

"Yeah, we do. She goes to school with us."

"She does?" I squinted at _AnnieOaky_'s profile pic. "No, she doesn't."

"Yes, she does. She's a grade behind us, but she totally goes to our school. She's smart, too. She was in my seventh grade algebra class, but I didn't know she was a sixth grader until halfway through the year because she got straight hundreds on everything. I think I only saw her get a 95 like once, and you know how Mr. Schaulk likes to loud cap everybody. If she got less than that, he would have called her out."

I squinted even harder at the pic. Our school was not that big, but I seriously did not recognize this girl. It didn't matter, though. I felt like I knew her, anyway. We were NewTubers. We had to stick together.

"I just want to ask her what happened," I said.

"This is what happened."

Dee nodded toward the screen. She had been busy typing in a new window. Until that moment, it looked like she had been typing gibberish in an old-timey screen. Now I saw what she was up to.

"That's _AnnieOaky_'s page?" I said.

"Yeah. Before she disabled the comments."

"How did you . . . ?"

Dee shrugged. "The Internet is forever. You just have to know how to look."

And be able to mix a little magic into your search, I thought. The faint red of Dee's magic was still around the keyboard.

"Wow. You are good." Luz stared over Dee's shoulder appreciatively.

Dee's brown cheeks blushed, but she kept typing.

"We're in," she said, and the comments expanded on _AnnieOaky_'s latest video like they had never gone away.

There were hundreds of them. They were horrible. I cried reading the stuff they wrote to her. And the more Dee scrolled down, the worse they got. None of them were about the video. Not really. They were all about her.

I didn't bother wiping away the tears. Othello rubbed his chin against my leg, but I shooed him away. I didn't want to feel better. "What kind of monsters would do something like this?"

Dee shook her head. "Not monsters. People. People say all kinds of stuff when they're upset. They feel better for, like, a second, but they don't think about how it piles up. How it's a person on the other side of whatever it is you doing. The funny part is if you ask them, they're gonna have a reason, like having a reason makes whatever you do OK. That's why I don't really mess with the Internet." Dee shrugged. "Everybody thinks they're the good guy. That's how the game works."

"Well, we know we're the good guys," I said. "We have to do something to help her."

"I'm trying," Dee said.

She was. Play the game 'til you know the game. Dee said that once at Belles Demoiselles, but at the time, I didn't really get it. Now I did. It's like math. You can't get creative with fractals and stuff if you don't even understand arithmetic. You have to learn how to play the game first, then you can put your own spin on it. Make it work for you instead of the other way around.

Dee's Belles Demoiselles charm was in a piercing at the top of her ear. I could see her shifting magic from her fleur-de-lis into what she was doing, but that wasn't what I was looking for. Our fleur-de-lis charms were shielded somehow. Probably a protection against getting your power sapped or stolen, but I wanted to add to Dee's power, not take away from it. Luckily, I had done it once before with the wildseeds in Vacherie, and I could do it again if Dee were wearing her dolphin charm. It took me a minute to find it. It was in a ring on her right hand. She was wearing a bunch of rings on that same finger, so I didn't notice it at first, but as soon as I did, I did things my way, channeling magic through it to boost her signal. It felt amazing. Like I was finally doing something right.

But Dee was the real MVP. Her tech skills were deep. I mean, super deep.

"But you didn't even have an IG account," I said. "How do you know so much about this stuff?"

"I know enough to stay off it."

Lowkey, we were all scared for Annie. I mean, you hear stories about kids who get bullied on the Internet. Some of them end bad. Real bad. So I just kept channeling as much magic into Dee's dolphin charm as I could, and she used it to try to undo whatever algorithm had tangled up Annie's YouTube channel.

I checked my channel stats. Views on the _AnnieOaky_ collab video were already over 300k with forty thousand new likes on that video alone. It wasn't helping, though. If anything, it was making things worse. _AnnieOaky_'s downvotes had tripled. And no one could leave comments, because they were disabled. It was bad.

Dee dove back into the code. It was impressive to watch her flying through screens and screens of stuff that looked like gibberish equations except she could read them like English. Sometimes it kind of looked like algebra, but that was wishful thinking. I loved algebra. If it had been algebra, it would have been easy.

Meanwhile, Luz looked up Annie's number in the school directory. Her mom's cell phone was listed. Luz called, but nobody picked up, so she texted her instead. Her mom texted back right away.

The text said: "Leave my daughter alone."

"She probably thinks we're the bullies," Luz said. "I texted her that we didn't have anything to do with it, but I doubt she'll believe me. I wouldn't believe me, either. Those comments were coming from people all over. If I were her mom, I'd be scared if a bunch of different people were coming at my daughter like that."

"Not a bunch of people. One person," I said.

Dee caught my meaning. Luz didn't.

"You think somebody made a bunch of different accounts to troll this girl?"

"Nah. The accounts are real, but Hasani's probably right. This is some type of campaign. It's too concentrated to just randomly come from a bunch of different people." Leave it to Dee to explain all that without talking about magic. "Somebody kicked this whole thing off. Other people are following behind whoever it is, but somebody is at the head."

"How do you know?" Luz leaned in.

"Like this," Dee said. She tapped a few more keys and the whole screen turned to code.

"Dang, girl. You are good," Luz said.

Dee blushed. "Miss Villere, our . . . er . . . camp director, taught me a few things. Everything on websites like this is done by algorithm. It's supposed to help keep things fair so people will see more things people like and less things people don't like. The companies that run the website try to keep the algorithms secret so people can't tamper with them, but if you know what you're looking at, you can follow them anyway, and, if you're good enough, you can mess with them, anyway. See this?"

Luz and I both leaned in closer. The whole screen was filled with words, but as if instead of leaving them in sentences, you chopped them up and made them into a salad.

Dee pointed at a random chunk. "This part shows where _AnnieOaky_'s videos weren't getting much interaction. So if nobody was messing with the algorithm, her post should have been being shown less and less, but something was making it get shown more and more. See right here? See how the code looks different? I can trace it all the way back to here."

"Where's here?" Luz said.

Dee tapped a few keys, the code went away, and the screen went back to normal.

"That's my mini-vlog. The one I did in the car with my mom on the way to camp." I blinked, hoping when I opened my eyes it'd be different. It wasn't. "That doesn't make any sense."

Dee shrugged. "That's where it starts. The comments are always linked to the algorithm. Links and uploads and all that. Plus if the commenter has a YouTube channel. But this one sticks out because it leads back to your page twice, even without a link in the comment. Everything before that looks normal, but everything after that kind of explodes."

I shook my head. "It should have done the opposite. I gave _AnnieOaky_ a shout-out in that video. When I got more likes, she should have, too."

Luz put her hand on my back. "It's not your fault," she said. "Some haters probably did it. People are always hating on successful people."

She didn't understand. I wasn't successful. Not then. I still barely had any followers. No one even knew who I was. I didn't have any haters. At least, not any haters on YouTube . . .

"Luz is right," Dee said. "Somebody was trying to sabotage you but got Annie instead."

Luz shook her head. "Who would do that? Like, who has the energy to hate on somebody that hard? And then how could everybody just follow along after a person like that? Like lemmings. Wait. No. Not lemmings. I heard they made the lemmings do that for the video, which is really messed up, but you get what I'm saying. Who has that kind of power where people just go along with whatever they do?"

I knew the answer to that, and from the look Dee gave me, she did, too. Angelique.

CHAPTER TWENTY-TWO

SILVER AND GOLD

*L*aToya answered on the first ring, but it was loud wherever she was.

"Hey. We're having a . . . uh . . ." Why hadn't we come up with a code word? We needed a code word. ". . . camp emergency," I finished. "Can you come over?"

"I mean, how much bigger do you want your little collab video to get, Hasani?" LaToya said, sighing. "It's heading to a million views and it's only been up, like, a day. Is that not enough?"

"It's not that. We need your help with . . ." I said. The talking in code thing was obviously not working. "Can you just come over?"

Luz made a face.

"Never mind," I said. "Dee and I will come to you."

Is it rude to just show up at someone's house? Yes. But I couldn't exactly say it was coven business in front of Luz. LaToya would understand when we got there.

"What's your prissy friend gonna do to help?" Luz said. "If we can't go to Annie's house, we need to be finding Annie's friends so one of them can do it. I think Annie is friends with Amy. At least, I saw Amy talking to her one time. And Amy is friends with Elise, and I know-know Elise. I say we call Elise, and—"

"We do need LaToya," I said. How could I explain it to Luz without explaining everything to Luz? I hated not explaining everything to Luz. "It won't help if Angelique is involved. Angelique is . . . special."

"Special how? I'm sure she thinks so, but let me tell you there is nothing special about a bully. They all do stuff the same way, and there is only one way to deal with them: Show them you're not scared and you're not alone."

"Bullies and Angelique aren't even in the same league. Angelique is pretty much Beyoncé with a mean streak, better skin, and more perfect hair. Angelique doesn't even really need to do anything to get what she wants. Everybody wants to be her friend so bad that they just do stuff for her. It's wild."

Luz's eyebrows shot up. "Dag. That's kinda cool. Now I kinda want to meet her."

"Trust me. You don't."

"You right. I don't," Luz said. "She sounds scary. But Dee couldn't fix whatever this Angelique person started on the Internet, so what do we do?"

"We get LaToya," I said. "With her"—magic—"around, we can combine our"—magical—"efforts and fix this thing."

"Dag," Luz said. "When did everybody learn to code? Now I want to learn how to code, too."

Dee's dad agreed to give us a ride. For once, I didn't feel bad about leaving my mom alone because, well, she wasn't alone. My dad was there. She looked a little sad, like maybe she couldn't count on him to stay after all his leaving, but Dad hugged her reassuringly as Dee and I left.

When we pulled up to LaToya's house, I finally knew how Annie felt when she saw Daddy Warbucks's house for the first time. LaToya's house was huge. Not as big as Belles Demoiselles, but Belles Demoiselles was a whole school and this was a house for just one family. There was a circular drive and the grass was so perfect it looked fake, and when we stepped out of the car to walk up to their massive front doors—no joke, there were two of them together—I also understood why LaToya could roll into Belles Demoiselles without being the least bit intimidated. This was how she lived all the time.

A tall blond guy in a tuxedo opened the door and gestured for us to enter. I didn't realize it was a party until we had actually walked in.

My Belles Demoiselles training snapped into place. Even though I was wearing a jean skirt and a slightly faded T-shirt, I made myself feel like I was wearing an elegant dress and party shoes just like everyone else.

LaToya came over to us. Her hair was freshly relaxed and flowing like Thuy's. She was wearing a gold headband that went across her forehead and a shimmery gold and silver dress that looked like it was from the 1920s. It probably *was* from the 1920s. LaToya was a flapper right down to a cigarette holder with what I hoped was a candy cigarette. Not just a party. A costume party. Great.

"Welcome," LaToya said. The warm magic of her greeting filled the space, and I leaned forward to return it with the half-Parisian air kiss, half-American hug that was appropriate for formal yet familiar events in New Orleans. She smelled amazing. The whole place did.

Dee gave a "wassup" nod.

"Everyone's in the salon," LaToya said.

Dee and I followed LaToya into another room off the main entrance area. It was decked out like a 1920s speakeasy with a stage and a piano player and bartender and everything. That much I could see from the entrance. As we walked closer, part of me hoped that we were walking into her parents' party. Of course it did not turn out that way. It was a room full of middle school flappers, and I knew every girl in it. They were all belles demoiselles.

"Make yourself at home. The bartender will make you anything you like. Mocktails, of course. You'll love them. Most of them are supersweet and I know how much you love sugar," LaToya winked at me.

That was a dig. At least I was pretty sure it was. I kept smiling and nodded.

"The piano player takes requests. He can turn anything into jazz or ragtime; it's great. The dance instructor has already left for the evening, but the Charleston, the Black Bottom, and the shimmy are really easy to pick up. The Lindy Hop and the foxtrot are a little harder, but I bet someone would be excited to teach you. Celeste and Ĉiela are both really good at them."

Ĉiela? I thought I knew everybody in the room, but it turned out I knew every face in the room, not every body. One of those faces was a double. Celeste had brought her twin. From their perfectly on-theme silver-and-gold flapper dresses, Celeste's with a yellow flower on her fascinator and Ĉiela's in red, it was clear Celeste and her twin had both been invited to this party. Dee and I had not.

Thuy came up and gave me a hug. "Where were you yesterday? I totally thought you were coming."

Yesterday? Dee didn't say anything. I shrugged.

"I mean, I flew in from California. You live in the same city and you couldn't make it?! I guess you have bigger things going on now. Are you cooking up something new with AnyaDo0dle?"

Did Thuy really not get that I wasn't invited, or did she get it and was trying to make me think she didn't get it? I couldn't tell. It didn't matter. I just played along, radiating as much of myself as I could through my smile.

"Well, everyone else keeps ordering the mock juleps, but I think the Flying Copper's the most authentic. Order one of those and join us on the dance floor!"

Thuy's enthusiasm was almost contagious. I smiled for real, despite everything.

"In a minute," I said. "I need to talk to LaToya."

LaToya was already lounging in a circle of chairs with Tyra, Danielle, Desirée, and Monique.

"Can I talk to you?" I said.

"Sure!" she said brightly.

"In private?"

"Really? Whispered side conversations are so juvenile. Just say whatever it is you have to say. We're among our dearest friends."

275

LaToya's voice had a tinge of British in it. It didn't match her whole flapper deal.

"OK," I said. "Since we're among our dearest friends, why didn't you invite us? We're a coven. What happened to all that talk about covens sticking together?"

"About that," LaToya said, trying to make herself sound bored. "Well, we never bonded our magic, so we couldn't truly call ourselves a coven, could we? And now I don't think it's a good idea anymore."

I know this sounds stupid, but that was the first time I really knew something was up. Until then, I was mostly thinking it was just LaToya being LaToya. Out for herself, yes, but, like, not in a bad way. Just in the way that people who want to come in first place have to be out for themselves. I know you have to be ambitious to be great, and I respected that. What was happening right then was not greatness. It was something else.

"Why not?" I asked. It was the best I could do and keep my charm in it. I was getting heated.

"I have a real coven now. We're bonded. The thirteen of us have already shared our magic."

"Thirteen?"

"Ĉiela, Celeste, Monique, Desirée, Thuy, Skylar, Casey, Valerie, Tyra, Danielle, Tanvi, Aarya, and I."

"So, like, everybody else?" I hadn't meant to say that out loud.

"Not everybody. Kalani couldn't make it. My dad was going to fly her in from the big island, but her parents said she'd already spent enough time on the mainland this year. We're gonna go see them in December, though, so it's all good. Fourteen might have been too much, anyway. Thirteen is a perfect number. My mom says my magic is already looking stronger. Daddy is so proud."

"Wow. That's cold-blooded," Dee said. I was so glad she was there with me. It would have been way worse on my own.

LaToya blinked innocently. "What? Leaving the two of you out? Like you wouldn't have done the same."

"We wouldn't," I said.

"Right. You *never* left me out. It's just that both of you suddenly found dolphins so charming that you had to both sneak out and get matching charms. On the same night. Without me."

I blinked. Had LaToya seriously been mad about that this whole time? I knew she was a little upset, but she hadn't mentioned it after the first time, so I thought she had gotten over it. Apparently not.

"It wasn't like that," I said, trying to figure out a way to explain it that wouldn't basically out a whole town of kismets and witches.

"Don't bother. It's too late, anyway. You have your coven. We have ours, but ours has all the cool kids."

"Cool kids," everybody sang back. This was clearly a thing. Some of them weren't even paying attention to know anything was going on, but they sang it back anyway like the next line in a song.

"We're sorry. We weren't trying to leave you out. I swear. I didn't even know what we were getting into when we left Belles Demoiselles that night. It was a family thing, not a coven. I didn't even know what a coven was until you told me."

LaToya's face didn't change. It was like she had woven an intention—not surprising since she was Miss Lavande's protégé and that was Miss Lavande's specialty. LaToya had told us that all the veils around Belles Demoiselles were woven from Miss Lavande's intentions, but they didn't block people out until those intentions were set. Hopefully LaToya's weren't. Maybe she just needed to see the real me to remember she could trust me. After all, I was wearing a mask. It wasn't a mask-mask, just a way of smoothing your face so that no one can tell what you're thinking if you don't want them to. I learned it from watching Miss LaRose, and I had put it up the moment we walked into LaToya's house, but at that moment I let it slip. No. I took it down. I wanted her to see me. I wanted her to see that I was being for real. That I had never meant to hurt her.

LaToya looked at me and smiled, but the smile was all Evilene, no Glinda.

She wasn't my friend. She never was.

"That's OK," I said. "If you want to be with the cool kids, that's fine."

"Cool kids," Skylar, Casey, and Thuy sang from the dance floor.

Not *that* cool. Angelique wasn't there. I wanted to point that out, to make LaToya explain. Saying it would hurt her, maybe as much as she was hurting me. But I wasn't there for myself or to argue with LaToya. I was there for _AnnieOaky_, and I still needed the "cool kids'" help.

"There's this girl with a YouTube channel," I started. LaToya cut me off.

"Which girl? Half the girls in here have YouTube channels."

I blinked. That was true. Thuy was SilverbellsandCockleShells. Tanvi was AR0sebyany0thername. Those were the ones I could remember. Everyone who had a camp makeover gave a shout-out to their channel on my page. Why had I never looked up their channels?

I shook off that thought. Everybody in this room was doing OK, even if I hadn't watched their videos. No one was trying to ruin their lives or make them want to disappear. That's what someone said to _AnnieOaky_: "You should disappear." And that wasn't even the worst comment.

"Someone is using their magic to bully this girl who hasn't done anything to anyone. It's all mixed into the YouTube code. We're trying get it to stop before something bad happens. We can fix it. We just need more power. Will you help us, LaToya?"

The piano player had stopped playing. The room was silent.

"It's probably you," someone said quietly.

Celeste. Of course it was Celeste.

"It's not me," I said. "I would never do something like that. That's horrible."

"It's definitely her." That was Celeste's sister. She didn't even know me, but no one contradicted her.

"It's not," I said, my voice softer than it should have been. Weak.

"No. I think it *is* you," LaToya said, perking up. "You wouldn't care so much if this girl weren't one of your followers. Did she send you some sad sob story when her rating started to tank? Is that why you did your next big collab with her instead of picking one of your actual friends who have supported you since day one?"

"No. That's not it."

"You're probably hoping something bad happens to that girl so you have something to cry about on camera," LaToya continued, really getting into it now. "We all know you love to cry on camera. It's the only reason anyone watches you. They want to be the first to see the next time you explode. And we also know how desperate you are to get a million followers. Who knows what you would do? You probably influenced that girl just to make her fail. It's pathetic, really."

That was horrible. How could she say that? I looked around the room, hoping somebody would speak up for me. I looked at Thuy. She looked sad, but she didn't say anything.

That's when we left.

Dee called her dad to pick us up. It was nighttime, but I swear sometimes it's hotter at night than it is in the day. Sweating in the dark on the sidewalk side of LaToya's ridiculous front yard only added to my misery.

A text came in from Luz.

Amy says she doesn't know her.

It took me a second to get it, but then I got it and got upset all over again.

"_AnnieOaky_ doesn't have any friends," I said.

Dee raised her eyebrows. I showed her my phone.

"Dag," she said.

"We have to go back in there," I said. "We have to charm them. Use magic. Whatever. We have to get them to help us."

"You're upset," Dee said. "Leave it. We'll figure it out. Just leave them out of it."

"Leave it? Are you serious? I mean, I don't want to deal with 'the cool kids,' either, but they have to help us. That girl is alone . . ."

I left that word hanging. No explanation needed. Nobody wants to be alone.

"You know how people say, 'Pick a struggle'? It's funny, but it's true. You can't do everything. You have to pick. We picked ours. They get to pick theirs, too." Dee shrugged. "We'll figure it out."

"What about Miss Villere?" I said. "We could ask her."

Dee shook her head. "Her help was giving us the charms. She's not gonna step in."

"What about Grandmé Annette?"

Dee shook her head. "Nah. She'll just tell us Annie shouldn't have gone on YouTube in the first place. Grandmé Annette doesn't believe in all that Internet stuff."

Neither did Dee. The only thing Dee's cell phone could do besides take grainy pictures was call and text, but Dee was helping. Why would that stop Grandmé Annette?

"OK, so maybe if I just talk to Thuy—"

"Hasani, leave it." Dee was loud. Dee never got loud. It hurt.

"I thought you were on my side," I said.

"I am," she said. "Listen. You don't have to play their game."

"What game?"

"The whole Belles Demoiselles game."

"You did," I said.

"Not like you. You look like you are taking all that to heart. Forget them."

Dee's dad was taking a long time. We sat on the curb, me hugging my knees, tears sliding down my cheeks. I was scared for Annie, but, in the quiet and the dark with my T-shirt sticking to my back, I realized something else was bothering me, too.

"They didn't have to trash me like that. They could have just said, 'no.' They were talking about me like I'm some kind of monster."

"Were they?"

"Yeah. They were saying it was my fault. Like I would do anything for fame. Like I would get some girl hurt just to get followers."

"Do you know who you are?"

I practically heard that in Miss LaRose's voice. She'd said it so many times. I nodded, but honestly, I wasn't sure. I was so tired.

"Then let it go."

I couldn't.

"I know Celeste never liked me. But LaToya was supposedly my friend and she was the meanest one. I would never influence a person, especially not like that. How could LaToya say that stuff about me when she knows it couldn't possibly be true?"

It wasn't really the kind of question that's supposed to get an answer, but I was still kind of expecting Dee to say something. Dee stared at the ground a long time before she said anything, and when she did talk, I wished she hadn't.

"You know it might be you, right?" Dee said. I shook my head. I could barely understand what she was saying. My magic, which had felt so weak, throbbed to life. Tiny bits of it flowed into my charm. "I mean, not YOU-you, but like, all the magic you're putting into your channel? The rant video? I'm on your side and everything, but, I mean, LaToya's not all the way wrong."

"How?" I croaked.

"All the bad code goes back to you, to that comment I showed you. I don't think you wrote the code, not on purpose, anyway. But you might have influenced it."

"You think I would influence people to be that hateful?"

"Not on purpose, but maybe you didn't know what you were doing. That's why I was trying to show you the code, to see if you saw what I saw."

"What did you see?"

"There's code on your page that's soaked in magic."

"I didn't write it. I don't even know how."

"Protective stuff," Dee continued. "Stuff that would stop somebody from downvoting your page or leaving a bad comment. It's like it can tell what's good or bad no matter what words are used. The good stuff stays and draws more good. The bad stuff gets . . . redirected. Which means it has to end up somewhere."

I shook my head.

"You're a witch, Hasani. Sometimes when you want something really bad, you can just make things happen. That's the dangerous part of being a witch. That's why my mom didn't want me to leave Vacherie if I couldn't become a belle demoiselle first. My father can't see my magic or keep it in check. She needed to know I could handle it myself before she let me go. Witches influence things."

"I couldn't have influenced all those people to do that. I could barely even get my dad to stay with my mom, and he loves her!"

"What?" Dee looked taken aback.

What did I say?

Her dad pulled up just then. I didn't figure out what I said wrong until we had climbed inside the car. My dad. In all my blubbering about not influencing people with magic, I had basically admitted that I had tried to do it. Now one of the best people I knew knew that I wasn't a very good witch, after all, no matter what I said.

Dee didn't speak to me the whole ride back to my house, and when I got out of the car, she didn't get out with me even though I was pretty sure she had left her stuff inside.

"Call me?" I said. It was more like a hope than a question. Definitely not a declaration. I didn't deserve that.

"I have to go to my mom's this weekend," she said.

That wasn't an answer, but I didn't press it. I got the message.

They waited for me to get inside, but I have literally never felt so alone as I felt on the walk up to my front door.

I opened the door, wishing it wasn't so late. Wishing my mother would be at the table waiting for me with a hug and a pot of tea. Of course I got my wish. I just wish that I hadn't.

CHAPTER TWENTY-THREE

HUGS AND KISSES

My mom was in the kitchen. It wasn't like her to be up that late. She was an early riser, which meant my mom was knocked out by 8:30 p.m. on a normal night, not still awake at 10:30 making a pot of tea like it was six o'clock in the morning.

"Where's Dad?" I said.

My mom was already pouring me a cup. I wrapped my hands around the mug, and the warmth felt good on my fingers. Not magic good, but good.

"Where's Dad?" I said again before taking a sip.

"Your father is not here," my mom said. "He's gone back to Sandy."

"He's gone back to see Sandy?"

"No. He's gone back to be with Sandy."

A tear rolled down my mom's cheek. She didn't bother wiping it away. "I told him he should. Eventually he believed me and left."

"You sent him back to her? Mom! No!" I shrieked. My magic wanted to rise to my fingertips or, maybe I wanted it to, but there was nothing there. It was like dry heaving into a toilet.

Othello was on my lap in an instant. He rubbed his head against my elbow. A little magic seeped in, but it wasn't enough. My mom hugged me. That wasn't enough, either. I felt empty.

"You don't understand," I cried into my mom's shoulder.

"I understand," she said softly. "I know how badly you wanted your father and me to get back together. I know how much you want us to be a family. But Hasani, we are a family, I promise you. Nothing and no one is going to stop us from being a family. We're connected, the three of us, no matter how far apart we are. Your father doesn't need to live here for that to be true, and living here isn't what makes it true. Your father will always be your father and he will always love you. Him falling in love with Sandy doesn't change that. And if we love him, too, we shouldn't try to keep him from being with another person he loves."

"He doesn't love her," I said.

"He does," my mom said, stroking the top of my head.

"No. She's just making him think he does. She's influencing him."

"Hasani? What are you talking about?"

"Mom, Sandy is a witch. She's influencing Dad with magic like he's a puppy or a dragonfly something."

I didn't feel bad about outing Sandy. Deep down, my mom must have known about her already, just the way she had always known deep down about me. I was just helping her put the pieces together.

My mom shook her head.

"Her perfect hair? Her Instagram following? The fact that Dad was willing to just ditch us and run off with her? Her stupid cold lemonade??"

My mom cocked her head.

"She literally had glasses of ice sitting on the back porch for at least ten minutes. None of it melted."

My mom cocked her head more.

"Mom! It was June! How else would ice not melt outside in June? It was hot! I was melting. The ice should have been melting."

"Maybe she put it outside right before you came and there was just enough shade to keep it solid. Maybe she's just lucky."

I shook my head. "She basically told me she was a witch at the ceremony, and it's the only thing that makes sense, because otherwise she couldn't have gotten in to the grounds. The closing ceremony is for belles demoiselles and immediate family only. And how else could she have gotten one of these?"

I pulled out my belles demoiselles charm.

"A fleur-de-lis charm?"

"Yes. Exactly," I said. My mom was getting it, thank goodness. Sometimes things take a while to sink in when you're in shock. "That's what makes her so dangerous. They literally teach us how to be sneaky with our magic. That's pretty much the only thing they taught us, and Sandy is using her sneaky magic to make Dad love her!"

"I don't know much about magic, but I don't think that's how love works, and, for the record, I don't think Sandy is a witch."

"Seriously? It only took two seconds for you to believe I was one."

"I could always see something in you. I never knew what it was, exactly, but I always saw it, and when Dee came, I could see a little of it in her, too. My grandmother had the same look. Maybe I can just see magic. Maybe I'm one of the lucky ones. A kismet. And my luck helps me see magic." It was my turn to cock my head. My mom had no idea what she was talking about. "Whatever it is, the little thing I used to see in my grandmother that you have so much of, I don't see it in Sandy."

I shook my head. This was all wrong. It didn't make sense. It was like my mom couldn't see basic facts that were sitting right in front of her. Maybe Sandy was influencing her, too.

If I'd had the energy, I would have given my mom a little pulse of magic. Just enough to get her back on my side. But the little bit Othello had given me was barely enough to stop me from feeling sick.

"And that charm you're talking about?"

The pulsing in my head was threatening to turn into a headache. Either my fleur-de-lis was empty, or it would not flow. I couldn't have burned it all off. I needed it.

"Your father gave Sandy that fleur-de-lis to welcome her to New Orleans," my mom said.

I opened my mouth to object. She cut me off.

"I know because I helped him pick it out from a jeweler in the French Market."

I looked at my mom. My mom looked at me.

"We can't just let Dad leave us," I said.

She hugged me again. She was quiet for a long time. I started to relax. I thought I was getting through to her. Then she said, "Your father didn't want to leave, Hasani. I made him leave."

I pushed back. I didn't want her to hold me. Not when she wasn't making sense.

"What? Why? Why would you do that?"

I had been trying so hard to keep us together, but we were falling apart anyway, all because my mom didn't know what we were up against.

"I knew if he went to see Sandy again, he would stay, but I thought he owed it to his wife to tell her in person why he wasn't coming back. I know that's what I would want." My mom wiped away another tear. And another.

I blinked, confused. "Your dad and Sandy got married. They eloped in Las Vegas the day before the ceremony. That trip to the beach was supposed to be their honeymoon."

More tears. "But your divorce isn't even final! Y'all said it would take a year."

"Baby, it has been two years."

Had it? It didn't feel like it.

"Neither of you said anything."

My mom took a deep breath. I thought she was going to say something helpful. Something that would make it better. All she said was, "It's hard."

No wonder Sandy had gotten into the ceremony. She was family, after all.

"I'm sorry." My mom was trying to wipe her face. Look normal.

The news didn't affect me the way I thought it would. I thought I'd be, I don't know, more angry? I was sick more than I was angry. I sat up straight. Disgusted. My dad was ripping my mom apart and here she was apologizing. I hated him for it.

"Mom, you have to stop saying you're sorry. I'm not just a little kid. I can do stuff. I can help. I have a lot of followers now. It doesn't matter if Sandy's a witch or not. If that homewrecker thinks she can just flip her hair and ruin our lives—"

"What did you say?"

"Huh?" I blinked.

"What did you call Sandy?"

I had to think. "A homewrecker?"

"Where did you hear that word?"

I shook my head. Where had I heard that word? A song? *The Parent Trap?* I wasn't sure.

My mom sighed. "I told your father it wasn't you," she said.

"What?"

"Somebody left a nasty comment on Sandy's Instagram page, and it set off a bunch of other nasty comments. I think she had to shut the whole thing down, which I'm sure is devastating for her, poor thing. I don't think she has any other business. Your father was going to talk to you about it, but I stopped him. I told him somebody must have hacked your account. I told him you're a YouTube star now, so people are bound to come after you, after all of us because of your success. I told him you didn't do it. Hasani, was it you?"

I nodded, not so much because I thought it was the time for the whole truth and nothing but the truth but because I could not imagine that my mom was on Sandy's side, caring whether or not Sandy got hurt. It seemed impossible.

My mom's face changed. She was obviously feeling some type of way. Disappointed. Sad. Something. But it was only because she couldn't see it my way. I had to explain.

"She deserved it." Honestly, there were way worse things I could have called her than a homewrecker. "Look how much she's hurt you. And Dad. All of us. He cheated on you and he just left me for weeks, all because of her."

I'd never said it so clearly before. At least that part felt good.

"Your dad made a mistake. It was hard, but I forgave him because we all make mistakes. Goodness knows I have. Maybe even ones that hurt him worse than his mistake hurt me. But his mistake did not involve Sandy, and his mistake is not the reason that we broke up. I am."

My mom looked at me like I was supposed to get it. I didn't get it.

"I love your father. I always will. But I don't want to be with him. I've known that for a while now, but it was so hard to bring myself to actually say it. It seemed like every time I got up the courage to do it, something would change my mind."

What was she saying? I wanted her to stop.

"When your father asked if we could try to put the pieces back together, I did because that's what you do when you're married. You put the pieces back together. You work things out. And we tried. Believe me, we tried. But somewhere along the way, I realized that in all that putting us back together, I still couldn't find me. That's when I said we should get divorced. Your father didn't want to, but he got his own place. He thought of it as temporary at first, to give me space to figure out what I really wanted. After a while, we both realized that it was for the best if we were apart."

I took a deep breath. This wasn't happening. I just needed to remember who I was and everything would be OK.

The words filled my mind. *I am a good witch. A good witch. A good witch.* The words bounced and echoed and filled me until they were replaced by a flood of magic. I reached out and touched my mother's hand. She needed to feel my magic as much as I did.

My mom's face changed again. I saw it click when my hand touched hers. Something in her eyes.

She gave a small smile. "But your father's right. He belongs here with you and I belong here with you, so I guess that means we belong together. Sandy sent him annulment papers in the mail. I told him he should talk things over with her in person. I was thinking that he would see her and not be able to sign them. He does love her. I know that. And I want him to be happy. But you're right. He'll be happy here, too. Of course he will. And so will I. Text him and tell him to sign the papers. Text him and tell him I take back the things I said. I want him to come back."

I was squeezing her hand. She squeezed my hand. I think that's the first time in my life that I ever actually understood my mother, which is wild because this whole thing was so well and truly messed up. I was looking at her, tears streaming down her face, tissue dabbing at her nose so she wouldn't sniffle, and I finally understood. She wasn't crying because she wanted to be with my dad. She was crying because she didn't want to be with him. She loved him and she didn't want to hurt him, but that wasn't what was making her change her mind. I was.

"Don't worry about me, baby. I'll be fine. Adults are allowed to be sad sometimes, too."

I was crying. Full on crying. I didn't realize it until my mom hugged me and walked me to my room and hugged me some more.

"Go ahead and text your dad." She kissed me on the forehead. "He'll come back if we want him to."

I waited until my mom shut the door, but that only made me cry harder. I wasn't crying about my dad being gone. I was crying because I had legitimately never asked my mother what she wanted or how she felt about anything, and it turned out I had been hurting her this whole time. It was me. I was the one who was hurting all of us.

My mom's phone rang. I didn't expect her to answer it. No one my mom knows would call her this late. But I heard her go into the kitchen to get it. All I could think was, *It was me. It was me.* The next thing I knew, my mom was back in my room saying my name like I wasn't a monster.

"Hasani?"

I didn't bother wiping the tears away.

"Do you know a girl named Anne Johnson?"

AnnieOaky. Why was my mom asking me about _AnnieOaky_?

I nodded.

"Was she at that party you were at tonight?"

I shook my head and shrugged to ask why. My throat felt dry. I didn't trust it to talk.

"I just got a call from your school's phone tree," she said. "Anne Johnson is missing."

CHAPTER TWENTY-FOUR

SWEET AND SUGARCANE

It was official. I was a monster.

My magic went quiet again. One moment, it was high water of the river being held back by a levee. The next moment, nothing. That was good, I decided. I couldn't be trusted with magic. Not after what I had done to my mom. I felt it happening this time, but it was so normal that I didn't even think to stop myself. The bridge wasn't the first time I had done magic. It was just the first time I got caught.

By then, it was past midnight and the only thing I could think of was how much I had screwed up. Every single thing that was going wrong was my fault and now everyone was miserable. My dad was miserable. My mom was so miserable that she probably wished she could run away, but she couldn't even do that, thanks to me. And, also thanks to me, _AnnieOaky_ was so miserable that she had actually run away. At least I hoped she had. The other things that could have happened to her were way worse.

I wished my mom had yelled at me about the Sandy thing. Sandy was horrible, and I didn't believe for one second that she wasn't a witch, but with everything staring me in the face, it was hard to think about all the stuff Sandy had done wrong when all the stuff I had done was just as bad, maybe worse. If Sandy wasn't a good witch, what did that make me? And now, when my dad came back, my mom was going to have to tell him that she was wrong. That I am exactly the kind of person who would leave that comment on Sandy's page. That I am exactly the kind of person who didn't regret doing it.

I checked our school's website on my phone. There was a post about Anne Johnson along with her school picture. Luz was right. I had seen her around. I had just never talked to her, or recognized her, apparently, even though she was literally my number one fan.

Had I always been that terrible? I must have. It's not really possible to become a destroyer of worlds overnight. How long had I been working my way over to the dark side? The bad code was my fault, even though I had no idea how I did it. But I didn't need to know how it worked, did I? In my mind, I was in the solarium and I could see the white flowers flickering again out of the corner of my eye. People were going to vote against me, but I felt the white flowers coming before they came, and I stopped them. Those screens went black instead. It didn't matter that I didn't know how I did it. I did it, and I had done this, too.

I ran over to my computer and pressed Ctrl+U the way Dee had to bring up the code. It stared back me. Why couldn't I control it now? I wanted to throw the stupid keyboard through the stupid screen, but then two things happened: 1. The code moved. It didn't, like, come to life or anything. It was more like when you delete one word in the middle of a paragraph, but it changes the spaces just enough that a bunch of different words shift? That's what happened. And 2. My phone pinged. I had a new YouTube comment. I swiped it open and read it. The comment was only one word: "Overrated." And while I was watching, two, three, nine people upvoted it. It might have been more, but I stopped watching.

It didn't matter. I deserved it.

don't know how much time passed. The next thing I knew, my mom was kissing me on the forehead, telling me I was going to go to the country with Dee.

"Dee was here?" I asked my mom. She looked normal. Too normal. Like she was trying not to show me how scared she was.

"She's worried about you," my mom said.

My phone chimed. It was Luz. Her AnnieAreYouOaky Instagram page had 13 followers. She wanted me to follow to get it 14. According to Luz, 13 was bad luck. I didn't know what an Instagram page with 14 followers was going to do besides show _AnnieOaky_ how unpopular she was. It was pointless, but I followed it anyway and shared it to my IG stories. I only had 84 followers there. It wasn't going to be much help. I thought about Sandy's Instagram and what her massive following could have done if she reposted something from @AnnieAreYouOaky. The page would have had thousands of followers and hundreds of "We miss you" and "Come back" messages in, like, a minute. If Annie found something like that, she was sure to come back. Too bad Sandy had to shut down her IG page. Not that Sandy would have helped me anyway . . . not anymore.

I looked up. My mom was staring at me, concern in her eyes.

"Dee thinks you should take a break."

"A girl is missing, Mom!"

"I know. And we're going to find her. But it won't do me any good for us to find her while I lose you. You were so calm and confident when you came back from camp, but that calm has all disappeared. I'm worried about you. I think the country will be good for you. Go. Get away from the Internet."

I didn't need a break. I didn't deserve a break.

But the next thing I knew, Dee's dad was dropping us off at her mom's house in Vacherie. Dee was quiet the whole ride.

We pulled up to a house right next to the levee. Dee's dad got out to hug her. He gave me nod, but he didn't help us to the door. Both of us had only brought a backpack, so we didn't really need help with our stuff, and I got the feeling Dee's parents didn't get along that well. Not that I knew for sure, but you can just add that to the list of things I was too caught up in myself to ask about. No wonder Dee hated me. She could finally see me for what I really was and, even with long hair and lip gloss, it wasn't pretty.

"Sunday at six," Dee's dad said.

Dee nodded and hugged him again. Then he got back in his car and pulled away while the two of us headed toward her house. It was nice, with a balcony on the second floor that looked right over the levee.

"You hungry?" Dee said when we got inside.

I shook my head. Dee wasn't having it.

"It's my night to make dinner, but I'll make you a snack first."

"You're talking to me?"

"Of course I'm talking to you."

"I thought you were mad at me because of my dad . . ." my voice trailed off.

"Not mad. Sad. You better than that, man."

Was I, though? Was I?

Dee put a platter of graham crackers and fresh peach slices in front of me along with a tall glass of milk. I was glad to have something to stare at since I didn't have a good answer.

"Why did you invite me? Aren't you afraid you'll be contaminated by a bad witch?"

Dee shrugged. "I know who I am. Everybody makes mistakes. That doesn't mean they deserve to be alone. I wouldn't leave you hanging like that."

"I know."

"You mind going to get me something from the store? I need more sugar. The walk might do you good."

Dee did not need more sugar. There was a whole canister of it on the shelf. But she was right. A walk seemed like a good idea. I needed space to think.

"OK," I said.

Directions to the store involved two different cane fields and taking a left at a group of old people who were always playing dominos outside of somebody's house, but I didn't pay close attention. If I really wanted to go to the store, I'd just use the map app, but I didn't need it. I knew where I was going. Belles Demoiselles: Pensionnat des Sorcières.

The river was right in front of Dee's house and so was the main road, River Road. I put a pin in the spot on my map app. Belles Demoiselles didn't show on the map, but I knew it was off River Road down past a sugarcane field. Sweat was dripping down my face before I got to the first cane field, and I severely underestimated the number of sugarcane fields one town could have, so it took me a really long time to find the right one. But eventually I found myself standing in the exact place where Mr. Paul had parked the car, right next to the house that I had mistakenly thought was the school.

I knew I was in the right place. I could feel it. But instead of a gauzy curtain of magic that I could walk right through, there was a solid wall of sugarcane. It was real sugarcane growing so thick together I would have needed a machete to cut a path.

I could feel my magic again. I had mostly been too scared to use it for the last few days, but getting through the wall of sugarcane was important. Help was on the other side. Tentatively, I let the magic fill me until I could feel it swishing in my fingertips. I didn't know any incantation for moving things, but sugarcane was basically just a locked door, and the thing that opens the most doors is knowing who

303

you are. Magic poured from my hands, splashing across the line of sugarcane in front of me. Morning glories grew along the edge, then slid off like they were butter on a hot pan.

That was it. I wanted to cry, but I pushed the feeling into my charm as much as I could and kept trying.

Eventually, I gave up and turned back, following a shortcut through a field that my phone showed me. Maybe Dee was right. Maybe we couldn't go back. Or maybe I just didn't know who I was.

I kept walking. There were paths cut in the field, some of them wide enough for cars. I kept missing turns, which seemed impossible since I was walking and there weren't that many turns to make, but by then I was too deep in the sugarcane to know which way was River Road and which way was the swamp. That was about when Dee found me.

"The store is down the first cut, not the third," she said. "This cut goes to the cemetery."

I nodded.

She laughed. "Let me guess. You were trying to go back to Belles Demoiselles."

I nodded.

"You were going to try to make Miss Villere help you unlock that code so we can find _AnnieOaky_."

I nodded.

"Did she?"

I shook my head. "I couldn't get in."

"I told you that. They keep it locked tight most of the year. Only Miss Villere, Miss Camille, and Miss Lafleur stay there year-round. I think it's because Miss Villere doesn't really like people, and Miss Lafleur can't keep the unicorns penned up all the time."

"Unicorns? Miss Lafleur never mentioned any unicorns."

Real talk, I would have liked Belles Demoiselles a lot more if they let the unicorns roam free.

"Probably 'cause you would have gone looking for them," Dee said. "Unicorns are mad judgy. They had to stop letting them roam free in the seventies. People kept getting gouged."

Miss LeBrun didn't teach us *that* in history, either.

"Anyway, the point is, you can't get in there. Come on," Dee said.

"Wait. Is this the right way," I said. My stupid map app made it look like she was heading away from the river, away from where her mom lived in Front Vacherie.

"Nah, this is right. Grandmé Annette lives in Back Vacherie."

"You said she couldn't help."

"She can, just not the way you think."

t was evening when we got to Grandmé Annette's house. She was sitting on her front porch, which I think was some kind of rule in Vacherie, because every house we passed had somebody sitting on the porch, many of whom had tried to wave us inside. Dee said, "Good evening," to every person we passed and kept walking, so I did, too.

Grandmé Annette smiled when she saw us.

"Still keeping the mosquitoes off you, I see," she said. "But all that jewelry got you sweating up a storm."

I was overheated because it was hot, not because I was wearing two tiny little charms, but I let Grandmé Annette send Dee inside to get me a glass of water.

"I see you not used to this heat, New Orleans girl. You should take all that off." Grandmé Annette gestured toward my necklace and its two charms. "Let yourself breathe. You working too hard."

"I like having them on," I said.

"Suit yourself." Grandmé Annette leaned back in her chair. She wasn't wearing any jewelry at all except a pair of hoop earrings. Her magic shifted and flowed smoothly beneath her skin, like water. "Just like my sister. I bet Marie-Claire went on and on about how it's not proper." Grandmé Annette scoffed.

"Who is Marie-Claire?" I asked, trying to remember if I had met that sister when the Vacherie coven gathered.

"Miss Marie-Claire Villere," Grandmé Annette laughed again. "That's not even she name. She got Villere off a commercial in New Orleans. That's how bad she didn't want to be from here. It's sad, sha." Grandmé Annette pulled the dolphin charm out of a little bag in one of her pockets and placed it against her skin. Her magic was drawn to it.

"See that?" she said. "These charms squeeze you tight like a brassiere. Now, why would anybody want to eat, sleep, and breathe in something like that they whole life? Sometimes you got to be free."

"Not me," I said. "Nobody in my family taught me about magic, so when mine came out, it came out wild. It felt good at first, but it hurt somebody and I don't know how to fix it. I guess that's why everybody hates wildseeds."

"Everybody hates us?" Grandmé Annette made it sound like a question, but I knew she was correcting me. I looked down, embarrassed. She called herself a wildseed and she was proud of it.

"Not you," I said.

"Not me, hunh? What about Dee? What about Evangeline and Regina, and all the people who poured their magic into you when you brought your needs to the circle?"

A tear stung the corner of my eye. I was going to dab it away, but Grandmé Annette reached out and lifted my necklace. Not much. Just enough so the fleur-de-lis wasn't touching my skin. It was as hot as an iron. Another second and it would have burned. The fleur-de-lis never got hot like that, but I pulled back and let it hit my skin again to choke back the sob that was threatening to come out.

"You not a robot, sha. You a real child with real feelings. You gon' make real mistakes and there is nothing that can stop it, not even magic. It don't do you no good to keep it bottled up in this thing, no matter what my fool sister told you, or my fool daughter."

Dee was there with the glass of water, looking at me like I was a stray kitten.

I shook my head. "Miss LaRose is right. My magic is too wild. It hurts people. I hurt people."

Then I couldn't help it. I poured it all out. Everything I had done wrong. All the people I had hurt: my dad, my mom, Angelique with the vines, _AnnieOaky_. I even hurt Sandy and maybe that was worse because I wanted to hurt her, I really had, and when I found out I did I wasn't even sad about it. I told them everything, including what I had done to my dad when I was trying to do something good. Maybe I could tell myself that dripping magic into my mom was an accident, but I couldn't convince myself about my dad. Dee knew it. I knew it. It was time I admitted it. That and everything else that made me a bad witch. The fleur-de-lis charm burned my chest. I left it there.

Grandmé Annette let me cry until the tears ran out and my breath was all hiccups. Then she said, "So, how you gonna fix it, sha?"

I looked up, amazed that she would ask me that since I so clearly had no idea what I was doing. "I'll just mess it up more," I said.

"Of course. You mess up. I mess up. Demi-Rose messes up. The whole world messed up. Now what?"

"I should tell them," I said. "I should tell everybody what I did." Maybe then they'd know to stay away from me.

"And who would that help?" Grandmé Annette laughed. I looked at her, confused. "Girl, you got to learn sweet from sugarcane."

I shook my head. That made even less sense than her telling me not to confess. That's what you do when you do something wrong, right? You confess.

"You think just going around pouring your wrongdoings on other people is gon' fix what you did? It might make you feel better, thinking you did something, but that's about as real as that ol' fake sugar. Supposed to be healthy, but that fake sweet don't do nothing but give you cancer. Learn better. Do better. That's real. That's sugarcane. So whatever you got to do to clean up the mess you made, you do it, but you keep it to yourself, you hear? Not making that mess again is the best apology you can give."

Maybe my Creole was getting better, because I finally understood what Grandmé Annette was saying. Not just the words, the meaning.

"You're a sorcière, a beautiful little wildseed ready to grow. Or would you rather me call you who you really are?"

309

"Who's that?" I said, thinking it was weird that Grandmé Annette was about to do that "First Daughter of a First Daughter" thing they did at Belles Demoiselles. I didn't think she liked that place.

"You're a witch with a plan, remember?"

"You heard that?"

Grandmé Annette winked. "Yeah, sha. I may be old, but my ears work good. And it sounds like you have a lot of mess to clean up. So what's your plan?"

My plans didn't work out. My plans hurt people.

"I don't have one," I said.

Grandmé Annette made a noise that was all m's and h's.

"I mean, I had one, but it isn't working."

"Why not?"

"Because I'm not a good witch, OK?"

I looked at Dee, expecting her to back me up. Expecting her to be looking at the ground, or turning away from me, or anything that would tell Grandmé Annette that I couldn't be trusted. But Dee was looking right at me. Not like I was a monster, but not like I was some girl she would blindly follow, either. She looked at me like I was just a person. A person who was right sometimes and wrong sometimes, but, like anybody, a person who could do their best to fix their mistakes, especially if they didn't try to do it all alone. Or maybe Dee wasn't looking at me like that at all, but I saw it anyway because that's what I needed to see.

I couldn't go back and fix what I had done to my parents. The best thing I could do for them was to do better. I felt sick thinking of what I had done, but I didn't try to get rid of the feeling. I needed to feel it and remember so that I would never do it again. But _AnnieOaky_ was different.

"I did have a plan," I said again. "I didn't want to drag Dee into it, but I couldn't do it alone. Even the two of us aren't strong enough, though. It won't work without more magic, and I probably shouldn't be trying to get more magic."

"Why not?" Grandmé Annette asked.

"I might hurt someone."

"You think you learned to walk without falling down? You're a witch. Witches use magic."

"We did. It wasn't enough."

"So get more help."

I looked at Grandmé Annette hopefully. I think some part of me hoped she was volunteering. Maybe she didn't know anything about coding, but she knew magic. If she joined us, there was no way things would get out of hand.

Grandmé Annette laughed again. "You don't want help from no old lady. You want somebody young you can grow with. Two will do in a pinch, but the real power is in three."

"We had three, Grandmé Annette," Dee said. "Didn't work."

"Must have been the wrong three. You can't share magic with everybody. Now that part I can help you with."

Grandmé Annette jumped up, took the glass of water Dee had brought me, and replaced it with a new glass for each of us. I thought it was a potion to make us more sensitive to our magic, but it was just lemonade.

"The powder kind," Grandmé Annette said. "It don't have power, but it'll still relax you. I'm saving the good stuff for the next good moon."

Then Grandmé Annette put on her dolphin charm and brought us and our glasses of powder lemonade out to her back garden. She held her dolphin charm out for us to see. "These charms link us, they remind us, but they don't define us," she said. "Your magic is free. Let it be free. Let it reach out for you."

I tried. Grandmé Annette stopped me almost before I started.

"You holding your feelings and you holding your magic and you holding everything too tight. You can't hold tight to everything all at the same time. You'll let go of something, but maybe not the some-thing you want. If you gon' use that thing," Grandmé Annette gave my fleur-de-lis a pointed look, "use it right. You trying to force your feelings in there with the magic. It wasn't designed for that."

Dee looked impressed. Grandmé saw and chuckled.

"I don't like it. That don't mean I don't know about it. Now close your eyes and let your magic flow so Hasani can see what to do."

Dee suppressed a smile, but then blue mist covered her body and flowed away from her hands.

I knew I wasn't doing it right. I tried to think of _AnnieOaky_ and the mess I made. I tried to think of my mom and my dad and what I could do to make everybody happy.

"That's your problem right there, sha. You can't make anybody happy. Your job is to stay out of folks' way so their own happiness can shine through. That's what any good witch does. We help people, but only when they ask. If somebody don't want your help, you just wasting magic."

"What if they don't ask for your help because they don't know you're the one who messed everything up in the first place?"

"In that case, it sounds like you just fixin' to fix yourself, and it's nothing wrong with that. Try again."

I did, and that time I thought about myself. I thought about who I was and who I wanted to be. I couldn't let go of all the things I had done wrong, but I tried to think more about what I could do right. I don't remember what I thought of. I only remember that it felt good and my magic started to flow. Not my fear. Not my loneliness. Not my anger. Just my magic. It felt like heaven.

"Good! Good!" Grandmé Annette said. "Now reach out."

My magic spilled out and filled a channel that went straight to Dee's. I knew it would, because we were connected. Dee had literally always been there for me, even when she barely knew me. I wanted to be there for her, too, even though I didn't know what she needed. The flow of my magic merged with hers, and I had the urge to ask her how I could be there for her, how I could truly be a better friend, but Grandmé Annette's voice cut in again.

"You find each other so easy because you already shared magic. Reach out again, both of you together. Find the one who can close your circle."

Our magic flowed together, a line of tiny roses and morning glories in the evening light. Grandmé Annette was right. There were so many witches at the moon gathering. We were so close to them. I tried to remember the faces I saw in the moonlight and wondered if the person we connected with would know it when our magic found them. Vacherie was filled with family I didn't know. Who knew who might show up? I was glad Dee was with me, if only because when one of my Vacherie relatives came, at least she would know their name.

Something stopped. Our magic changed direction. Instead of flowing out, it turned in, spiraling round and round like it was filling an enormous pool. Dee looked at me. I looked at her. The morning glories had connected with another flower. A Louisiana phlox. I didn't need Dee to tell me the name of the girl whose magic had created it.

Angelique.

CHAPTER TWENTY-FIVE

SHIFTS AND COILS

The thought of having to go crawling to Angelique was horrifying. I almost didn't do it. But it wasn't about me; it was about _Annie Oaky_. I couldn't leave her out there like that. That's not who I was. I had to do something, even if it meant begging Angelique to help me.

"You OK with that, Dee?" I said.

"I'm good," Dee said. "You good?"

"I'm good."

"Good." Grandmé Annette smiled. "Now either come inside and eat dinner or go home and eat dinner, but I don't want to waste any more magic on these mosquitoes tonight."

"My mama's probably looking for us," Dee said. "I left dinner on the table."

Grandmé Annette nodded like she knew that's what Dee was going to say, but before we turned to leave, I had one thing I needed to ask.

"Grandmé Annette, why a dolphin? Is it like a French royalty thing?" The Dauphin was the best I could come up with for a Louisiana dolphin connection, but that didn't seem right.

Grandmé Annette waved me away. "Psssh. You're not old enough for that one yet. Young people always in a rush, but that's why you have us old people to remind you. One story at a time. Now go head back. If you don't call that girl soon, she'll soon be calling you."

Angelique did call, Dee's phone and mine. I was the one who answered, even though I didn't know the number. It was a 504 number. I thought it might be someone from school calling about Annie.

I felt Angelique radiating through the phone before I even said hello. She didn't say hello back. She said, "I knew it was you, Hasani."

"You called me," I said.

"Before that. I knew we were going to make a connection. That's what I told LaToya when she kept trying to push that coven on everybody. You can't force a connection. It's either there or it isn't."

I was speechless. Literally speechless.

"I didn't know Demi-Rose, but I definitely knew it would be you."

"You did?" I stammered. "But you were so mean to me."

"I was. That's why I changed the words of that toast."

I raised an eyebrow.

"I was supposed to say, 'To the charmed girls and their fleurs-de-lis.' I changed it so you wouldn't feel excluded even though I knew Miss LaRose was trying to keep you out. LaToya told her you'd been bragging about your dolphin charm, but I stood up for you. And who do you think got you invited to the Vacherie coven in the first place?"

"That was you? But you made fun of me."

"You literally stared at me everywhere I went like I was some kind of circus freak, and then you attacked me on the first day of class. What did you expect me to do?"

"I'm sorry," I said.

"I apologize, too," she said.

And that was that. Angelique was in.

We got on a Hangout and started working on cleaning up my mess.

Turned out, both me and Dee had stuff in common with Angelique. Not her room. Dee played it off better than me, but I knew she was as impressed by Angelique's room as I was. It was all white with little accents of gold and not a single thing out of place.

"I just like order," she said. "That why I love algebra so much."

I gasped.

Angelique rolled her eyes. "Spare me the math hate. I've heard it before."

"No!" I squeaked. "I love algebra, too!"

She grinned. "When you take something super complicated and work it down to something totally simple like x = 3.98, it's just emotionally satisfying. I'm not even sorry. It is."

"Right???" I exclaimed. "It's not even about the grade. It's about the satisfaction."

Not only was Angelique a math geek like me, but she was also a coder like Dee. She started talking about Java and pythons and RWBY, which I legit thought was an anime, not a coding language, but when they worked together for an hour and hadn't made much progress, I had to interrupt their lovefest.

"It's my mess. I think that's why whatever you're doing is not working."

"We went over this," Dee said. "You can't do everything by yourself. That's why people have friends."

"I know," I said. "I meant that since my magic locked the code, I think we have to use my magic to unlock it. Like, me and Angelique boosting you won't work because—"

"My magic is the wrong key," Dee finished.

"Exactly. So . . . do you think you can teach me?"

I'm not gonna lie. Dee left me hanging long enough that I started wondering how good the coding tutorials on YouTube would be. But then she laughed and said, "All right, but you owe me, bruh."

We worked on it for hours. Obviously I did not learn all of coding in one night, but Dee and Angelique got me to the point where I could recognize the starts and ends of commands. From there it got way easier.

I had no idea if using my magic in the code again meant I was being a good witch or a bad witch, but, weirdly, that didn't make me afraid to use it. My magic is a part of me. I used it gingerly at first, the way you get up after you fall off your bike. But slowly, I started to see the parts where the code went bad.

"It doesn't look like there's anything wrong with the code," Angelique said. "It looks like it should be working as it was designed, so I don't know what you could do besides coding all of YouTube again from scratch."

"Maybe the problem isn't the code," I said. "Maybe the problem is my magic."

Dee gave me the side-eye like I was beating up on myself again, but I wasn't. I didn't understand much about the code, but what Dee and Angelique taught me was just enough to help me see it instead of just looking at it. That meant I could finally see my magic in it, too. It made the code shiny like leaves after a rainstorm, but the coating wasn't like water, something that would evaporate when the sun came out. It was more like armor. My magic was trying to protect me. Correction: *I* was trying to protect me, but I didn't want that kind of protection anymore. I didn't need it.

There was a line of text that looked more like me than YouTube.

"How do I delete this one?" I said, highlighting it on the screen.

"You just did," Dee said.

I looked again. The only thing highlighted was a single space. Then the text on the screen shifted again and again.

"You're doing it," Angelique said. "Don't stop."

How had she known I was going to stop? Not forever. Just for a second to understand what I was doing. But how did Angelique know? Then I remembered. Angelique could see my magic. Maybe even feel it. We were connected. That meant that, even though it needed to be me doing it, I wasn't alone. I drew on both their magic, Dee's and Angelique's, and when I forgot to do it, they gave me more, amplifying it through my dolphin charm and filling the fleur-de-lis with the extra, and code shifted and changed until, suddenly, it came to a complete stop.

Angelique broke off first. I could hear her keyboard clicking through the screen. Then my phone dinged.

"That one is a comment from me. I figured you would have your notifications off, so I gave that one a little extra zing."

"Glitter makeup is killing the environment?" I read.

Angelique smiled. "That's the one!"

I rolled my eyes.

"Well, we needed to test to see if negative comments could get through or not. Mission accomplished. You're welcome."

I laughed. The real test was whether or not someone who wasn't a witch could leave a thumbs-up on _AnnieOaky_'s videos. I texted Luz, who texted back like a second later that she could. Five minutes later, she texted again that she had left a like on every one of Annie's videos and a bunch of other people had, too.

"_AnnieOaky_'s doll eye shadow video is up to 22 likes!" I said.

"Too bad she doesn't know that," Dee said. "Anybody heard from her yet?"

"No," I said. I had just texted Luz asking the same thing.

"Does she have a phone?" Angelique asked.

"Yeah. Her location services are off," Dee said.

"That doesn't matter," Angelique said. "It's tech. If _AnnieOaky_ has a phone, we can find her. How do y'all think I found you?"

"Fair," Dee said.

"What do we have to do?"

Angelique was already typing. "It'll take me a while. It'd be better if you were both here. In person. Since _AnnieOaky_'s not a witch, finding her will take more energy. When do y'all get back to town?"

"Tomorrow night," Dee said.

I started to correct her, but then realized that we had stayed up through the night, so it was already Saturday.

"OK. The two of you get some sleep. I'll keep working on it until you get back."

"Angelique?"

"Yeah."

Angelique had just stayed up all night helping two girls who she just made friends with help another girl that she didn't even know.

"I just wanted you to know that the only reason I stared at you is because you always look so beautiful. Especially your hair. It's always perfect."

Angelique blushed.

"You have to coil the ends," she said, extra cool. I don't think she was even putting any charm in it. That was just her voice. "It's just a twistout, but that's the difference. Most people twist all the way to the bottom. The secret is to coil the ends. Comes out perfect every time."

"See you in the city," I said.

"See you in the city," she said.

Then I closed the chat screen, but instead of getting ready for bed, Dee and I both jumped at a loud banging on the front door.

"We have a bell," Dee said, heading down the stairs.

Miss LaRose stopped us from coming all the way down with a look. Then she looked through the peephole and opened the door.

It was my dad. He didn't look happy.

CHAPTER TWENTY-SIX

REAL AND FAKE

y dad was mumbling something to Miss LaRose about him not knowing I was out here and not giving permission for me to go out of town as I came back down the stairs with my one bag that I hadn't even unpacked. When he saw me, my dad smiled a little bit at Miss LaRose and Dee, but not at me, and as soon as we got in the car, he went all stone-faced.

I expected him to yell or at least say what he was mad about. To be fair, he had plenty to be mad at me about, I just didn't know which part, so as soon as he pulled onto River Road, I started talking, telling him how cool Dee was and how she had been teaching me coding, and how we had connected with another girl from camp, Angelique, who was super rich but really nice and liked algebra and had amazing hair.

"You'd like her, Daddy. You really would. Everybody likes her."

My phone chimed, but I ignored it, not wanting to leave too big a gap in the conversation, if me chattering on into the silence could be called a conversation.

My phone was already on silent mode, so I turned it off and on again just to be sure. That was too much quiet. My dad filled it.

"Sandy and I split up," he said. He sounded tight like a TV dad. He kept his eyes on the road.

My magic bubbled to the surface. I wanted to put my hand on his and let the extra magic drip through to calm him, make him more like himself. I didn't. I remembered a bunch of things Grandmé Annette had said all at once and tried to sort them out.

That's your problem right there, sha. You can't make anybody happy . . . You're holding your feelings and you're holding your magic and you're holding everything too tight . . . fix yourself.

I was holding too tight. I exhaled, doing my best to relax. Something softened just enough for me to feel the gap between my magic and my anger. The magic was sitting right on top of it, riding it, but they weren't the same thing. I separated them, steering the magic into my charm and letting the anger float right to the top. It prickled my skin and made me feel jumpy. I breathed out again, trying to soften it up.

"Don't go huffing with me, young lady," my dad said.

I hadn't huffed, and he never called me "young lady," not like that, so I turned to look at him to see what was going on.

"I know you don't care that Sandy and I split up. You don't have to be so rude about it. Is that what they taught you at that camp?"

"I'm sorry, Dad." I did my best to keep my voice calm with the anger stinging the backs of my eyelids.

He snorted. "Yeah, well, that's not what I wanted to talk to you about."

I know he didn't believe me, but I was telling the truth and I really wanted him to believe me. "Really," I said, holding back the magic from my voice, hoping he would hear the truth without it. "I'm sorry about Sandy."

He scoffed again. "You don't need to worry about that. She won't even pick up when I call her. Probably blocked me."

"I'm sorry, Dad." I didn't know what else to say.

"Stop just saying sorry, Hasani. I'm trying to talk to you. I'm trying to get through to you. You think that just because you're a child, you can do whatever you please. Well, you're wrong. What you do matters. What you say matters. How you treat other people matters. Here your mother and I were raising you to be a good person, a kind person, and as soon as you get a little freedom with that phone and that channel, you start acting like a—"

"Witch," I said.

My dad looked at me, shocked. To him, I said a curse word. I knew he would hear it as bad, but I didn't. Witches aren't good or bad, we just are. And sometimes we make mistakes, just like fathers.

"That's not . . ." my father began.

"That's OK, Dad. You didn't say it. I did. I shouldn't have left that comment on Sandy's page. It was mean. I made a mistake. I'm sorry."

He looked like he wanted to say more, but my apology took the wind out of whatever he was going to say. Another thing I learned from Miss LaRose, no magic required. The way he was working his jaw, I knew he wasn't ready for what I was going to say next, but I had to say it, anyway.

You're holding everything too tight . . . fix yourself.

"Your turn, Dad."

"My turn for what?"

My magic moving to the surface. I folded it neatly back into place and let my anger do all the work.

"You left me," I said.

"I didn't."

"You did."

My words radiated through the car. They were filled with who I was, even without magic to carry them. Those two words held my power, my pride, my confidence, my creativity, my love, and my knowledge that I deserve to be loved right inside them. Maybe they always had. Charm, not magic.

"I'm sorry for ever blaming Sandy. She's not my family. I blame you."

My dad was quiet for a long minute. We were in the city again, or close to it. Jefferson Parish, only a few blocks from Uptown. His jaw was so tight that his veins popped. We crossed over the railroad tracks and he pulled the car over in an old gas station on Oak Street.

"I was going through some things," my dad said.

He kept talking, but I don't remember much of it, just bits and pieces. Lonely. He said lonely a lot. And sad. And sorry. I mainly remember that whatever he was saying didn't stop me from feeling angry and hurt, but it also didn't stop me from loving him. I could love him and be angry with him at the same time. I could love him but not want to hear his excuses.

"I was wrong, baby. I'm gonna do better."

"It's OK, Dad." I didn't say I forgave him. That would have been fake. Maybe he would do better, but that's not what mattered. Whatever he was going through, it was up to him to fix it. I couldn't do it for him no matter how much magic I had. I could only do me. That was real.

"I love you," I said. That was real, too.

My phone chimed again, then again in a different tone. It should have been on silent.

I looked down at it. It was Angelique.

"Are these getting through?"

I scrolled up through the earlier messages.

"Check your messages."

"Cutting through."

"If you don't answer in five minutes I'm cutting through."

"Wake up!"

"Why aren't you answering your phone?"

"Dee's on her way."

"Where are you?"

"I think I found your friend. If this is her, her phone is at three percent. We need to get it to five percent to be sure. How soon can you get here?"

She had dropped a pin of her house and sent that, too.

I looked up at my dad.

"My friend is in trouble," I said. "I have to help her."

He snapped into Adventure Dad mode. "Roger that. Want me to take you over there?"

"No," I said. "I need Mom."

CHAPTER TWENTY-SEVEN

LOST AND FOUND

My mom was waiting in her car when we pulled up at the house. She glared at my dad with her we're-not-going-to-talk-about-this-now-but-we-are-going-to-talk-about-this-later face, and the two of us headed to Angelique's house. On the ride there, my mom didn't mention my dad and neither did I.

Angelique lived Uptown, too, but in a much fancier part than we did. Her house was right on the avenue. My mom parked her little electric car right out front like we lived there.

"This place has good energy," my mom said, which surprised me. She was not usually impressed by fancy houses.

Angelique answered the door. My Belles Demoiselles training kicked in.

"Mom," I said, addressing her first because she's older and more important, "this is Angelique Hebert, a friend from summer camp. Angelique, this is my mother, Nailah Schexnayder-Jones."

"Helen Schexnayder," my mom corrected. "You can call me Miss Helen."

"Thank you, Miss Helen. Please, come in. We're all in the study."

Angelique led us through several formal rooms to a slightly less formal room that could have doubled as a computer lab. Dee was already typing away on a computer, and so was a woman with very dark brown skin and hair shaved so short it showed off the perfect shape of her head as much as the fleur-de-lis charm she was wearing on a thin silver chain showed off her graceful neck.

"Mother, this is Hasani Schexnayder-Jones, my friend and linked sister, and her mother, Helen Schexnayder. Miss Helen and Hasani, this is my mother, Angela Hebert."

Linked sister. I liked that.

"Please, call me Mrs. Hebert," Angelique's mom smiled. "Now, Angelique, why don't you bring everyone up to speed while Mrs. Schexnayder and I see what we can do to manage some of the chaos on the parent group pages."

"Yes, ma'am," Angelique said, nodding to her mom.

Angelique's mom and my mom went to a table on the far side of the room.

Angelique pulled me behind the desk where Dee was working.

"I've been working on a trace. I went backward from what I could gather of Anne Johnson on YouTube, but traces are easier when you know the person in real life, so I had to abandon that. Then I realized I didn't have to trace _AnnieOaky_ directly; I could trace you. Your magic was all over her page, so I traced it instead, until I got to an account that's been inactive for the last two weeks and has marks of your magic leading to a phone that is not connected to an active YouTube account. The phone also has traces of your magic in it, so I think we have an eighty or ninety percent chance that it's her phone. Below five percent battery, the phone is in a protective lock mode that's pretty hard to penetrate, even with satellites, so the first thing we need to do is charge the phone enough to get it out of safety mode. Then we can get inside of it and see who it belongs to and, if it's Annie, we can boost it enough for the satellite to locate it."

All that was assuming that Annie was still with her phone, but I stopped myself from thinking that. I didn't want to be the one to mess up the good energy my mom mentioned before.

"So, what do we do?" I said.

"We link and try to connect one of our phones to that phone to give it a battery boost. It'll be easier if the three of us start together, but then you and Dee will need to hold the connection while I figure out whose phone it is. We can use my phone to do the boost."

"No. Use mine," I said.

Neither of them argued. I pulled out my phone and the three of us held hands. So much magic passed through us that it felt like we were swimming in it. Dee sent her magic through her dolphin charm before sending it around our circle, but I was surprised that Angelique did, too. My phone blinked on. The screen was all letters and numbers. We held it like that, Angelique directing our magic into my phone. After a minute or two, she let go of us and went back to the computer.

"Seven percent. Hold steady," Angelique said. "This will take a minute."

Dee picked up my other hand. She kept the flow directed at my phone, but the power between just the two of us was more like a puddle than a pool.

"It dropped to four percent," Angelique said, grabbing our hands again. "That was too fast. If it goes to zero, we might not get it back."

We all concentrated. Angelique and Dee were both moving magic from their fleur-de-lis through the dolphin charm. That seemed backward to me. The fleur-de-lis was more powerful. If anything, they should have been moving magic from the dolphin to the fleur-de-lis, not the other way around. But in any case, magic flowed around us enough to swim in. It wasn't quite as high as it had been the first time, but it was amazing that we were able to produce so much when we had already used so much. This time we held on longer. When Angelique finally let go, she excitedly reported that phone was at ten percent, but it almost immediately dropped back to four.

"We need a third while Angelique is working," I said. "Two is good, but three is better, right? Who can we call?"

Names floated through my head. Thuy. Danielle. Monique. I wasn't sure whose side any of them were on. Calling them might be a waste of time, and we didn't have time to waste.

"Mrs. Hebert?" Dee asked tentatively.

Angelique shook her head. "My magic came from my father's side and my mother's magic isn't compatible with mine, which means it isn't compatible with yours, either," Angelique said. "We'll have to push it higher next time so when it crashes, it will hopefully stay above five percent."

"That enough?" Dee asked.

"I'll have to work faster." Angelique went to take up our hands.

"I have another idea," I said. "Mom? Will you?"

My mom looked up, startled.

"Will I what?"

"Will you link with us?"

My mom shook her head. "I'm not a witch," she said.

"You're a kismet," I said.

"No, I'm not. Am I?"

But even as she was wondering, my mom came and held our hands. I couldn't see her magic before we started, but I knew it was there. I felt for it, the luck that was always around her. Sure enough, as soon as she held our hands, there it was. Her wisps of magic clicked right into place just like I knew they would. She gasped at the feeling of it, but for me it felt familiar, more like a memory. My mother had been boosting me with her kismet ever since I could remember. Maybe she didn't call it that. Maybe she called it tea and cleansing the air and filling me with love with kisses on the forehead, but that didn't stop it from being what it was. Only kismet could have protected her from me and my wild magic before I knew what I was doing.

Her magic made mine flow even stronger. I couldn't understand it at first. I probably would never have understood it if I hadn't been able to see it with my own eyes. My mother's luck was flowing through my dolphin charm and dragging my magic along with it. Sprinkles of magic went in and came out like a full-on storm. I was wrong about the dolphin. It was meant to amplify magic, not store it. I was wrong about my mother's magic, too. Kismet wasn't just weak magic. It was different magic, magic I might never be able to do. Even with my fleur-de-lis, I had to *think* for my magic to do the right thing. My mother's kismet just knew what to do. Before I knew it, our magic was waist-deep and rising.

"Got it," Angelique said. "Anne Johnson. The phone is definitely Anne Johnson's."

ngelique tethered my phone to _AnnieOaky_'s and we followed the connection, going straight when it got stronger, turning when it got weaker. My mom called the police and tried to tell them what we were up to as we zigzagged across the city. Eventually we got to a place where the signal seemed to end. It was an old, dilapidated warehouse on St. Claude Avenue, not too far from the bridge to my dad's house.

"It's either in that warehouse or the woods behind it," Angelique said.

Neither place was good. None of us said that, but I know we all must have been thinking it from the way everyone jumped to action.

Mrs. Hebert called the police again, my mom called Annie's mom, Mrs. Johnson, and Dee, Angelique, and I tapped out a message to Annie. It said, "Please let us know you're safe."

"I'll force her phone to chime," Angelique said. "That way if it's on silent or something, she'll still hear it."

We pressed Send. The connection dropped. We waited a full minute. No response.

"Dang," Dee said. She looked defeated. Dee never looked defeated.

A tear ran down Angelique's cheek. "I don't know what else to do," she said. "Should we go in there?"

"No," both our moms said at the same time.

"You girls stay right here where I can see you," my mom said.

"The police are on their way," Mrs. Hebert added.

"So what do we do?" I said, praying they wouldn't say exactly what they said.

"We wait."

ee, Angelique, and I hugged. I wished Luz was there. We took a pic and sent it to her so she'd know we were where the signal ended and that we had all tried and done our best to make this OK and that none of us were alone because we all had each other. Luz's brother took a pic of her holding up our pic. She posted it on the @AnnieAreYouOaky Instagram page with the caption "We're here for you."

I liked the post and added a comment: "Love your #1 Fan."

My comment seemed so small compared to what was in front of us, but I wanted to flood Annie, wherever she was, with as much love as we could send her. Maybe it would help her get through whatever it was she needed to get through. I didn't know. I couldn't control that part and I couldn't control whatever happened after, but I could send her love. That much I could do.

I looked at my mom and Angelique and Dee. They all nodded. I linked us together again. My first thought was to open the post up to love. I could have gotten it a thousand likes in a few minutes. It would have been easy. But I had barely thought the thought before I pushed it aside and used our energy to just offer up love and hope that some of it got to _AnnieOaky_.

A message came in from Luz.

"She's checking IG!!! She just hearted one of AnyaDo0dle's stories!"

Angelique laughed, relieved. "What else is she going to do while she's hiding out in the woods and/or an abandoned warehouse?"

I wasn't ready to laugh or smile or anything. I needed to see her. She came out at the exact moment her mom pulled up. Her mom leaped out of the car. She didn't stop to turn the engine off or close the door. She just ran and scooped Annie up, saying, "We checked in there," over and over again through her tears.

Annie was crying, too. "I'm sorry, Mama," she said.

"We were so worried." Her mom squeezed her tighter.

"I'm sorry, Mama," Annie said again. "I just thought everyone would be better off without me."

"How could you think that? How?" Annie's mom was yelling, but I understood why she was. I think Annie did, too.

When her mom calmed down a little, she turned to my mom and Mrs. Hebert, and said, "I don't know how you did it, but thank you for finding her."

Mrs. Hebert nodded and smiled, but my mom went in for a hug. I know that hug. It's healing. It's magic. Just like my mom.

Annie watched them for a second, then turned to us. "I don't know what you did to get those messages to come through while my phone was dead," she said quietly, "but thank you. I didn't know so many people cared. And that Instagram page, @AnnieAreYouOaky? It has 19 followers. That's a lot!"

"It is?" I said.

Dee nudged me.

Annie didn't seem to notice. She bobbed her head up and down. "Yeah. A ton! Do you think all of them are into carving dolls? I couldn't fit that many people in my room. Even this place only has enough equipment for ten people at a time."

"This place?" Dee said. "The abandoned warehouse?"

"It's a maker studio," Annie said. "They didn't get enough kids to enroll for camp, so they just closed it down for the summer until the college students come back to town. They were mostly the ones using it."

"Ah. Artsy, not creepy," Dee said.

"Well," I said, "I just want you to know that you're an amazing artist and the only reason your YouTube channel had so many down-votes and stuff was because of—"

"Spambots," Angelique said smoothly. "Dee and Hasani have been working to shut them down for days, and now they have."

"With help from you," Dee said to Angelique.

Angelique nodded graciously, then both of them looked at me hard, practically daring me to contradict them.

"I just thought you should know. It'd be a shame for you to shut your channel down because of some . . . bots."

"I can't believe y'all did that for me. As soon as my mom lets me back on the Internet, I'm going to watch all of your videos on repeat so you get a million more views just from me."

"Actually, I was thinking of shutting my channel down," I said.

Annie gasped. "Why would you do that? You're my favorite YouTuber."

I shook my head. "I just . . . well . . . my page had a weird boost. It didn't grow organically and—"

"I found you organically," Annie said. "I was your second follower."

"I know, but it's not like my channel is doing anything important, so it's not worth it if it's hurting somebody . . ."

"Oh. You don't like doing makeup anymore. I get it."

"God, no!" I said, and Mrs. Hebert gave me a look. "Goodness, no," I corrected. "I love doing makeup videos."

"Then why stop? I don't care what anybody says. I love your videos, and it's not just about the makeup. It's about seeing somebody who's not afraid to just be themselves where the whole world can see. Besides, I'd miss your content so much, and I'd miss you, too, even though we're not friends."

"Not yet," I said. "Give it time."

CHAPTER TWENTY-EIGHT

ARE YOU A GOOD WITCH OR A BAD WITCH?

nnieOaky_'s YouTube page was shut down again and she didn't respond to any of our messages even though my mom assured me that she had talked to Annie's mother every day and Annie was safe.

When I pushed, Mom just said, "Their family has some things to work out. Let's give them a little time to do it."

My mom was right, but she did give Annie's mom a message from me, Luz, Angelique, and Dee that whenever she was ready, Annie would have a group of friends waiting for her.

y dad started texting and calling me every day. I told him all about my new plan. The whiteboard in my room was filled with it. Some of it was the same as my old plan. I mean, you can never stop loving your subscribers, especially not when your goal is to hit one million, but now that I knew about the code, I resolved to get there without using magic to mess with the algorithm. I didn't know how to weave my intentions like Miss Lavande, but I had a goal and I was determined to get there the right way, no matter how long it took. I didn't think it would take too long, though. The lessons I learned at Belles Demoiselle—Introductions, Greetings, even The Art of Arranging—would all help MakeuponthecheapCheap grow, and I had a whole string of collabs set up to help share the love, including some with a few of the "cool kids" who were actually cool. Thuy had reached out to say how she had been too shocked to say the right thing at the party, and how LaToya was really just hurt and I should give her a chance. I honestly wasn't trying to hear all that about LaToya, but I was glad to be Thuy's friend again. My dad listened to all of it. He didn't try to tell me what to do or give advice when I didn't ask for it. He just listened, and I listened to him, too. The day Sandy unblocked him, I don't think I have ever heard him so happy. Real happy, not cartoon happy. A few days later, he came to pick me up and brought me to our favorite burger place to tell me that he and Sandy had decided to get married again, but this time he wanted me to be the first to know.

I wasn't upset. I mean, don't get me wrong. I wasn't happy, either. Well, maybe I was a little bit. I was happy for my dad and sad that our family wouldn't be the same. And if he married a witch, so what? Witches deserve love, too.

I was still suspicious of Sandy. I mean, she knew way too much about Othello to not have been watching me on the monitors in the solarium. Then Dee casually reminded me that I had literally made an entire video series about training my cat, and I felt stupid. As much as I didn't want to, I knew I had to apologize, and I did. Sandy was cool about it. Not cool, like, chill. Sandy has no chill. But she didn't try to make me feel worse.

"You know what would mean so, so much to me?" Sandy asked. "If you would take a picture with me and your dad at the wedding."

I let out a breath. I was scared she was going to say "be in the wedding." I wasn't there yet, but a picture I could do.

"Can my mom be in it?" I asked.

"Of course!" Sandy sang, then she flitted off the way Sandy does, hair trailing in the wind. She came back a moment later with a little package topped with seashells instead of a bow and handed it to me.

"My mom always hoped I'd get into Belles Demoiselles, so I was so excited when you did," she said.

I knew it. I knew Sandy was a witch. But she didn't get into Belles Demoiselles? Dang. Sucks to be her.

I fixed my face into a soft smile.

"Don't worry. I told your dad about me, but I won't tell him about you. That's your story to tell, but I do think it's precious that in his world girls randomly get scholarships to summer etiquette schools," she laughed. "This was supposed to be your graduation present. I've seen your cat videos, so I know you're already good with them, so I thought maybe you might like this. Open it."

I unwrapped the package. It was a book with a banana leaf cover. There was nothing written on the front, but the title was printed elegantly on the first page: *Spells, Meditations, and Incantations for Freeing the Mind, Body, and Spirit.*

"Freedom is kind of my thing," she said. "But the book is only half-filled on purpose. You can fill the other half with whatever works for you."

I had some ideas.

"Thank you, Sandy," I said, and I really meant it.

On the day of my dad and Sandy's wedding, Luz, Dee, Angelique, Annie, and Annie's mom sat together in the audience, but I sat with my mom in the front row. Was I excited about it? Not entirely.

Did I sit with my back straight, knees together, chin parallel to the ground, and a soft but pleasant smile? Absolutely. But I didn't put any charm in it. If there was any charm at that wedding, it came from my dad's smile. His real smile. I was happy for him. So if any flowers grew on the St. Claude bridge that day, I can promise you, it wasn't me.

After the vows and before the reception, we took a picture with the four of us. I still have it. I used it in my 500k Get to Know Me video. Sandy posted it on her new IG account, @HitchedandFree, which had almost as many followers as her old one two days after she opened it.

It's a great picture. We all look happy, and I don't think it's by magic.

Acknowledgments

All fiction writers are liars, but let me hit you with a little bit of truth: I could not have written this book by myself. A book? Sure. This book? Nope. Not at all. I needed a lot of help from people who were generous enough to offer their time, expertise, and support. Thank you to my editor, Maggie Lehrman, for all her lovely insights. Thank you to Bigger J, Candace, Jennifer, Rebecca, Samantha, and my personal Steve Trevor who, separately and combined, make the most cutting, gentle, helpful, and inspiring critique partners a person could hope for. Thank you to all the aunts who inspired parts of various characters in this book, including my very own Auntie Nette, who grew up in Vacherie, where this story is set, speaking Louisiana Creole.

Louisiana Creole, also known as Kouri-Vini, is the endangered Creole language of Louisiana that was formed during the French Colonial period in the eighteenth century. Many people still speak

Louisiana Creole today, thanks in part to the efforts of people like Clif St. Laurent and Jonathan Mayers, who advised on the words and phrases used in this book.

Some links to learning resources:

My Louisiana Historic and Cultural Vistas: mylhcv.com/kouri -vini-its-sister-languages. This is Dr. Christophe Landry's site, which is *full* of articles and resources. There are audio courses, flashcards, and maps that can be purchased in Kouri-Vini here, too.

Ti Liv Kréyòl: om.conlang.org/learnlouisianacreole/learn louisianacreole.html. A Louisiana Creole language primer that can either be downloaded for free, sans illustrations, or purchased with images.

Mythologies Louisianaises: arthurrogergallery.com/wp-content/ uploads/2018/11/Mythologies-Louisianaises-Project-Catalogue -Arthur-Roger-Gallery-Web.pdf. Trilingual Publication in Kouri-Vini, Louisiana International French, and English, featuring artwork by artists connected to Louisiana culture. The exhibition opened for White Linen Night at Arthur Roger Gallery in 2018.

About the Author

Marti Dumas is a mom, teacher, and creative entrepreneur. She is passionate about promoting childhood literacy and for the past fifteen years, she's worked with children and teachers across the country to encourage an early love of reading both in and out of the classroom. Her stories combine science, humor, family, and magic, while adding much-needed diversity into the children's book landscape. She lives in New Orleans with her family.